'TIS THE SEASON FOR MURDER

It was bedtime for this business owner. I swung my feet onto the floor when my phone rang again, but this time it was Abe.

"Hey, handsome," I said, smiling. "Are you working on those lines that caused the fire across town?"

"Am I ever. We finished restoring power only a little while ago to the four square blocks that lost it."

"I saw the house on the news at about seven-thirty. Adele called me. At least nobody was home."

"Right. Nobody living, anyway."

What? "What do you mean?"

"They had to cut through the roof of the part that wasn't burning to get to the fire."

"I saw that on TV."

"I have to get back to work, but I wanted to tell you what I saw. I was up in the bucket looking down into the attic. Several guys inside were staring at something on the floor. When they mo̶v̶e̶d̶ ̶a̶part, you wouldn't believe what I saw. I don̶'̶t̶ ̶k̶n̶o̶w̶ ̶how it got there, but I saw a skeleton. A h̶u̶m̶a̶n̶ ̶o̶n̶e̶.̶"

A Country Store Mystery

Candy Slain Murder

MADDIE DAY

KENSINGTON BOOKS
KENSINGTON PUBLISHING CORP.
www.kensingtonbooks.com

KENSINGTON BOOKS are published by

Kensington Publishing Corp.
119 West 40th Street
New York, NY 10018

All Kensington titles, imprints, and distributed lines are available at special quantity discounts for bulk purchases for sales promotion, premiums, fund-raising, educational, or institutional use.

Special book excerpts or customized printings can also be created to fit specific needs. For details, write or phone the office of the Kensington Sales Manager: Attn.: Sales Department. Kensington Publishing Corp., 119 West 40th Street, New York, NY 10018. Phone: 1-800-221-2647.

Kensington and the K logo Reg. U.S. Pat. & TM Off.

First Printing: October 2020
ISBN-13: 978-1-4967-2317-8
ISBN-10: 1-4967-2317-1

ISBN-13: 978-1-4967-2318-5 (eBook)
ISBN-10: 1-4967-2318-X (eBook)

10 9 8 7 6 5 4 3 2 1

Printed in the United States of America

*For my brilliant, talented, quirky, and generous
New England friend Sheila Connolly, who was always
my role model in writing multiple cozy mystery series.
May your spirit rest easy, dear Sheila.
We all miss you.*

Acknowledgments

Many thanks to Christopher Huff and Pamela Vandewalle Huff for inspiring me to write about birth children (and parents), reunions, and adoption. Expanded families rock. We love you and your brood!

Thank you again to Terri Bischoff, independent editor extraordinaire, for helping me fix and enrich this story in all kinds of ways. Gratitude to D. P. Lyle, MD, for help with facts about body decomposition in an attic. I also consulted the *Book of Poisons* by Serita Stevens and Anne Bannon. Brown County Sheriff Scott Sunderland once again provided me with an important detail about Hoosier County police procedure—thank you, sir.

Kelly Braun chipped in one of Buck's more colorful phrases—thanks, Kelly! Jan Grape first mentioned "Oh, my stars and nightgown"—I had to include that, as well as the Dan Rather quote about the too-small bathing suit, which I heard on the *Wait Wait . . . Don't Tell Me!* radio show.

Author Julia Spencer-Fleming kindly put me in touch with her daughter, Virginia Hugo-Vidal, who converted to Islam as a teenager. Virginia was generous enough to share her experience of the faith with me. She explained what it's like for her to live as a convert, so I could portray my character Marcus Vandemere in more depth. Any misrepresentations are of my own doing. Also, thanks to Julia for teaching me the word "eldritch."

Longtime friend Tim Mundorff turned me on to the Columbus—his hometown—architecture as well as the Gom sandwich.

My young friend James Tanona is now age eleven—with a fourteen-year-old sister—and is a voracious reader who loves this series. He reviewed all the scenes that include teen Sean and gave me a few pointers on how teenage boys behave.

Gratitude, always, to my agent, John Talbot, to my editor, John Scognamiglio, and the rest of the talented crew at Kensington, including publicist Larissa Ackerman and talented cover artist Ben Perini. To my Wicked Authors blogmates—seven years and going strong—I couldn't do this without you. Readers, please find us at the blog and on Facebook. Finally, love always to my family, my Hugh, my Sisters (and Brothers) in Crime, and my family of Friends.

Chapter One

I frowned as I stood at the hot grill in my country store restaurant. I was beset by a vague sense of foreboding, a gray film creeping over the light in my psyche.

Everything in my life was rosy. Pans 'N Pancakes, my business, was thriving and in the black, and right now it smelled like meat grilling and contentment. My employees, Danna Beedle and Turner Rao, seemed happy with their jobs. I was solid with Abe, my electrical lineman honey. Aunt Adele was healthy. It was December first, with white lights twinkling and the aroma of fresh evergreen wafting from the tree Abe and I had cut and set up in the corner yesterday. Most important? Our small town of South Lick, Indiana, hadn't seen a murder in a year. So whence this sense of looming doom?

Danna carried over a load of dirty dishes from our biggest table. We still had a few diners finishing their meals, several waiting for their food, and one couple intent on their chess match at the game table. But at one-forty-five, the lunch rush was over. My right-hand woman took a second look at me after she deposited the dishes in the wide sink. "What's the matter, Robbie? Did you hear bad news? Did a ghost walk over your grandma's grave?"

"No." I mustered a smile. "Everything's fine. I got a funny feeling something might happen. A not-good something."

"You?" she scoffed. "I thought you didn't believe in woo-woo stuff like that. Me, on the other hand, I listen hard when I sense something bad's up."

"I don't really believe in woo-woo." Although that palm reader out in Santa Barbara last February had been onto something when she'd warned me of danger. Danger I should have paid more attention to. "Anyway, all's good here, right?" I waved my arm around at the country store where I'd made my dream come true. Tables of different sizes filled the restaurant area. Shelves filled with antique and vintage cookware lined the store section, almost all of it for sale. I also offered skeins of Adele's wool and her knitted hats, a local Amish farmer's honey, and other homey products. I even had a pickle barrel. A big menorah sat ready on a windowsill for when Hanukkah came around next week, and tomorrow Abe was going to bring Sean, his teenage son, to help decorate the tree.

"Yes, it's all good." She pointed at the grill. "Except you just burned that turkey patty."

"Shoot!" I flipped the patty. "It's not too bad. I'll eat it when I get a chance. And there's only one more order waiting, right?" Our order carousel had a single slip hanging from it. I grabbed another disk of ground turkey and laid it on the grill.

"Yep, for that two-top. I'm going to take a quick break, okay?" Danna asked.

"Go ahead."

She slid out of her blue store apron and tossed it in the dirty laundry box, then headed for the ladies' room. I examined the slip. We'd run out of our lunch special, and this was a straightforward order of two hamburgers—one medium rare with the works and one well done with nothing—a coleslaw, a fruit salad, and two brownies, with a milk and a ginger ale to wash down the meals.

I also offered one kind of soup every day, plus turkey and veggie burgers, a couple of wraps and sandwiches, and a Caesar salad on the regular menu. Customers could also order breakfast all day long until we closed at two-thirty. With such a small crew and kitchen, I stuck to the first two meals of the day. And today Turner was off. Tuesday tended to be our slowest, customerwise. Turner was taking one class per semester at a new culinary institute in Blooming-ton, the university town in the next county. The class was held on Tuesdays, and I'd told him Danna and I could manage without him for a day.

After I finished the turkey burger order and delivered it, I filled the hamburger plates and carried them over to Tanesha and Bashir, a couple holding hands at their table. They were staying in one of my B&B rooms upstairs and had said they were on their honeymoon.

"Enjoy your meal." I smiled at them. They looked

more or less my age of twenty-nine. Geez, that meant I'd be thirty next May, which was kind of hard to believe.

"Thanks, Robbie. We love it here," Tanesha said in a clipped accent that pegged her as being from Minnesota or maybe North Dakota.

"I'm glad. I do, too." Despite being a native mid-coast Californian, I did love the distinct seasons and the relaxed pace of life in southern Indiana. South Lick was nestled in the hills of scenic Brown County, so I could get a strenuous workout when I took my bicycle on the roads to work off the stresses of being a solo entrepreneur.

I turned back to the grill. The cowbell hanging from the heavy old front door jangled as a tall man younger than me walked in with light brown skin flushed from the cold. He closed the door but stood with a tentative air, gazing around as if searching for something or someone. I'd never seen him before.

"Welcome," I called. "Are you here to eat? You can sit anywhere, and we'll be right with you." I walked toward him, rubbing my hands on my apron. "I'm Robbie Jordan. This is my store and restaurant."

"Thanks." He didn't smile and a tic beat at the corner of a brown eye. He was slender, over six feet tall, and his short-cropped dark golden hair was as curly as his dark lashes, almost kinky, in fact. A chinstrap beard lined his jaw, and he looked to be in his mid-twenties. "Um. Does somebody named Danna work here?" When his voice shook, he cleared his throat. "Danna Beedle."

At that moment, Danna emerged from the rest-room. I glanced her way.

Was this guy on the up-and-up? He looked innocent enough, and was clearly nervous. But strangers coming in and asking for Danna, who had only last month turned twenty-one, made me nervous, too. "And who might you be?" I found something a little familiar-looking about him but I couldn't figure out what it was. Or maybe he was the cause of my uneasy woo-woo feeling a little earlier.

"My name is Marcus Vandemere. Can I please talk to her?" His gaze followed Danna to the kitchen area where she donned a clean apron. "That's Danna, isn't it? I would have known her anywhere."

What? Well, what could go wrong in a public place like this in broad daylight? "Yes, it is. Danna?" I waved her over. When she drew close, I said, "This gentleman would like to speak with you."

She cocked her head, her reddish-blond dreadlocks covered today in a red-and-green scarf in honor of the Christmas season. "Hi. I'm Danna." My assistant, almost as tall as Marcus, held out her hand to him.

He took a deep breath and blew it out, then took her hand in both of his. "I'm Marcus, and I'm so glad to meet you. I've been looking for you."

"You have?" She scrunched up her nose. "Why?"

"I'm your half brother."

Chapter Two

Danna gaped at Marcus. "You, you're . . . what? I don't have a brother." She slid her hand out of his, frowning. "I'm an only child. Always have been."

I stared at him. Had Danna's late father, whom she'd never known, had a child with another woman?

"I know this is a big shock." His voice was stronger now, and his tone gentle. "Our mom gave me up for adoption."

Whoa. Corrine Beedle, Mayor of South Lick, had a past I hadn't had a clue about. And neither did Danna, judging from her reaction.

"She did?" Danna's voice rose. "She never told me. How old are you?"

"I'm twenty-six."

She narrowed her eyes. "I'm twenty-one, barely. So Mom . . ." She shook her head. "I'm sorry, it's super hard to get my head around this."

"I understand," he said.

"Where do you live, Marcus?" I asked.

"In Bloomington. I'm in grad school at IU, but I grew up in Indianapolis."

A customer raised her hand across the room. I gestured that I would be right there.

"Why don't you two sit down over by the desk?" I pointed to the small sitting area in my office corner where they could talk without diners hearing. "I can handle things, Danna." As long as a tour bus didn't show up.

She looked wary but finally nodded. "Come on." She slowly added, "Marcus," as if trying on the word for size.

I busied myself with delivering the ticket to a four-top. The total was under thirty-five dollars, and they'd ordered—and consumed—a lot of food.

"We sure love your prices, hon," one of the women said.

"Thanks. I need to meet my expenses, but I'd hate to have them so high folks felt they couldn't afford to eat here." In fact, what I charged for meals was under the going rate in Nashville, but I sure made up in quantity what I might have earned with a pricier menu.

I refilled the drinks of the honeymooners and checked with the chess players to see if they needed anything. I shot a glance at Danna and her brother on my way back to the sink. They sat at right angles, neither of them smiling or looking relaxed, but talking. What an astounding piece of news for her to get out of the blue. He probably wanted to meet his birth mother, too. What would Corrine do with that? Meeting a birth family had to be a minefield to navigate on either end. Marcus could be welcomed with open arms—or treated coldly. Had Corrine ever looked for him and not found him? A lot of people used Ancestry or other DNA services these days to connect with birth families. Marcus's sibling relationship to Danna must have been what I'd thought looked familiar.

All the customers had paid and left, with the newlyweds also buying a vintage muffin tin before heading out for the afternoon. I was loading the dishwasher when Danna and Marcus approached.

"Get this, Robbie. Marcus loves to cook, too." Now Danna was smiling, and her eyes sparkled, too.

When a wide smile split Marcus's face, I definitely saw the resemblance between the two.

"I sure do, especially international foods," he said. "My parents always took us to weird restaurants—at least they seemed weird to a kid—and we traveled a lot, too, when I was growing up."

"Maybe cooking is in our genes," Danna said.

"Robbie, I need to get back for a seminar," Marcus said, holding out his hand. "Thanks for not kicking me out."

"Hey, I'm glad to meet you." I shook his strong, smooth hand. "I hope you'll come back and eat here."

"He promised to," Danna said.

I watched as she walked him to the door. They exchanged a hug, and after Danna closed the door behind me, she stood rooted in place, shaking her head as if in wonder.

"Hey, turn the sign to 'Closed' while you're there," I called to her. "It's two-thirty."

She flipped over the sign in the window and locked the door, then nearly skipped back to me.

"Robbie, can you even believe what just happened?

I have a brother. I always wanted a big brother, and now I have one."

"That's great. Can you come down off your cloud a little and scrub the grill? I turned it off and it should be cool enough."

She laughed. "Yeah, sure. Sorry." She grabbed the scraper and started.

"How did he find you, anyway?"

"He read an article about finding birth families. He'd never felt like he needed to before, since he grew up happy and loved. When he finally asked his parents—his adoptive parents—they told him Mom's name. It wasn't like in the old days of closed adoptions and locked records. They knew about my mom all along, but had agreed after they adopted Marcus as a newborn not to tell him until he asked."

"And he asked."

"Yes. He'd done Ancestry, but neither Mom nor I have, and my grandmother hasn't, either, so he couldn't find us, and I don't have any other siblings." She paused in her cleaning and drew her light brows together. "That I know of. Man, I am *so* having a talk with my mother tonight."

"Do you wish she'd told you about him earlier?"

"Of course! I could have had a brother years ago."

"Yeah." I loaded detergent into the dishwasher and pushed the On button. "Unless she'd also agreed not to tell you until he looked for her."

"I guess. Whatever. I'm just glad I know about Marcus. And he's only over in Bloomington! I can, like, see him all the time."

"I'm happy for you."

She smiled to herself as she worked. Her hand

slowed. "So that's who it was," she murmured. "Robbie, one time when I was about eight I caught my mom looking at a picture. She was sitting on her bed and she had this really sad look on her face."

"You think it was a picture of Marcus?"

"I bet it was. I went in and asked her who was in the photograph. I only caught a glimpse but it was definitely a little baby."

"What did she say?" I asked.

"She stuffed it into her nightstand drawer, hugged me, and said she loved me."

"Which didn't answer your question."

Danna resumed scrubbing. "Not at all. Next chance I got, I went and looked for it, but she'd hidden it somewhere else. I asked her again and she told me it didn't matter."

"You'll get the whole story tonight, I'm sure." I also planned to google the heck out of this guy to make sure he was who he said he was. I wasn't letting anybody hurt Danna.

Chapter Three

The wind was an angry banshee by seven that night. I sat in my small apartment at the back of the store and listened to it roar like the Wabash Cannonball through the big fir outside. The one antique window I hadn't gotten around to replacing rattled something fierce, and the gale was a lewd Father Nature whistling through a crack in the door.

Still, I was snug with my feet up on my couch, tuxedo cat Birdy rolled into a ball at my side. A half-completed crossword puzzle was on a clipboard on my knees and a half-empty glass of a hearty red wine sat on the end table next to my elbow. Abe couldn't be with me because he had been called into work. Electrical wiremen were much in demand when branches were coming down onto wires all over the county.

Something went *thud* outside my back door. I groaned, but laid down the puzzle and padded through the kitchen to the door. I switched on the porch light and peered through the glass. As I'd thought, it was my trash can, rolling toward the back of the property.

Heck, let it roll. Today had been trash day, so it was empty. And it would either lodge against the barn or the tall trees. The heavy plastic barrel wasn't going to escape. The store trash cans were in an enclosure at the side of the building, so they were safe, too.

I got snug on the couch again. I frowned when sirens raced by out on the road. The rumble that accompanied one sounded like it had to be a fire engine. I hoped if it was a conflagration, they caught it quickly. This was wind without rain, and it had the potential to carry sparks far and wide.

Sipping my wine, I pictured Danna at home grilling her mother about Marcus. Would the discussion go smoothly for her? Would Corrine welcome Marcus into their lives? Or would she want to keep him at a distance? Maybe he'd be a painful reminder of a past she had left behind. Of course, Danna could have her own relationship with her brother even without her mom. She'd sounded excited about that. Too, perhaps Marcus only wanted to meet Corrine but not get close to her. He had adoptive parents he probably loved, after all. Twisty situations with many threads could get smoothed and sorted out, or they could become even more tangled.

I also had two half siblings, except they were younger than me. I hadn't been given up for adoption, but my mom, now almost four years gone, had never told Roberto Fracasso she was pregnant. He'd been a visiting scholar here when they'd fallen in love and I was conceived. He'd gone back to Italy, and Mom had moved to Santa Barbara. After I'd found him almost two years ago through luck and digging,

I'd gone to Pisa to meet him, his wife, and his two adult children, even a little nephew. Although my half sister hadn't warmed up to me, I'd loved meeting everyone, Roberto most of all. My short hefty-hipped build was Mom's, but my brown eyes, Mediterranean skin, and lush dark curly hair were a hundred percent my father's. Gazing at his face was almost like looking in a mirror.

My cell rang with my aunt Adele's ringtone. I connected and greeted her.

"Turn on the local news, Robbie," she said in a rush. "Quick."

I grabbed the remote. The screen filled with footage of fire enveloping a two-story house. Gushes of water from the firefighters' hoses formed arcs into the flames. One end of the house was not on fire but the roof gaped open. I glimpsed an REA cherry picker truck at the edge of the scene, REA being the county electrical cooperative and Abe's employer.

The camera cut to a reporter with her back to the fire. "In breaking news, the South Lick home of a local man caught on fire earlier this evening after a tree blew onto a live wire, sparking the blaze. No one was at home, but the firefighters had their hands full battling the flames so they didn't spread. The fire chief told us they currently have the fire ninety percent contained and he's confident the neighboring homes are safe. Teams from Monroe and Johnson Counties also responded to the call. Power is out in the neighborhood, but an REA spokesperson says they will repair the lines as soon as it is safe to do so.

Back to you, Clint." She signed off and the station returned to its usual programming.

I hit the Off button. "Wow," I said to Adele. "Do you know whose house it is?"

"That's William Geller's. Doctor over to Columbus Regional. He's lived in South Lick since God made dirt."

South Lick sat about halfway between Columbus Regional Hospital to the east and the Indiana University Hospital in Bloomington to the west. "It's a good thing he wasn't home," I said.

"Yep. Musta had to work late or something."

"Does he have a family?"

"Nope. Wife upped and left him about a decade ago, and they never had any kids."

"That's a blessing, anyway. And that the firefighters contained it despite this wind. Is it howling out at your farm, too?"

"Like a pack of hungry wolves." She whistled. "But my sweetie Samuel and me, we're cozy inside. And I took and trimmed my trees last fall so they aren't anywhere's near the wires or nothing."

"Good. I still have power. The fire must be on the other side of town."

"All righty, hon. You have a good night now. We'll be in for lunch tomorrow, I reckon."

"Give my love to Samuel," I said. "And to you."

"Will do. Love ya, sugar."

I shivered after I disconnected. That guy Geller was awfully lucky not to be in a house on fire. I'd never experienced a blaze like that, and wasn't planning on it, either. I picked up the puzzle again.

An hour and a half later, the puzzle was finished

and so was the wine. I yawned wide. Five-thirty this morning was a long time ago, and my alarm would go off at the same time again tomorrow. With a breakfast restaurant that opened at seven, I had to be in the store working by six every day except Sundays, when we opened at eight, and Mondays, when we were closed. It was bedtime for this business owner. I swung my feet onto the floor when my phone rang again, but this time it was Abe.

"Hey, handsome," I said, smiling. "Are you working on those lines that caused the fire across town?"

"Am I ever. We finished restoring power only a little while ago to the four square blocks that lost it."

"I saw the house on the news at about seven-thirty. Adele called me. At least nobody was home."

"Right. Nobody living, anyway."

What? "What do you mean?"

Voices sounded through the phone. "I'll be right there," Abe said away from the phone. "Robbie," he said to me. "They had to cut through the roof of the part that wasn't burning to get to the fire."

"I saw that on TV."

"I have to get back to work, but I wanted to tell you what I saw. I was up in the bucket looking down into the attic. Several guys inside were staring at something on the floor. When they moved apart, you wouldn't believe what I saw. I don't know how it got there, but I saw a skeleton. A human skeleton."

I gasped. "Really?"

"Yes. Hey, love you. I'll be by in the morning." He hung up.

A human skeleton? My mouth drew down in horror. *Wait.* Adele had said the dude who owned the house was a doctor. Maybe it was simply an old demonstration skeleton made of some kind of material that wouldn't melt. Abe wouldn't be able to tell from up in the air. Because if that thing was real, in Ricky Ricardo's words, somebody was going to have some 'splaining to do.

Chapter Four

Danna trudged through the front door right on time at six-thirty the next morning. I already had the coffee on and biscuits in the oven, and it was smelling delicious in here.

"Good morning, Sunshine," I called to her.

She mumbled a greeting as she hung up her parka. She slipped an apron on over her knee-length flared black skirt and a yellow vintage bowling shirt and washed her hands.

"Late night?" I asked.

She only bobbed her head before clomping her Doc Martens into the cooler to bring out the condiment caddies for the tables. We always left the tables set the day before, with our blue cloth napkin silverware rolls, but we couldn't leave things like sugar packets out in case of mice or ants. I would wait for her to raise the subject of talking about Marcus with Corrine.

I cracked eggs into the dry whole wheat pancake mix I'd prepared yesterday, added buttermilk and oil, and switched on the mixer. We'd decided on a spinach–red pepper egg bake for a breakfast special, which I'd prepped several big pans of yesterday afternoon. I sprinkled grated cheddar over one and slid it into the preheated second oven. It would look Christmasy with the reds and greens.

"Can you write the egg bake on the Specials board, please?" I asked my sleepy assistant, who'd finished with the caddies.

"Okay." She had a clear and artistic hand with the colored chalk, and she added a little flourish of green holly with red berries next to the name. She headed into the cooler, emerging with her arms full of bacon and sausage packages. As she laid a dozen links on the grill, Danna said, "Heard about the fire last night. News said they found a dead person in the attic."

I whipped my head in her direction. "It was a real skeleton?"

"Yep. They don't know whose."

"Wow. Abe was working there last night, and he saw it. The dude who owns the house is a doctor, so I was thinking maybe it was a teaching skeleton or something." I shifted the pancake mix into a pitcher and washed the big bowl as I wondered who had died in his attic. Had Geller known? How could he not? I shuddered involuntarily. "I hope this isn't another violent death. We don't need any more of that in South Lick."

"Like, ever." This morning Danna's dreadlocks were in a fat braid down her back and she'd tied a blue scarf over them.

Me, I threaded my messy ponytail through a blue store ball cap every day. Although I loved Danna's style, at work I didn't even try. I wore a long-sleeved store T-shirt with jeans in the winter, short-sleeved when it got warmer.

"So, I talked with Mom last night." Danna stashed the rest of the meat in the small fridge under the counter and started cracking eggs into the mixer bowl for scrambled and omelets. "She was pretty surprised Marcus had found me. She also apologized for not telling me."

At least that part of his story was true. "Good. Does she want to meet him?"

She laughed. "She was kind of tentative on that, but yeah, she finally conceded she would. We're going to ask him to dinner in a day or two. I texted him and he's coming here for lunch today. I really want to get to know him better."

I wrinkled my nose. "Uh, you know we're going to be busy at lunch, Danna. Especially with news of human remains found in an attic." My store had become the community watering hole and nothing could make me happier. When something newsworthy happened in town, people flocked here to learn and to share what they knew, which one had to be careful about, of course. Lots of gossip was unfounded and could be dangerous. "You probably won't have much time to talk."

"I know. He wanted to eat here, and he has the afternoon off. We might hang out after I'm done with work."

At a knock on the door, I glanced at the clock. "It's already seven. You ready?"

She gave me two thumbs up, so I hurried over, unlocked the door, and turned the sign so it read CLOSED toward the inside. I pulled open the door to none other than Buck Bird, second in command of the South Lick police force. Behind him under the porch light was my beloved Abe O'Neill and a few other customers.

"Good morning, Buck, Abe." I smiled at them.

"Mornin', Robbie." Buck pulled off his regulation hat. "It surely smells better than heaven in here."

"Come on in, everybody." I stepped back to let the crowd in. "Sit anywhere you'd like." Before I shut the door, I peered out to see what damage the wind had wreaked, but the sun wouldn't be up for another forty-five minutes and I couldn't see a thing.

A circles-under-his-eyes Abe waited for me. "You look lovely, as always, darlin'." He kissed my cheek.

So did he, although "hunky" was more accurate. I laid my hand against his face. "You're really tired, aren't you? Did you work all night?"

"Until about two. And we have a lot more to do today. What can I get to eat that's fast?"

"Everything's ready and we have a yummy egg bake. I'll bring you a plate right away."

Danna was already pouring coffee and taking orders, so I made a beeline to the kitchen area and hauled the bake out of the oven. A minute later I carried a plate full of the casserole, two biscuits, and three sausages to where Abe sat with Buck.

"How come he rates?" Buck asked in a hungry, plaintive tone.

Abe waggled his dark eyebrows. "I have a direct line to the chef, Buck. Thanks, sweetheart." He dug into the bake.

"Danna will take your order, Buck. I have to get back to the grill."

"All righty, then. But come on back when you get a sec. We got us some news going on in town I think you might could be interested in."

"Will do." News about a skeleton, or about its identity?

Chapter Five

It took me half an hour to get back to Buck. A steady stream of hungry would-be diners had filed in. At least Danna and I were a well-choreographed team, so we could handle it. Turner breezed in early even though he wasn't due on shift until eight o'clock. I thanked him.

"Sure. Want me to do the front?" The slender twenty-three-year-old slipped on an apron and washed his hands.

"Perfect. Danna, can you take over cooking?" I asked.

She straightened from loading the dishwasher. "You got it."

I told her which orders were already on and which were up next, then headed for Buck. Abe had eaten quickly and left, saying he'd see me at four with Sean to decorate the tree. Buck sat bent over his phone, stabbing at it with his index finger. His usual gargantuan breakfast was down the hatch, leaving only a smear of syrup on his pancakes plate and a dab of sausage gravy on the dish he'd wolfed biscuits and gravy from. His extra-long legs, also as usual, were stretched out nearly to Indy. I sank onto the chair opposite him.

"I only have a minute, Buck. What's up?" I lowered my voice. "Is it the skeleton?"

"I'm not even gonna ask how you up and heared about that. But you're right." His accent was more Kentucky than Indiana, and he drawled the word "right" into almost three syllables. "Human remains in the attic. Sounds like the title of one of them Nancy Drew books. But in this case it's a hundred percent real life."

"Do you have any idea whose it was? And did the owner of the house know about the skeleton?"

"We're still trying to determine the answers to both those questions. It's a puzzle, I have to admit."

"What did the coroner say?" I thought back to the body I'd found right here in my store two years ago. The county coroner had been a man. What was his name? It came to me in a flash. "Does Coroner Mayers know how old the skeleton is? How could Doctor Geller not know about it?"

"Slow yourself down there, Robbie." He held up a hand. "You're more full of questions than one of them robots on the phone. At least you ain't asking me to press one for this and two for that." He drained his coffee. "See, it's this way. Geller's wife, Kristina—we all called her Tina—went missing about a decade ago. Geller said she left him. Nobody never heared from her again. Her twin sister, Beltonia? Toni wasn't so sure. So, yes, Mayers is keeping that detail in mind. And it was, in fact, female remains."

Yikes. "So it might be his wife?" I heard my voice

rising and slapped my hand over my mouth. I checked around, but nobody seemed to have noticed.

"Might could be. Thing is, the doc's got one of them false legs."

"You mean a prosthesis?"

"Yup. Got the limb blown up in eye-rack."

"In Iraq?"

"That's what I said. Stepped on one of them mines or whatnot. He told us he don't never venture into the attic. Can't manage climbing up and down the pull-down steps. It's what he claims, anyhoo."

I wrinkled my nose. "How in the world could someone die in your attic and you don't know about it? That doesn't make sense. I mean, bodies must smell as they decompose. A lot."

"Yes, they do. However, 'spose it was the wife and she had herself a accident up there during a cold winter. The process would go slower and not be so odoriferous."

Buck, who so often sounded like a country bumpkin, once in a while threw in words like "odoriferous," and it made me smile. "And maybe the husband has a bedroom on the first floor, so he wouldn't have noticed. I still think it's strange."

"It's got strange written all over it."

I thought for a moment. "Oscar must be starting an investigation." Oscar Thompson, the state police homicide detective I'd had dealings with before.

"No, actually Oscar's on a case down to Evansville. You might not want to hear this, but Octavia Slade has been assigned to figger out this here case."

"Really?" Octavia was pretty much responsible for ending my budding relationship with Jim Shermer two years ago, or at least she shared the responsibility with him. I didn't have a lot of warm fuzzy feelings for the woman, no matter how competent a detective she was.

Buck bobbed his head. "She got herself some special training in cold cases last year, and if this one ain't cold, I'm a donkey's great-granddad."

"That means they think it was a murder."

He shrugged. "It's unexplained human remains. How the woman got dead is still to be determined along with who she was and all like that."

I grimaced. "Well, it's just awesome that Octavia will be around town for a while."

"Now, Robbie. I know you two ladies got yourselves a small itty bit of history." He gave me a kindly avuncular look. "Seems to me you're a heck of a lot happier with O'Neill than with that scoundrel Shermer. Would I be wrong?"

"Of course you wouldn't be wrong." Of course I was happy. Very happy. It didn't change the fact that as soon as Jim laid eyes on Octavia, the two had decided to resume a prior relationship, leaving me in the dust. It still hurt in a residual kind of way. Lucky for me, Jim had moved out of town a couple of months later so I didn't have to run into either him or Octavia around South Lick.

My B&B guests trotted down the interior stairs. The bell on the door jangled as more than a dozen people filed in all at once. Danna gave me a panicked look from the grill. I stood.

"Looks like we have a tour bus invasion, Buck. I'd better get to it. Will you tell me what you can?"

"Sure thing, hon." He handed me two twenty-dollar

bills, more than double what his breakfast cost. "Here."

"Buck, that's way too much," I protested, even though he did this all the time.

"Put it in the tip jar. All y'all earn it, and more."

I shook my head. "Thank you, my friend. Good luck today." I tucked the cash into my apron pocket and made my way to welcome the newcomers. As long as talk of murder didn't spread, my bank account was going to be happy. Or maybe even if it did. Unlike last Christmas, neither my cooking nor products I sold could possibly be suspected in that poor woman's death. I didn't even live in Indiana ten years ago.

Chapter Six

"That was a busy morning," I said to my employees at eleven-fifteen. We sat around a table eating our early lunch before the midday rush hit.

"Those tour ladies cracked me up," Danna said after she swallowed her bite of the last piece of egg bake.

"Yeah, they'd heard about us all the way down in Georgia." Turner laughed. "They were all 'bless your heart' this and 'Lordy me' that. And, man, could they ever eat."

Danna laughed. "One was a little tiny thing, and she ate as much as Buck does."

"Maybe they'll come back every year," I said. I swiped up the last bit of fried egg with the crust of my rye toast.

"Are we all set for the quesadillas?" Danna asked.

We'd decided to offer a dish I'd had in Santa Barbara last winter, a flour tortilla folded in half over cooked chicken, a smear of refried beans with mild green chilis, and cheese, then lightly fried. "I think so. People can choose to have them with or without chicken. I think they'll go together fast, and we have plenty of sour cream to top them with, and salsa to offer on the side. The guacamole is ready, too."

Turner snorted. "Hope the salsa is mild. Hoosiers don't go much for hot peppers. I learned the hard way when I made lamb vindaloo for some high school buddies. Those dudes about died. Insisted we go on an ice cream run after to cool off their mouths. They downed a pint apiece."

Turner's father, Sajit Rao, was from India, and Turner had learned to prepare that cuisine from his Indian grandmother. He made a mild Indian potato dish for the restaurant as a breakfast special from time to time.

"The salsa is mild, don't worry," Danna said. "I was the one who put in that order."

"Perfect."

"Robbie, is it true they found a human skeleton in that house that burned last night?" Turner asked, hazel eyes wide.

"I'm afraid it's true. And the guy who lives in the house claims he knows nothing about it."

"Earlier you told me he's a doctor," Danna said. "What's his name?"

"Buck said it's William Geller. He's an anesthesiologist at the hospital in Columbus."

"That guy?" Turner's mouth turned down.

"You know him?" I asked.

"He was a total fail when my mom had her knee operated on a few years ago. She'd chosen to be pretty much awake because it was only a meniscus repair. Geller hadn't given her enough of the right kind of anesthesia and the surgeon's instrument went beyond the numbed area. Mom's leg jerked and it nearly ruined the procedure. She said later she'd never felt such a pain, not even giving birth to my sister and me."

"Ick. That's criminal," Danna said. "I hope they put her under after that."

"Yeah, immediately," Turner said. "I'll tell you, I wouldn't let anyone I loved go within a hundred miles of the dude."

Geller sounded incompetent. Maybe the truth was more nuanced than Turner's story. "But he's still practicing." I carried my plate and fork to the sink.

"Apparently." Turner shook his head and brought his plate over, too.

"Danna, you'll fix the Specials board?" I asked. "I'm going to take a quick break."

"You got it," she said.

I could take a half hour off and they'd be fine, but all I needed was a quick pit stop. After I emerged from the restroom, I wanted to turn around and go back in. Detective Octavia Slade was seated at a two-top perusing a menu. I took a deep breath and mustered my inner adult.

"Welcome back to South Lick, Detective," I said when I reached her table. "What can I get you?" I didn't have an order pad and pen in my hands, so I clasped them in front of me to keep from fiddling nervously.

She glanced up. "Hello, Robbie." She tilted her head. "You're looking well." A few more threads of silver streaked her dark cap of hair than had two years ago, but her face was still largely unlined and her eyes as inquisitive as ever behind dark-rimmed glasses.

"Thank you." I wasn't interested in small talk with her. "Our lunch special is a chicken or cheese quesadilla, if you're interested."

Her eyebrows went up. "I love quesadillas. I was in San Francisco recently and had a delicious Mexican lunch."

"San Francisco is lovely."

"Yes. I was on my honeym—" She bit off the word as her neck reddened.

My gaze dragged itself to her left hand, now bearing a gold band on the ring finger. So she and Jim were married. *Awkward.* "Congratulations. Would you like the chicken or the cheese?"

"I'm still a vegetarian, so the cheese, please." She swallowed. "Listen, Robbie . . ." Her voice trailed off.

No. Just, no. I was so not getting into anything personal with her. The past was the past. "I'll put that order in." I headed for our cooking area. "A quesadilla for Detective Slade," I told Turner at the grill. "Hold the chicken."

"Got it. A detective, huh? She here for the body in the attic?"

"That's what Buck told me this morning." Turner hadn't been working for me in the late fall and winter two years ago when Octavia had worked those murders.

Danna came out of the restroom, shot a glance at Octavia, and joined us in the kitchen area.

She scrunched up her nose and whispered, "Isn't she the one who—" Danna, who had been with me since I opened the business, knew all about the Jim fiasco.

I held up a hand. "Yes. And now she's here to investigate that skeleton."

"What happened to our buddy Detective Thompson?" Danna asked.

"Buck says he's working on a case in Evansville. Octavia is who we've got. She told me her lunch order but I didn't ask what she wanted to drink. Can you take care of her, please?"

"I'm all over it, Robbie. Don't worry." Danna hustled to Octavia.

Turner raised a single eyebrow. "History with the lady?"

I bobbed my head once. "But it's all good." When the bell on the door jangled, it was a relief to see four hungry diners walk in, cheeks ruddy from the cold wind. Customers I'd never seen before. My life was almost perfect. I aimed to keep it that way and stay firmly in the present. I'd read about a meditation guru from the sixties who was all about "Be Here, Now." That was going to be me, in spades.

Chapter Seven

"Bro!" A smile wider than Lake Lemon split Danna's face after Marcus walked in a few minutes before one o'clock. Today he wore a kind of rounded skullcap. She hurried over to him.

I was on the grill and smiled, too, as I watched them embrace. My smile slid off when I realized I'd never gotten around to running a search on him last night, what with the fire and all. I shook off the nagging concern that Marcus might not be who he said he was. I flipped two meat patties and a chicken quesadilla, then laid on two turkey patties. We were having a busy lunch service. Customers kept coming in that door, and the word "skeleton" resurfaced in conversations over and over.

I hadn't interacted with Octavia again, who'd consumed her lunch while working on a tablet. She'd paid and left. Would she come in to eat again while she was in town? I didn't care. At least she'd had the decency to realize her faux pas when she started to mention her honeymoon.

Turner arrived with both arms full of dirty dishes, which he rinsed and loaded into the dishwasher.

"Can you take over the grill?" I asked.

"Of course. Hey, who's the dude with Danna?" He tilted his head in their direction.

Should I let Danna tell him? We didn't really have time for that right now. She wouldn't mind. "He came in yesterday saying he's her half brother. Apparently Corrine gave him up for adoption before she married and had Danna."

His eyes went wide. "Whoa! She looks super glad to see him. That's cool."

"She is."

"She didn't know about him before?"

"Nope." I still had that nagging worry about if Marcus was who he said he was, but I couldn't address it now. "I'll deliver Adele and Samuel's lunch." I brought him up to speed on the rest of the orders before grabbing the two quesadilla plates I'd topped with a dollop of sour cream and a scoop of guacamole. I set them down in front of my aunt and her octogenarian beau. "Lunch, straight from Santa Barbara." I smiled at both of them.

"Thanks, Robbie," Samuel said. "You're a peach."

"The little cups have mild salsa to put on top," I added.

Adele studied her plate. "Got any hot sauce?"

"Sure." I tilted my head. "I didn't realize you liked spicy food."

My no-nonsense aunt scoffed and tossed back her pageboy-cut hair, which was the color of the slate roofing shingles on the century-old South Lick Library. "All the work we've done in India, we've both come to right enjoy some spice in our lives, haven't we, Samuel?"

He blushed right through his dark skin. "Indeed we have. Robbie, she's talking about hot peppers, you know."

"Of course." I swallowed a laugh. I knew these senior citizens were intimate, but I didn't need any more detail than that. "Let me get the hot sauce."

When I returned, Adele beckoned for me to lean down. "Who's that fella Danna's all starry-eyed about?" she whispered, pointing at Danna. "She dump Isaac for him?"

I glanced at the table where Danna sat across from Marcus. She did look a little like she was crushing on him. "No, that's actually her half brother. He showed up yesterday and introduced himself."

"You don't say." Adele nodded knowingly. "The baby Corrine had."

"You knew about him?" I asked.

"Well, sure. Nothing I don't know about this town, hon. I'm not aware of the particulars, don't you know, but Corrine was clearly pregnant at one point. She'd been hanging around with a black jazz musician in Nashville. By the looks of this young'un, I'd guess he was the daddy."

I looked at Marcus again. An African-American father would explain his nearly kinky hair and the light coffee tint to his skin.

Samuel tilted his head. "I remember that cat. Died in a plane crash twenty-odd years ago."

"Corrine disappeared for some months and did not return with an infant," Adele went on. "She musta went off to an aunt or somewheres, had the baby, and gave it up for adoption."

"When she came back from being away," Samuel said, "everybody gave her space, and next thing we knew she married that good-for-nothing Beedle."

"Danna's father," I said.

"Yep," Adele said. "He was meaner to poor Corrine than a hungry fisher cat in March. Upped and got himself killed in a hunting accident when Danna was only a small little thing."

When I'd first opened my store, I'd heard gossip that maybe Corrine had engineered the fatal accident, but the story had never gone further than that.

"His death turned out to be a blessing to both Corrine and Danna," she added.

"May his soul rest in peace," Samuel, a devout Christian, added.

"Anyway, Danna is delighted to have a sibling, at last, and a big brother, to boot," I said as Turner hit the Ready bell. "Enjoy your lunches." On my way to the grill, I stopped by where Danna and Marcus were talking.

"Welcome back, Marcus." I smiled. "Danna, sorry, but I'm afraid we need you to bus tables."

She stood. "I know. We're going to hang out after we close today."

"You go work, Sis," Marcus said.

"I'll be right back to get your order," I told him.

"Thanks."

By the time I'd delivered the orders that were ready and made change for two satisfied diners, a woman had joined Marcus at his table. Looking to be in her late forties, she was about my height and had a trim figure, with professionally dyed and streaked shoulder-length hair the color of chestnuts. I wasn't sure I'd seen her before, but then a lot of customers came through my place every day. If she was local, she might have eaten here.

"Good afternoon, ma'am. I'm Robbie Jordan and the proprietor."

When she smiled at me, her lip caught on one prominent eyetooth. "Nice to meet you, Robbie. I've actually been in a couple of times since you opened. Great food, great atmosphere you've got here."

"Thanks. Sorry I didn't remember you."

"No worries. I'm Beltonia Franklin, but please call me Toni."

I blinked. Buck had talked about Beltonia this morning. Toni, whose dead sister Tina might well be the skeleton in the attic. I mustered a smile. "Welcome back, then. I gather you know Marcus?"

"We're in the same karate dojo." He drummed long fingers on the table and didn't smile.

"He's quite good," Toni added.

He blinked. "I'm not, actually. I'm still a white belt."

Toni ignored his protest and went on. "I was going to grab a bite to eat, but when I saw Marcus here, I asked if I could join him."

Marcus looked away, as if he wasn't particularly happy about dining with her.

"What can I get you both?" I asked. I took their orders and headed for the grill. Was there a way I could steer conversation to Toni's twin's disappearance? I had a few minutes to figure it out.

In the kitchen area, Danna was rinsing plates.

"Who's sitting with Marcus?" she asked me in a murmur.

I stuck the order on the carousel for Turner. "Somebody he studies karate with. Do you know her? Her name is Toni Franklin."

Her eyes flew wide. "The twin of the lady who disappeared when I was like eleven."

"Apparently."

"I've heard Mom mention her name, and I've seen her around town, but I don't know her."

"He doesn't seem very happy she joined him. He must be too polite to say no." I glanced at Marcus again. "Danna, that cap Marcus has on is interesting. It reminds me of one that Muslim men wear."

"It is. He told me he converted to Islam last year. He really respects their principles and finds it a comfort to pray regularly." Danna straightened from the dishwasher. "What's funny is that he was raised as Quaker. But he says he finds both faiths suit him and nourish his spirit. He told me Quakers as well as Muslims believe people can have a direct relationship with God. Interesting, isn't it?"

Chapter Eight

The rush had let up ten minutes later but the three of us were still at full speed servicing every table. When the doorbell jangled, I groaned but kept it silent. And then let out a relief-laden breath. A man came in alone and hung his coat on the rack. When he swiveled to face the seating area, he seemed almost to lose his balance. I made my way over to him, surveying the status of several smaller tables as I went. Adele's and Samuel's plates were empty and they looked like they were getting ready to leave.

"Greetings, sir. I'm Robbie Jordan and this is my store. Are you here for lunch?"

"Yes." In a rumpled suit and tie with the smell of a recently smoked cigarette around him, he looked to be in his sixties, but was still at least six feet tall. His white hairline was creeping back toward the crown of his head. Permanent frown wrinkles coursed between his eyebrows. He wore wire-rim glasses, with hair tufting out from his ears, and had a marked overbite.

"I'm afraid all the tables are full, but several parties

are finishing up." I gestured to the sitting area. "Would you like to sit while you wait? It won't be long."

"Thank you, Ms. Jordan. I will be glad for a seat." He lowered himself and set the leather bag he'd brought in on the floor.

Before I could resume delivering food, Adele and Samuel were at my side. Samuel pressed bills into my hand.

"That Mexican food was a joy," he said. "Wish we'd brought beer to go with."

"Why, William Geller, as I live and breathe," Adele exclaimed, gazing at the man.

Interesting. The owner of the house with a skeleton in the attic. I wasn't surprised Adele knew him. She knew everyone.

"I haven't seen you since Gerald Ford was president," she continued. "Where you been hiding yourself?"

Geller made as if to stand.

"No, you sit, now. No need taxing your bum leg."

When she bustled over and sat next to him, his smile looked distinctly uncomfortable.

"You know Samuel MacDonald, of course," Adele continued. "We're a thing these days, don't you know?" She winked at Samuel.

"Is that so?" Geller's nostrils flared as he gazed at Samuel. "Afternoon, MacDonald."

What was that expression about?

"Good afternoon, Doctor Geller." Samuel smiled at him with his usual kindly, sincere expression. "How are things in the medical world?"

"Fine. The usual." His voice was terse.

Turner waved to me from a two-top he'd just cleared.

"I have a table for you, Doctor, if you'd like to follow me," I said.

"We'll catch you later, Roberta." Adele stood and bussed my cheek before sweeping Samuel toward the door.

"Have you been in before?" I asked Geller as he boosted himself to his feet.

"No, I'm normally at work when you are open and I don't dine out often as I am alone. But I have some, ah, matters to deal with today."

"I heard it was your house that burned last evening. I'm very sorry."

His response was a grunt. When we passed Marcus's table, where he was digging into a hamburger and Toni had started on a quesadilla, Geller paused. I did, too. Toni had been his sister-in-law—or technically still was, I supposed.

"Afternoon, Toni," Geller said, but didn't smile at her.

She gazed up at him. "I heard about your fire, William, and the skeleton they discovered. Who do you suppose it could be?" Her words were innocent but laden with a cutting tone.

"As I've told more than one investigator, I haven't a clue." The doctor didn't meet her gaze.

"I have some ideas," she murmured. "Want to hear them?"

Marcus looked from her to Geller and back in bewilderment.

"Not particularly. My table, please, Ms. Jordan?" Geller looked at me with what-are-you-waiting-for expression.

"Sure. Excuse us," I said to Toni.

But Geller didn't move, now staring at Marcus's distinctive hat. "Don't you know gentlemen remove their hats indoors, young man?"

"My *taqiya* is a sign of respect for my faith." Marcus touched his heart. "Peace be with you, sir." He didn't touch his hat, but his hands clenched on the table and the corners of his mouth drew down.

"Leave the man alone, William," Toni said, sounding annoyed.

Geller pressed his lips into a line.

"Doctor Geller?" I gestured toward the empty table, which was blessedly on the other side of the room. And blessedly he followed me.

He chose the seat facing Marcus and Toni and lowered himself into it. "I'm surprised you allow terrorists like that in your establishment." He pointed his chin toward Marcus.

Terrorists? I cleared my throat. "I serve any paying customers who behave themselves, regardless of religion or anything else. Do you still want to order lunch?"

"I suppose so, since I'm here," he grumbled. "Not the clientele I was expecting, though."

"I'll give you a minute." I made a beeline back to the kitchen area. That was way too much drama for one afternoon.

Things quieted down over the next twenty minutes. Marcus left, telling Danna he was going for a walk and would be back at three to meet her. Toni left, too, without speaking to her brother-in-law again. Geller had taken what looked like might be a medical journal from his bag and perused it as he ate.

I glanced at the door when it opened at two-fifteen. Phil MacDonald pressed the door open with his back, his arms full of two wide pans. I hurried to his side.

"Is this a brownie delivery?" I asked, holding the door for him.

"You got it. I have a couple trays of cookies in the car, too." Phil, Samuel's grandson, was a good friend and also the baker of yummy desserts for the restaurant.

"Let me take those." I baked sweets when I needed to, but not having to make sure we always had a treat for dessert took a big load off my shoulders. I carried the trays to the counter, then rushed back to hold the door for him again.

He set them on the counter and high-fived Danna, who was finishing up the last lunch orders. "How are things, today?" he asked.

"Kind of dramatic, actually," I said. "Can you stick around until we close, or at least until customers clear out?"

"Sure." He glanced at the Specials board. "Can I get a quick quesadilla while I wait?"

Danna shook her head. "No can do. We ran out of tortillas two minutes ago. It was more popular than we expected."

"No worries. How about a turkey burger, instead, with extra coleslaw?"

"I'm on it," she said.

William Geller raised his hand, gesturing for the check. Phil looked in his direction, then back at me, his startlingly blue eyes wide in his dark face.

"Surprised you let that dude in here," he muttered.

"Why?"

"He's a known white supremacist. Attends KKK meetings, the whole nine yards."

"Ouch," I murmured in return. That might explain Geller's look when he saw African-American Samuel.

"It's true. Grandpa told me to steer clear of him whenever possible."

"Well, as I told Doctor Geller when he complained that a diner wearing an Islamic hat was a terrorist, I serve anybody who behaves himself or herself. So far, the doc has behaved himself, mostly."

Danna whipped her face toward us. "He called Marcus a terrorist?"

"He did." I grimaced.

"Just. No." She shook her head in disgust. "That man better not show his face in here again."

"Who's Marcus?" Phil asked.

I held up a finger, signaling for him to wait. "Hey, girl," I patted Danna's arm. "Doctor Geller's a paying customer minding his own business." *Mostly*.

Chapter Nine

We were an empty restaurant by two-fifteen, so I turned the OPEN sign to CLOSED and locked the door. Phil still sat at the table he'd taken as far as possible from Geller, who had left without incident. I bused the table next to my friend and came back with a rag to wipe down the top. He was bent over his phone. An image flashed through my mind of a booming chiropractor industry in ten or twenty years treating all the neck and shoulder problems that would arise for our bad-posture small-device-centric generation.

Phil glanced up, then looked around the restaurant. "Everybody's gone. I hadn't even noticed."

"Lost in a novel?"

He pulled his mouth to the side. "I wish. No, I'm reading the latest bad news from Washington. I wish Congress would get its act together for once."

"Yeah. It's ever thus, right?"

He frowned at Danna scrubbing the grill. "So, who is this Marcus dude she's all concerned about? Some new boyfriend? Did she drop Isaac?" He and Danna were good friends, and he looked worried.

"No, she and Isaac are good." I smiled. Adele had been concerned about the same thing. Sure, Danna was young, but she and Isaac had had a solid relationship for a year and a half. "Marcus is, well, Danna should tell you. Hey, Dan," I called. "Take a break and come talk to Phil."

She gave a last swipe to the grill. Turner pushed the Wash button on the dishwasher and moseyed our way, too.

"Looks like a party. Who wants a beer?" I asked.

When three hands went up, I headed for my apartment. By the time I set down four open bottles, Phil had leaned his elbows on the table. He still looked worried.

"Danna, have you checked this guy out?" Phil asked. "What if he's a scam artist?"

"My mom acknowledges having him." Danna tapped her finger on her pilsner. "She even said she was sorry for not telling me."

"Yeah, so she had a baby boy out of wedlock," Phil said. "How do you know this dude is the one?"

I piped up. "They do share a resemblance. Turner, you saw Marcus. Did you notice it?"

"Now that you mention it," Turner said, "I think I did, but I didn't get a really close look at him."

Danna stood. "Phil, you're being ridiculous. How else would Marcus know to find me?" Her voice rose. "His parents told him Mom's name, for goodness' sake! Google easily takes care of the rest."

"Okay, okay." Phil was only a few years older than Danna but had been her babysitter when he was a teenager. He held out a hand. "Sit down, Danna. I asked because I care about you."

She ignored his gesture. "If you stick around until three, you can judge him for yourself. I have cleaning to do." She stalked back to the kitchen area.

"Now I hurt her feelings," Phil murmured, his gaze following Danna, his finger tracing the condensation on the bottle.

"She'll be all right. Tell her you're happy for her before you leave." I took another swig of beer.

"I recently started studying karate," Phil said. "There's a tall dude named Marcus in the dojo. He's pretty good. I wonder if it's Danna's Marcus."

"Possible," I said. "A woman was in earlier who sat with him and said they are in the same dojo, too."

"Marcus isn't a very common name, is it?" Turner asked.

"No, I don't think so." I shook my head. "On a different topic, I want to know more about Geller. How did you find out he belongs to the Ku Klux Klan?" A shiver ran through me at the thought of the organization's white robes, pointy face-covering hoods, and burning crosses.

Phil gave me a look. "Robbie, if you're black, it's common knowledge."

"And they're here in Brown County?" Turner asked.

"They're pretty much everywhere, but especially from here on south. Dangerous folks, and they've gotten bolder in recent years." Phil drained his beer. "I have to run. Afraid I can't wait and meet the half brother of mythical proportions." He pushed to standing. "Thanks for the brew."

"Sure. Take care, and thanks for the desserts. The check's in the mail." I sent him a check every month for his baking, but part of our ritual was for me to say it was in the mail every time he delivered.

"See you, dude." Phil and Turner exchanged a fist bump. Before Phil left, he spoke to Danna where she was wiping down the stainless counter with way more vigor than it needed, and it looked like they made peace.

"Turner, has your dad ever had a run-in with the KKK?" I asked.

He shook his head. "I don't think so. If he has, he hasn't told me. He's a pretty light-skinned Indian, and lots of people think he's Italian or maybe Greek. I sure haven't had any problems, but my skin's even paler than Dad's, although my sister's is darker. She takes after my *dadiji*, my grandma."

"Sound like you might want to avoid Doctor Geller for more than one reason."

"I promise."

Chapter Ten

Turner and Danna left at three o'clock. Marcus had shown up right on time, and the two of them sailed off together.

I stayed working in the restaurant. The place was clean, tables were set for tomorrow, and I'd already thrown the laundry in the washer in my apartment, taking a minute to freshen up Birdy's food and water. Of course he followed me back into the store. I didn't mind the company, and he was good about staying off the tables and the kitchen surfaces. He explored the antique cookware shelves for a minute, then settled in next to the pickle barrel in a perfect Sphinx pose, watching me through slitted eyes.

I'd felt like using the same eyes on William Geller after both Turner and Phil had divulged that the man had unsavory aspects about him. Could he have killed his wife and left her in his—their—attic for a whole decade? Had he harmed her and left her for dead? Maybe instead she'd gone up there to hide from him and had tripped and hit her head. She'd died alone, and he'd never gone up to look for her.

And, if not his wife, who in the world else would the female skeleton be? Was the doctor a serial killer? Perhaps he'd buried other women's skeletons in the back garden or in the basement.

Geez. I shook my head. I wasn't usually so fanciful in my musings. And anyway, I needed to leave this to Detective Octavia Slade. It was her circus, her monkeys. It occurred to me that Buck hadn't come in for lunch. Which was odd, but maybe the case of the skeleton in the attic was keeping him too busy to eat, although that was unlikely. He must have picked up a meal elsewhere.

Abe and Sean would be here in an hour for our tree-decorating party. I'd better get busy. I set to work whipping up some cheesy muffins as a snack. Sean had a legendary appetite despite being an increasingly lanky string bean of a teen. This summer he'd shot up to five foot ten, making him an inch taller than his father, and he didn't seem finished with growing, either. I'd love to see an eating contest between Sean and Buck. I imagined Sean might edge out the lieutenant for the trophy.

Once the biscuits were in the oven, I mixed up tomorrow's biscuit dough, since the counter was already covered with flour. *Shoot.* We hadn't brainstormed a Thursday special. I wrapped the biscuit dough in plastic wrap and stored it in the walk-in cooler. I stood there surveying what we had in stock. I did have a couple of gallons of frozen turkey stock left over from cooking down the carcasses from our Thanksgiving extravaganza. I pulled those out to defrost for a lunch soup.

But what about breakfast? We were out of tortillas,

so breakfast burritos wouldn't fly. I spied a tall stack of bagged pita bread next to a big container of feta cheese. What had we gotten those for? I couldn't remember. I might as well use them for a stuffed breakfast pita with a Mediterranean touch. We always had pitted kalamata olives around. A feta-olive omelet stuffed into a half pita and grilled made a perfect breakfast special with a Christmasy touch—if you stretched the concept a little. Jesus was born near the Mediterranean in the land of sheep, olives, and flat-breads, wasn't he? I smiled. Coming up with creative dishes was one of the most fun parts of being a cook.

At a knock on the front door, I hurried over to open it. "How are my favorite men?" I stood back to let them in.

Fifteen-year-old Sean blushed. "Hi, Robbie."

I knew better than to over-hug the kid, so I patted him on the arm, instead. "Glad you could come, Sean."

Abe, on the other hand, knew a big hug was exactly what I wanted. He ended with a quick kiss. "Hey, darlin'. We bring offerings." He handed me a paper sack, the nice kind with handles.

"What's this?" I asked.

"Grandma's gingerbread people and holly cookies," Sean said. His voice had finally stopped cracking and was an almost alarmingly low baritone. "I mean, you know, holly-shaped cookies."

"Thanks," I said. "Not exclusively gingerbread *men*?"

Abe laughed. "Mom's an equal rights baker."

"She starts her baking early, doesn't she?" I asked.

"Uh, you could say that again." Sean shook his head. "She says I eat so many cookies she has to start early so she'll still have some left for Christmas."

"She would be right," Abe agreed.

"Cocoa's not with you?" I asked the teen. Abe's parents had given him a chocolate Lab puppy for Christmas a year ago.

"He's still at doggy day care," Abe said. "Sean's mom is working late this week. We'll get him later. He's good there until six."

"He totally loves it, Robbie," Sean said. "The other dogs are his buddies. It's so funny. It's almost like he doesn't want to come home."

"Awesome," I said. "Hey, come on in, guys." The timer dinged, so I hurried over to draw out the biscuits. I slid them onto a wire rack. "Hungry, Sean?"

His eyes lit up brighter than a full moon. "Obviously. Those smell amazing, Robbie."

"Thanks. Come on over and grab a few. You want milk with them?"

"Yes, please." By now Sean knew where the plates were. A minute later he sat at the closest table layering butter onto three split biscuits.

"What am I, chopped liver?" Abe mock-whined.

"Help yourself, sweetheart. You want milk, too, or something more interesting to drink?"

"I think I could handle one on the interesting spectrum. Do you have any stout?"

"I do. Back in a flash." By the time I returned from my apartment with two thick, dark stouts in glasses, the guys had finished their biscuits, and Sean's milk glass was empty, too. He was bent over his phone, doing what teens do. I handed Abe his beer and clinked glasses with him.

"Cheers, darlin'." He rolled his eyes at his son with an exasperated look.

"He's fine," I mouthed silently, and took a sip.

Sean rose and scuffed over to the tree. "Awesome noble fir." He leaned in, inhaling. "Nice."

"Smells great, doesn't it?" I joined him. "How did you know what kind of tree it is?"

"I kind of love trees. I, like, study them, and I'm in a Junior Foresters club at school."

Abe moseyed over and slung his arm around Sean's shoulders. "He's thinking of studying tree science."

"Yeah. Or math." He ducked out of his dad's reach and lifted a small box of ornaments out of the big box I'd set on a table next to the tree. "Okay to get started?"

"Sure," I said. "I already strung the lights. Have at it."

We dug into the glass balls, carved wooden figures, and souvenir ornaments I'd collected. Naturally, Sean handled the top branches while I took charge of the lowest ones. I made sure not to put anything breakable down there. Birdy had joined us and was already batting around a painted wooden snowman I'd hung.

While Sean was around the back of the tree, I murmured to Abe, "Hear anything about who the, uh, person was?"

"No. But there's a lot of buzz that it might be Kristina, the ex." He kept his voice low, too.

"I heard that, too. Her twin sister came in today."

"Toni? She's a tough nut. She owns a duplex and doesn't treat her tenant at all well."

"In what way?" I asked.

"Doesn't fix things that are broken. Keeps raising the rent. I know the renter, Shirley Csik. She's not a happy camper."

"Someone named Shirley comes in to eat every once in a while. Dark hair, athletic?"

"That's her."

I tilted my head. "That's a funny last name. Chick, like in chicken?"

"That's how you say it, but it's Hungarian. Spelled C-S-I-K. We went to high school together. She was the captain of the soccer team."

"Is the other side of the duplex empty?" I asked.

"No, that's where Toni lives. She keeps up her side just fine." He shook his head.

Sean rejoined us. "Dad, at school kids were saying that the skeleton in the burned-up house is a lady who disappeared when I was little, and that her husband killed her. Is that true?"

So much for keeping our voices down.

"I have no idea, Seanie," Abe said.

Sean rolled his eyes at his dad using the childish nickname but he didn't object verbally.

"The police are looking into it," I said. I glanced at Abe, who was well aware of my history. "In fact, Detective Octavia is back doing the investigation."

"No kidding," Abe said. "Did she come in to eat?"

"She did, and she let slip that she and Jim got married, too." I held up a hand. "I'm fine with it. Frankly, I'm glad she took him off my hands. I wouldn't be with you otherwise." I slid my arm around him and squeezed his firm waist.

He kissed the top of my head. "That makes two of us." His voice was husky.

"Hey, dudes, cut it out," Sean said.

I laughed and let go of Abe to open a green box. "This is the angel for the top. Whoever puts it on gets to make a wish. Sean, want to do the honors?"

"A Christmas wish?" Abe asked.

"Any wish." I smiled but was hit with a wave of sadness. "It was my mom's ritual." I watched as Sean mounted the step stool carefully. He took the angel from the box and slid it onto the tippy top of the tree.

"Perfect," Abe said.

Sean climbed down and peered into the ornaments box. "Looks like we got them all."

I snapped my fingers. "Nope, one more." I hurried to my desk and returned with two new ornaments in my hand. I handed Sean one. "I had these made. One for you and one for me."

"Sweet," the teen murmured as he examined the wooden gingerbread dog with a collar reading "Cocoa." He looked up. "You even got his name painted on it."

"A crafter at that new artisan co-op in town customized them for me."

"You're awesome, Robbie. Thanks." He extended his fist for a fist bump.

I bumped, then handed him the matching dog. "Here. Hang this one for me."

He obliged. "That reminds me. What's that corny thing you say, Dad? Great minds think alike?" He slid his hand into his jeans pocket and handed me a small flat red envelope. "Open it."

I drew out a wooden skillet-shaped ornament. It was painted blue on both sides, with Pans 'N Pancakes neatly lettered in white, and had a loop of string attached to a hole in the handle. My throat thickened. "I love it. Thank you so much, Sean." I gazed up at him.

"I made it in shop class. Well, they call it 'Maker Space,' but it's still shop."

Abe beamed at both of us. I swiped a tear from the corner of my eye.

Sean peered at me. "Are you crying?"

I sniffed. "It's such a sweet thing to do for me, that's all. They're happy tears, kid."

"All right, enough sweetness from you two," Abe said, but his voice was gentle and full of love. He found the switch on the light cord and flipped it. The tiny colored and white lights on the tree glowed and made the glass ornaments sparkle.

"Cool," Sean said in a soft voice. "I really like Christmas."

I did, too. I wished a mysterious skeleton hadn't intruded on the cozy season. But it was an old mystery, and if Octavia couldn't solve it, no one could.

Chapter Eleven

The Mediterranean breakfast sandwich was making people nod in approval after their first bite the next morning. The lit and decorated tree elicited oohs and aahs, too. To a one, customers told me how pretty it was. The contrast to outdoors might have had something to do with it. Even after the sun ostensibly had risen at eight, it was still dark out there. Rain rapped insistently on the west-facing windows, and hungry diners came in wet, cold, and miserable.

Buck pushed through the door. He shook off his hat and coat before hanging them. "Guess we should oughta count our lucky hens it's thirty-six degrees out and not twenty-six, because this would be some kind of snowstorm if it was any colder," he told me.

"You're right about that. Hey, missed you at lunch yesterday."

He shook his head. "Some kinda big work powwow I had to attend. The mucky-mucks and their meetings. Wastes everybody's time." He sniffed. "Goldarnit, it smells good in here, Robbie."

I laughed. "Sit yourself down, then. The usual?"

"Yepperoozy." He squinted at the list of specials. "What in Joe Hill's backyard is a Mediterranean sandwich?"

"An omelet with feta cheese and black olives in pita bread, then grilled."

"You lost your marbles, Robbie? Olives don't belong in no breakfast, and I don't have any idea what fatal cheese is. Gimme a regular American breakfast, okay?"

I snorted. "You got it." I headed over to Danna at the grill. "Buck doesn't want olives or fatal cheese."

She laughed out loud. "That's classic Buck. Let me guess. He asked for an American breakfast."

"Exactly."

"Coming right up." She turned a couple of sausages, still smiling to herself.

I surveyed the restaurant. Buck had snagged the last open table. My upstairs guests sat holding hands and gazing at each other as they ate, dreamy expressions floating on their faces. The newly minted husband was apparently left-handed, because he held her left hand with his right. After the doorbell jangled, a tall man made his way in. He flipped down the hood of his rain jacket and looked around. I made my way to his side.

"Good morning. I'm Robbie, and this is my store." I held out my hand.

He shook it with a hand that dwarfed mine. "James Franklin. I've been meaning to try this place for a while." About forty, he also had an enormous head, with a receding hairline and a brow that bulged above bushy dark eyebrows. Right now his forehead was lined and his eyes downturned as if he was super worried. About what, I couldn't guess.

"I'm afraid all the tables are full right now," I said. "But you're welcome to wait. It won't be too long."

He glanced over my head. "Buck Bird has a spot at his table. I'll go see if he minds company."

"That's fine." I watched him. *Franklin.* Where had I heard that name recently? I snapped my fingers. That was Toni's last name, too. Connected? Likely, in a town this size. I busied myself pouring coffee, delivering plates, and fending off questions.

"What do you think, Robbie?" a daily regular asked. "Are those bones Tina Geller's?"

"Tina?" I asked. "Do you mean Kristina?"

"Sure. We always called her Tina, though. You know, Tina and Toni, the twins."

"Anyway, I couldn't tell you whose remains they are."

"Seems to me they have to be hers." She shook her head, making a *tsking* sound. "Boy howdy, the doc is in trouble now."

"More coffee?" I wasn't going there with her, or with any other customer, the lieutenant excepted.

I carried Buck's triple-sized breakfast to his table, where James had settled in. "I guess you two know each other. Can I get you some breakfast, Mr. Franklin?"

"'Course we know each other," Buck said. "Don't I know everybody?"

I laughed. "Apparently."

"Please call me Jamie," the newcomer said. "I'd like the Mediterranean special, please. Despite my name, I'm half Greek. And a side of fruit salad."

"I'll get that over to you. Are you related to Toni, by any chance?"

Jamie's nostrils flared and he looked like he'd tasted a moldy strawberry. "She's my stepmother. Or was. Since my father died, I don't have to call her that anymore."

His stepmother? She couldn't be more than five or ten years older than him. "I met her only yesterday," I said. "I'm sorry for the loss of your father."

"It's been a few years, but thanks. If you ask me, she killed him."

Whoa. I glanced at Buck, who gave a little shrug as if he already knew Jamie's views.

"Everybody knows Toni married Dad for his money, and he had a lot of it," Jamie went on. "He was thirty years older than her. Why would she pull something like that if not to get rich?"

Because she loved him, maybe? On the other hand, if she had a lot of money, why was she living in a duplex?

"Franklin here was asking me about the skeleton," Buck said. "Wondered if it was Tina's."

Along with everyone else in town.

Jamie lowered his head into his palm for a moment. He straightened with full eyes. "Kristina was nothing like her evil twin sister." His voice was thick with emotion. "Nothing." He swallowed hard.

Was he about to start crying? I'd let Buck deal with that. "I'll put in your order." I bustled off. I needed to give Adele a call when I could and get the scoop on Jamie and Kristina. Something was definitely going on there.

Chapter Twelve

I'd just sat down at ten-thirty with an overdone sausage and a breakfast special when Adele breezed in carrying a big paper bag. The restaurant was only half empty, which was more crowded than usual for this time of day, and my crew and I were switching off taking breaks. I waved to my aunt, who set down the bag on my desk before sauntering over. After she planted a kiss on my cheek, she plopped down in the chair opposite mine.

"How's my favorite niece?" she asked.

"Glad she's sitting down for a minute. We've been busier—"

"Than a mosquito at a nudist colony?" She chuckled at her own joke.

I smiled. "Pretty much. I wouldn't want to live at a place like that today, though. Brrr."

"You and me, both." She inhaled. "It smells as good as heaven's own kitchen in here, hon."

"It does, doesn't it?" Danna had slid a fresh pan of biscuits out of the oven not a minute ago, and the current batch of sausages were maple cured.

Combine that with the lingering aromas of sautéed onions and peppers, crisp bacon, and banana-walnut pancakes, and it was pretty darn divine.

"I brought you a new supply of hats." Adele gestured toward my desk with her chin.

"Thanks. Christmas shopping is in full force already." All kinds of diners browsed my cookware and gift-item shelves after they ate, more times than not leaving with one of my handled paper bags holding their purchases. I almost needed another employee for ringing up hats, honey, and hot plates. Last December I'd also sold custom packets of Mexican hot chocolate mix. That hadn't worked out so well, unfortunately, what with the police confiscating them to check for poison. "And your hats are popular."

"That's dandy, then." Adele slipped out of her coat and leaned back in the chair.

"Do you want to eat?" I popped in the last bite of sausage.

"I will, by and by. Me and my waist never say no to an early lunch." She patted her solid midsection with a satisfied air.

"Adele, what do you know about James Franklin?"

She cocked her head. "What are you curious about Jamie for?"

"He was in for breakfast a couple hours ago. He seems to hate Toni Franklin, and almost broke down when he talked about how different her twin Kristina was."

My aunt nodded like a wise old owl. "I had my suspicions about them two, Tina and young Franklin, back before she went away. You can pick up looks between lovers, don't you know? Even if they weren't together, weren't touching or talking but were in the same place out in public, you could almost reach out and grab the electricity between them, they had that much of a spark."

"But she was still married to the doctor."

"That she was."

"Did you think that was okay?" I asked.

"Plenty of South Lickites muttered about what a scandal it was. But hey, hon, you don't live as long as I have without learning that everyone has their own ways of being. I don't know what goes on in anybody's private lives except my own, and that's fine with me."

That was my aunt, a portrait of tolerance. "Kristina had to be almost a decade older than Jamie, right?"

"So what?" Adele lifted a shoulder and dropped it. "Her sister went and married a geezer near old enough to be her grandpop."

"Jamie mentioned that. Said she snagged him for his money." I finished my Greek breakfast sandwich, every bit as delicious as I'd thought it would be.

"There was no shortage of affection between Toni and old Tug, mind you. But I think he was starting to lose his marbles. By the time he shuffled off this mortal coil he wasn't the sharpest tool in the shed, if you get my drift."

"Jamie claimed Toni might have killed her husband herself."

"He's not the only one who says that. Maybe she slipped Tug a little something, maybe she didn't. Don't much matter. He was about gone, anyhoo. Fact is, he didn't make no provision for his boy in his estate. Left his fortune to his wife and that was that."

"Ouch. Did Jamie try to contest the will?"

Adele wrinkled her nose. "He surely did. But that Toni, she hired herself a hotshot lawyer. It was a legal signed will, witnessed and notarized. Jamie didn't have a chance."

"What does he do for work? Is he hurting for money?"

"He's some kind of writer. I think he writes stories for newspapers and magazines. Like one of them freelancers."

"Unless he's written a major bestseller, I can't imagine he's rolling in dough with a job like that," I said.

"No, indeed." Adele shook her head with a baleful look.

"He's as much of an independent businessperson as I am. It isn't always easy going it alone." No wonder he was upset about his father leaving all his money to Toni and not even including Jamie.

Adele gave me one of her big auntie smiles. "You ain't anywhere's near alone, darlin'."

"I know, and I'm glad of it." I spied a woman at the cash register literally tapping her foot. Two red-handled rotary beaters and a cast-iron skillet sat on the counter. "Duty calls." I stood. "What can I get you to eat?"

She glanced at the Specials board. "Still got the special?"

"I think so. Want that?"

"Please, Roberta. And a couple few slices of bacon, too."

"Coming right up." I hurried over to the impatient customer and rang up her items. I wrapped the skillet in blank newsprint, packed the beaters in its cavity, and slid it all into one of our larger bags. "Have a lovely holiday," I said as I handed her the bag.

"Merry Christmas," she said pointedly.

I gave her a smile. I was sticking with wishing customers happy holidays. Not everybody celebrated Christmas. Plus, today was only December third. I headed to the grill.

"Let me cook and you take a break," I said to Danna.

"Sure, thanks." She stripped off her dirty apron as she filled me in on the order status.

I poured out Adele's omelet and laid three strips of bacon next to it. "How was your visit with Marcus yesterday?" I asked. I hadn't had a chance to ask her earlier.

"So awesome. We went for a walk in the state park."

Which was sparsely populated with visitors at this time of year. I mentally let out a breath of relief. Marcus had clearly not attacked Danna or anything, but he was in essence a stranger.

"Can you believe I actually have a brother?" She smiled to herself, leaning against the counter. "And speaking of that, Mom and I are having him over for dinner tonight and want you and Abe to come, too. Can you? Josie is going to be there. She's his grandma, too, after all." Danna stuffed some feta, a few olives, and a slice of tomato into a half pita and took a big bite.

I thought. "I'm free, for sure. I'll check with Abe and let you know, okay?" I'd first met Corrine's mother a year ago and had liked her a lot. A type A seventy-year-old who still ran her own consulting business, Josephine Dunn had provided a key piece of eyewitness information in a murder investigation.

"Great."

Turner approached with a tray full of dirty dishes. "I can't believe how busy we are." His thick dark hair was mussed, even though he wore it short, and one acne-scarred cheek had a smudge of ketchup on it.

"You look pooped, Turner," Danna said. "Let me finish this and do a high-speed trip to the you-know-where, and you can break, okay?" She popped in the last bite of her sandwich.

"Thanks." His shoulders relaxed.

"That won't be much of a break, Danna," I said.

She batted away the thought. "I'm solid." She headed for the ladies' room.

I loved my employees and the way we all took care of each other.

"I mean, I know this is great for the business, Robbie, but wow." Turner blew out a breath. "We almost need a fourth person for the holidays."

"I know, to take care of retail." I sprinkled feta and olives on Adele's omelet and folded it over. The other three outstanding orders were ready, too, so I slid everything onto four plates. "We're caught up for the moment. Sit down and I'll deliver these."

"Thanks." Turner plopped onto a chair.

After I delivered the other three plates, I took Adele's to her table.

She looked relaxed, knitting something out of a soft-looking green yarn. When she saw me, she stuffed it into the bag at her feet.

"Boy howdy, that looks good, hon." She glanced at

the door when the bell jangled. "Why, if it isn't Clive Colton himself."

A thickset man not much taller than me entered and glanced around. He wore workman's jeans and boots and had a square head covered with a fuzz of thinning blond hair.

"He's been in before a few times," I said.

"He's Beltonia Franklin's husband. You didn't know that?"

"I didn't. So she remarried." South Lick had a whopping population of about seven hundred, but I'd only lived here a couple of years. I was always learning new bits about the local residents.

"Indeed she did, but it's common knowledge they aren't getting on so good lately. Fact, I think he moved out last month." She waved her hand at him. "Yo, Clive. Come on over here and set with me."

He wove his way through the tables. "Thanks, Adele. Good morning, Miss," he added, smiling at me. His cheeks were ruddy in a way that made me think he might make a habit of hitting the booze hard after work.

"I'm Robbie Jordan. Welcome. I don't think we've met."

"Clive Colton, Miss." He held out a beefy hand.

I shook it, the palm thick and callused. "Please have a seat. You and Adele clearly know each other."

"We go a fair ways back," Adele agreed. "And you two have a lot in common, Robbie. Clive here is a plumber. Can fix near about anything that has water going through it. Clive, my niece Robbie is a skilled carpenter, learned the art from my late sister, who was a cabinetmaker and creator of fine furniture."

Clive's smile split his broad face. "Couple of girl woodworkers. I like it."

My mom had been an artisan, not a girl wood-worker, but I let the comment pass. I knew Clive didn't mean any harm. "Coffee?" I asked him.

"I'd appreciate that. I don't have long before I have to get back to the job site. Could I get two fried over easy with biscuits and gravy and a double order of sausages, please?"

"Coming right up. Toast too?"

"Yes, white, if you've got it, with extra butter."

"You got it." I scribbled the order and took it to the grill.

On my way back to the table with the coffee, the doorbell jangled again. This time it was Buck. Back for lunch so soon? He surveyed the restaurant. As I watched, his gaze landed on Clive and his expression turned to dead serious. *Uh-oh.* Something was afoot, to paraphrase Shakespeare. I arrived at Adele's table at the same time as Buck.

He held his hat in his hand. "Clive, I'm afraid I have some bad news."

Clive looked up at him, blinking. "What do you mean?"

"There's no easy way to say this." Buck spoke in a low tone. "I'm very sorry, but Toni has been found dead."

Chapter Thirteen

Adele frowned. My eyes widened. Clive's mouth dropped open and the color went out of his face.

"What are you talking about?" he asked, his voice rising. "How? When? She can't be dead. I mean . . ." His voice trailed off.

Buck laid his hand on Clive's shoulder. "Her housecleaner found her not an hour ago."

"But she's so healthy," Clive murmured. "She's always doing karate and such. She's not a fat slob like me."

Buck cleared his throat. "It's possible her death was not a natural one."

No. Not another homicide. Poor Toni. Nobody deserved such an end. But why would they think that?

"We have some questions we need to ask you," Buck went on.

Clive stared at him. "What do you mean?" He sounded bewildered. As he stared, light appeared to dawn. He struggled to his feet. "If it wasn't natural, that means someone upped and kilt her?" He spoke in a harsh whisper.

"That is one possibility," Buck said.

Adele and I exchanged a glance. Turner emerged from the restroom. After he caught sight of our group, he frowned and hurried to the grill to confer with Danna, who had taken over cooking while she watched the proceedings. Some customers ate and chatted, but several locals were paying close attention.

"And you think because we'd separated that I did it," Clive said, his tone bitter. "She wasn't nice to me. She insulted me and kicked me out of the house last month. But I loved Toni, warts and all. I would never in any lifetime lift a finger against her or any other woman." He raised his chin.

"Now, Clive." Adele patted his arm. "Nobody said you did. Buck wants to ask you a couple few questions, that's all."

Turner arrived at the table with Clive's hearty artery-clogging breakfast and shot me an inquiring glance.

"Can I at least eat?" Clive asked Buck.

Buck turned his hat in his hands. "Well, now—"

Clive interrupted him. "Never mind. I'm not hungry. Let's get this over with." He grabbed the jacket he'd slung over the back of his seat. "Sorry, Ms. Jordan."

"Don't worry about it," I said. "I'm so sorry for your loss, Mr. Colton."

Adele stood. "As am I. Don't you worry, now. Everything's going to be fine."

Mute, Clive preceded Buck out the door.

"Whoee, don't this just beat the band," Adele muttered, watching them go. "One sister's skeleton found ten years after the fact, and her twin knocked off two days later. Buck and Oscar are going to have their hands plum full."

I shook my head. "Oscar's on another case. Octavia is back, investigating the remains in Doctor Geller's attic. I imagine she'll take on this one, too."

Adele looked straight into my soul. "You okay with her being in town, darlin'?"

"Yes. I have to be, don't I? Turner, why don't you take that order back to the kitchen? One of us can eat it, or we can toss it."

"Sure," he said. "I'll down the eggs and toast right now."

"Good." I smiled at my vegetarian helper.

"I don't mind helping out with them sausages," Adele offered. "I never mind extra meat in my diet. I live for the stuff."

"They're yours." Turner slid them onto her plate and headed back for the kitchen area.

Adele sat again. "Some news. No shortage of folks Toni rubbed wrong, that's for sure."

I glanced around. Things seemed under control, so I sat, too. "Jamie and Clive for starters, right?"

"That's it."

"Abe told me Toni's tenant wasn't very happy with her, either."

"Shirley Csik." Adele nodded, setting the tiny silver bells on her dangling earrings to tinkling. "She used to be a soccer star around here. Strong girl."

I set my chin on my hand. "I wonder how Toni died. Why do they think it might have been a homicide and not a heart attack or something?"

"She was youngish. Don't they have to investigate when somebody who ain't old ups and dies?"

"I suppose so. Did Toni ever have children?" Who would grieve for her besides Clive?

"No," Adele said as if it was a silly suggestion. "First off, I doubt old Tug coulda provided her with the necessary ingredient, if you catch my drift. He was already old and sick when they tied the knot." She snickered. "Plus, Toni wasn't exactly the maternal type, may she rest in peace."

"Ms. Jordan," a customer called to me.

"Enjoy your meal, Adele, if you can." I stood.

"Me?" she scoffed. "I can always eat."

"Did Buck just arrest Mr. Colton?" the woman two tables away asked me when I got there. The local's eyes were wide and her expression excited. The woman sitting opposite her looked eager for dirt, too.

Down, ladies. "No. There was an unfortunate incident earlier and Buck needed to ask him some questions."

"What was the incident? Did somebody die?"

Her friend picked up the thread. "Buck looked super serious when he took Clive away."

"I don't know the details, but I'm sure it will be in the news later on today." I plastered on a smile. "Can I clear those dishes for you?"

People could be awfully morbid. How could anyone get excited about someone dying?

Chapter Fourteen

The restaurant was abuzz with the news as the true lunch rush set in. We didn't have a lot of tourists on an early December Thursday—they would show up on the weekend—and word had spread fast among the locals. Because my reputation for working on past homicides preceded me, I was pestered with questions.

"I heared Beltonia was murdered in cold blood in her bed this morning," an older gentleman said when I delivered his hamburger—well done, no lettuce, extra sauce—and chicken soup.

"Did you? I'm sure the authorities are on the case." I smiled and turned away before he could ask me for details.

One of my chess-playing regulars beckoned me over. "Are you helping the detective on this one, Robbie?" she asked. "Poor old Toni. She never could get a break, and took it out on everybody but old Tug."

"I'm not involved. More coffee?" I wanted to ask what she meant by "a break" but really didn't want to engage in speculation, plus all three of us were flat out simply trying to run the place.

At around a quarter to one, Shirley Csik came in. A two-top had vacated, and Turner had cleared it. No one else was waiting, so after I wiped down the table, I beckoned her over. With dark hair pulled back in a thick ponytail, she was shorter and more trim than me and walked with a fluid grace like the athlete she'd been. For all I knew, she still played soccer or some other sport in an adult league. We'd never gotten to know each other during her occasional visits for breakfast or lunch.

She greeted me and sank into the chair. The buzz quieted around us. Shirley cast her gaze right and left. "Why are people staring at me?" she asked in a low voice, pretending to study the menu.

"I guess you haven't heard the news."

She looked up. "What news? I've been in Nashville all morning at the gift shop where I work."

"Your landlady was found dead this morning."

Shirley's breath rushed in with a rasp. "Toni?"

I bobbed my head.

"That's terrible. The poor thing." She brought her hand to her mouth, but looked more pensive than sad. She blinked. "Do you know how she died?"

"I don't."

"She seemed too young and healthy to have a heart attack," she said. "It must have been some undiagnosed weakness."

"You must have known her well, living on the other side of the house."

"You're Robbie, right?"

"Yes."

She frowned and cocked her head. "How do you know where I live?"

"Abe O'Neill is my boyfriend. We were talking about Toni because it's possible her sister's remains finally turned up, and he mentioned you in passing."

The suspicious cast went out of her expression. "Abe's a sweetheart. Always has been. Lucky you to snag him."

"Thanks. He's the best. So you didn't hear anything odd this morning from Toni's side of the house?"

"What do you mean?"

"I don't know. Like a thud if she fell or something?" Or a cry of protest, a struggle, anything to indicate a violent death, but I couldn't say that to her.

She shuddered. "That would be an awful thing to hear. Anyway, no, I didn't. It's a crappy building—or at least my side is—but it actually has pretty good soundproofing between the two halves."

"I see. Well, can I get you some lunch?"

"A turkey burger with no bun, please, a side of sausages, and a chocolate milk."

I jotted down the order. "Coming right up." I headed for the kitchen area where Turner had taken over on the grill. Danna was at the sink.

"Danna, let me know what I can bring tonight, okay?" I pointed to her. "Oh, and Abe texted me that he can come, too."

"Bring a bottle of white wine and yourselves," she said. "Mom and I have a menu all planned."

"Cool. Will do." The doorbell sounded, signaling a hungry-looking Buck's return. Of course, he always looked hungry. I gave Turner Shirley's order and made my way to Buck, checking for an empty table as I went. He was going to have to stay hungry a little while longer.

"Hey, Buck. Sorry, every table is full."

"I am plum starvational. Took me this long to deliver Colton to Octavia. The man did not want to talk."

"He just lost his wife and he seemed to be genuinely broken up about her death. What did you expect?"

"All right, I'll grant you that." He glanced at the full restaurant. "Got anybody fixing to leave soon?"

"That table of four might be." I gestured with my chin. "Or I can pack up a takeout lunch for you."

"I need to set my bones down and be out of the station for a piece. I can wait." He narrowed his eyes. "Say, is that Shirley Csik back there at my usual spot?"

True. The two-top I'd sat her at was Buck's preferred seat, because it was at the far end and next to the wall. He always liked to have a view of the entire restaurant while he ate. I sometimes felt like Pans 'N Pancakes was his second office.

"Yes, that's Shirley. She came in a couple minutes ago." I lowered my voice. "And she hadn't heard about Toni's death. I gotta tell you, she didn't seem too broken up about it when I let her in on the news."

Buck scratched his chin. "She didn't, huh? Interesting. She's on my list of folks to interview. Maybe I'll go see if she wants to share the table."

"Buck, no." I grabbed his sleeve. "You're not going to grill her in my restaurant while she's eating. She came in for a nice quiet lunch and she's going to get it. Nab her on her way out if you want, but I can't have my customers disturbed during a meal like you did with Clive. Unless you're going to arrest her?"

"No arrest, Robbie. But all righty, I'll be a good doobie and bide my time."

That sounded ominous, but worrying about it would be as useless as two buggies in a one-horse town, to quote Adele.

Chapter Fifteen

By one-thirty things were marginally quieter. Shirley had finished her carb-free lunch and sat reading something on her tablet. I cleared her dishes.

"Is it okay if I occupy the table a little longer?" she asked.

"It's fine. Nobody's waiting and the lunch rush is over. Take your time. Can I get you anything else?"

"No, thanks."

I handed her the check, then moseyed over to Buck, who had basically inhaled a double bacon cheeseburger and a mound of ruffled potato chips. Only a forlorn shred of tomato and one crispy chip crumb remained on his plate. He was on the last bite of his second brownie, but his gaze was on Shirley.

He spoke in a low voice. "I'm going to talk to her now, Robbie, so please don't obstruct the law."

"I guess I can't stop you." I watched as he unfolded his extra-tall frame and went hat in hand to Shirley's table.

She glanced up at him and stashed her tablet in her bag. So much for leisurely reading. The table next to hers happened to need clearing, and if I could do a little listening, too, well, it was my restaurant. I headed in that direction.

"Yes, I know who you are, Lieutenant." Shirley stood. "What can I help you with?"

"I have a couple few questions for you regarding the demise of your landlady, Beltonia Franklin."

Shirley caught sight of me. "Robbie told me after I came in that Toni had died. It's terribly sad. I don't know how I can help you."

"Welp, I need to clarify a few little small things. Would you like to set down and talk here or come on over to the station?"

Her mouth turned down, as if the thought of going to the police station tasted bad. "Here would be fine, sir."

"Very well." Buck glanced around. Nobody was sitting in the immediate vicinity. "Robbie, if you could manage not to seat anyone new next to us, I would appreciate it."

"That should be fine." Unless a big group came in, in which case we'd need every available seat and then some.

"This should cover my meal, Robbie." Shirley handed me the check and enough money to pay for it and a tip, too. "I don't need change."

"Thanks." I gave one last swipe to the table behind them and reluctantly moved on. If I scrubbed it any more I'd take off the finish.

My next ten minutes were full with delivering tickets, taking money, busing tables, and helping a customer find exactly the right gift for her mother. I visually checked Shirley's table every chance I got. So far her conversation with Buck looked like it was peaceable. Harmonious. No voices were raised, she hadn't stormed away, and he hadn't escorted her out, either. I didn't know what I'd expected and was glad it looked more like a casual chat than a police grilling of a suspect. Abe had said Shirley didn't like Toni at all. If this morning's death had been at someone else's hand, the tenant could easily acquire the label of suspect, or at least person of interest.

I'd finished ringing up a man who bought three of Adele's hats and three small jars of honey when Octavia Slade pushed through the door. I thanked him and greeted her in the next breath.

"We're still open for lunch. You can sit anywhere." I gestured toward the emptying restaurant.

"Thank you." Her gaze was on Buck and Shirley. "I'm going to join my colleague over there."

"They've both eaten already. He's interviewing Shirley."

Now she looked at me. "Yes, Robbie." She spoke with the kind of slow, borderline-impatient tone adults use to children. "I'm aware of that."

I made a little *fine, be that way* face at her back as she wove through the tables toward the policeperson and the person of interest. If the detective wanted to order food, let her ask for it. And if she didn't order it before we closed at two-thirty, tough toenails.

Danna signaled to me from the kitchen area.

"What's going on over there?" she asked, pointing her head toward the officers and Shirley.

"No clue, except Detective Slade was just a teensy

bit rude to me." I shut my mouth before I said something rude, too.

"Think Shirley is okay?"

"No clue about that, either. Do you know her?"

"She coached my soccer team when I was in elementary school," Danna said, still looking at the threesome. "She's really good at the sport. She was also great at helping energetic little girls learn how to work together."

"Do you think Shirley is a good enough player to make it onto a professional team?" I asked.

"I'd say so."

"Shirley said she works at a gift shop in Nashville. That doesn't sound like much of a career."

"Right? But she'd have to move to Chicago to play on the Red Stars. She must have something keeping her in Brown County."

A sick mother? A troubled sibling? Or a child, possibly. If anyone knew Shirley's story, Adele would. I'd ask her when I got a chance.

Turner showed up with a load of dishes. "Something's going on over there," he muttered. He faced us and made a gesture backwards with his thumb in front of his chest.

I looked. Octavia hadn't sat. She stood with hands clasped in front of her talking to Shirley, but they were too far away for me to hear. Shirley shook her head, hard. Buck made a conciliatory wave of his hands. Octavia gestured in the direction of the door. Shirley shook her head again. Buck patted her arm, then stood. Octavia reached for Shirley's elbow, but she shook her off and rose, arms folded tight over her chest. The three of them started for the exit. I headed over to intercept them.

Octavia lowered her chin, giving me a look signaling *Don't you dare interfere*. I ignored it.

"Shirley, are you all right?" I asked.

Her neck and cheeks were aflame. "Yes. They want my fingerprints, if you can believe it."

"I can, but I'm sure it's only to eliminate you," I said. From being a suspect, I would guess, but I didn't say it to her.

Octavia pulled open the door. Buck hung back.

"Dang it, Robbie," he murmured. "I gotta pay you."

"Bird?" Octavia said sharply.

"Don't worry about it, Buck," I said. "I'll start a tab for you." Actually, I wouldn't. He'd overpaid so many times I literally owed him a week of meals, not that he would take me up on it.

"Sorry about all this" were his last words to me. "Ms. Csik, if you'll kindly come with me." He ushered her out the door with gentle moves.

Octavia let the heavy door close. "I will not have you interfering in my investigation, Robbie." The tautness of her mouth carved a dozen tiny wrinkles above her upper lip.

"And I'd appreciate it if you didn't haul any more paying customers out of their chairs. It's not good for business, Octavia." I turned on a dime and made a beeline for the kitchen. She might have seen the smoke coming out of my ears before the bell jangled and she was gone. I didn't care.

Chapter Sixteen

I hurried toward Shamrock Hardware at a little after four. I was clean out of trash bags, and all the sponges in the restaurant were looking pretty grotty. In addition, a bracket had broken as Turner had tried to clean it after we closed. The bracket held our recipe book stand, which was important so we could consult the store recipes hands free. Abe's brother's store should have a replacement, since that was where I'd gotten it in the first place.

I smiled to see the store staff all wearing Santa hats. Danna and Turner and I could start doing same, but it was a little early. Last year we broke them out for only the final pre-Noel week. I rounded the end of a row and nearly ran into Sean, equally outfitted in headgear. He had his foot on the bottom rung of a step stool and held a box of lightbulbs. He worked here after school a few days a week and had probably ramped up his hours for the holidays.

"Hey, Robbie."

"Hi, Sean. How's it going?"

"Good. Can I help you find something?"

I held up the broken bracket, which I'd unscrewed before I left the restaurant. "I got this here when I was renovating my store, and it broke this afternoon."

"We can definitely replace it at no cost."

"That's not necessary. We're pretty hard on our appliances because we have to clean so often, and this sits right near the grill."

Sean shook his head. "No, my uncle is, like, really clear about the policy. Replacement of a store item if it's broken. No questions asked."

"Sounds like a great deal to me. Don's a good man."

Sean frowned. "That Doctor Geller doesn't seem to think so."

"Oh?" Geller's name sure was popping up a lot this week.

"He was in here a little while ago. He brought in a part that was broken and wanted the free replacement. He and Uncle Don got in a major argument about it."

"Why?"

"Because we don't sell that brand. My uncle said he never has. What kind of a tightwad tries to rip off a local businessman?" He shook his head.

I frowned, too. "That's crazy. It's not like Don doesn't know what he sells."

"Right? The doctor even let loose a bunch of swears. Uncle Don finally had to say he was going to call Buck before the dude would leave." He set down the box of bulbs. "Come on, I'll show you where the brackets are."

I thanked him and followed him down the next aisle to the end. New bracket in hand, I said, "I'll let you get back to work. Thanks for the help. I need a few other things, but I know where they are."

"Wait." Sean touched my arm and lowered his voice. "I've been trying to think of what to get my dad for Christmas. Can I ask you what you think about an idea I had?" His tone was touchingly sincere, especially for a teenage boy.

"Of course."

"You know how nuts he is about cooking."

I nodded.

"And he lived in Japan for a while. So I found a Japanese restaurant in Bloomington, and guess what?"

I wanted to hug this kid right now. Instead, I said, "What?"

"They give cooking classes! I talked to the lady, and based on what I told her about his experience, she'll let him into the advanced class. I've been working all the hours I can to pay for it."

"Sean, you are the best." Now I did hug him, but for only a second.

His cheeks flamed. "No, I'm not. I mean, you know, sometimes him and me, we kind of butt heads. But he's, like, a super good dad."

"What teenager doesn't butt heads with his father? Abe's going to love that gift. And, seriously, if you come up short on the amount, I'm happy to fill in the gap for you." Abe was so going to appreciate Sean's gesture, and he would enjoy the classes, too.

"That's really nice, Robbie. I hope I won't need that, but if I do, I'll pay it all back."

"Deal." We exchanged a fist bump. "See you soon."

I was on the verge of calling him "sweetie" but closed my mouth in time. We were nearly on that basis, but not quite. Geller, on the other hand, didn't sound like anybody's sweetie. Someone fighting with mild-mannered Don was almost laughable.

Chapter Seventeen

As Abe and I walked over to Danna's house at a little before six o'clock, I filled him in about Shirley being taken away earlier for fingerprinting and, I assumed, grilling, by Octavia.

"That seems logical," he said. "Their apartments do share a wall, and everybody knows Toni didn't treat her tenant very well. Folks also know Shirley was unhappy about it."

"I hate that they took her away like that in my restaurant with other diners looking on."

"I hear you."

"Abe, Adele told me Toni inherited all his dad's money. If she's well off, why in the world is she living in a duplex? That can't be where she lived with her wealthy husband."

"Exactly. I heard Toni blew through a lot of the money early on and mismanaged much of the rest. She had to sell the big house in Nashville. The duplex was all she could afford, because she could rent out the other half."

"Wow. Jamie must resent her even more for losing the house he grew up in and wasting his dad's money."

"You got that right."

We passed Corrine's vintage Jaguar in the driveway. I rang the doorbell of the modest ranch house.

"Come on the heck in, you two." Corrine pulled open the door. She gave Abe a hug and I got one, too, inhaling her cloud of perfume as she leaned down to reach me. Corrine didn't go halfway on anything. "We're setting in the family room."

I handed Corrine two bottles of wine. "One red, one white."

"You didn't have to bring a thing, hon, but I do appreciate it."

"Thanks for having us, Corrine," Abe said.

"Hey, you and Robbie are family, like."

We followed her down a hall to a comfortable room where Danna and Josephine sat side by side on a long sofa. We greeted them. Josephine had insisted I call her Josie last year when I'd met her, so Josie, it was.

"No Marcus?" I asked.

"He texted me he's running late," Danna said. "He'll be here soon."

Corrine pointed at armchairs. "Now set yourselves down, kids. Wine for everybody, or beer?"

Abe held up a hand. "Beer for me, please. We walked over, so we can both indulge a bit."

"You got it." She pointed at me. "Robbie, I got a chilled white open."

Josie held up her wineglass. "It's a very nice pinot gris, my favorite."

"I'd love a glass, thanks."

Corrine bustled off toward the kitchen from which emanated some delicious aroma I thought might be beef stew. My stomach growled audibly and Danna laughed.

"Help yourselves." She pointed at a dish of multi-colored olives, a bowl of carrot sticks next to one of hummus, and a plate of cheese and crackers.

"Thanks." I selected a fat green olive and bit around the pit.

"I'm excited to meet this young man," Danna's grandmother said. "Now I have two grandkids instead of one."

Right. Danna had said Corrine didn't have siblings.

"You're going to love him, Josie." Danna beamed.

"I'm surprised Isaac isn't here," Abe said, referring to Danna's sweetheart.

"He couldn't make it. He teaches a metalworking class on Thursday nights. Plus, I think he's a little suspicious of this new man in my life. I keep telling him he's my brother, not a boyfriend." The little ring in her right eyebrow went up. "He'll come around." She sipped from her glass of seltzer.

Corrine came back with my glass of wine and Abe's beer in a frosty mug and sat next to me, tapping her right foot. For once she wasn't wearing heels, instead clad in flat-soled red tennis shoes. Her tennies, as we called any athletic footwear back in my home state of California, were of red leather but were flat, nonetheless. The layers of her flaming red hair were more subdued tonight, too.

"Are you nervous to meet Marcus?" I asked her.

"I guess I am, a little." Her red-painted lips quavered. "I'm afraid I'm going to blubber all over the boy."

Wow. I'd never seen a vulnerable side to Corrine. We all have our weaknesses, of course, but some hide them better than others.

"You're good, Mom." Danna leaned forward, elbows on knees. "He's looking forward to meeting you and Josie, and he told me he doesn't blame you for giving him up."

Corrine inclined her head, but didn't speak.

"Robbie," Josie began. "Will you be investigating Beltonia's death? I heard talk of suspicious circumstances."

Skipping over the investigating part, I asked, "Oh? What did you hear?"

"My friend whose daughter works dispatch told me they called the crime scene team to the apartment. What with Toni's death coming so soon after the discovery of her long-lost sister's bones, and all."

"I'm not the least bit surprised," Corrine said. "Toni had more enemies than Judas and Nixon put together."

Abe let out a laugh at the image. I filed away that piece of information.

"Corrine and Josie, Danna and I were talking about Shirley Csik today," I said.

Danna picked up the thread. "Yeah. She should be playing pro soccer, but she'd have to move to Chicago or another big city to be on a team."

"Do either of you know if there's something keeping her here?" I asked. "A retail job in a gift shop doesn't exactly seem like a compelling reason to stay."

"Not really," Corrine said.

Josie shook her head. "You might ask Adele. She pretty much knows everything."

I smiled. "That's for sure."

Corrine glanced at the clock on the television. Danna saw her do it.

"I'll text Marcus and see where—" She was interrupted by the chime of the doorbell. She leapt up. "I'll get it."

Corrine stood, smoothing down her black sweater.

"It's going to be fine, sugar," Josie murmured. "You'll see."

Danna nearly dragged Marcus into the room. He was dressed neatly in a white oxford shirt and green V-necked sweater with a big bunch of red carnations in his hand, but a tic beat in his upper lip and his smile was a nervous one.

"Mom, Marcus. Marcus, my mom, Corrine, and my grandma, Josie Dunn."

Marcus stepped forward and held out his hand to Corrine. "I'm so glad to meet you, ma'am."

"Hey, there, I'm no ma'am." Corrine looked like she wanted to bear hug him, but held out her hand, instead. She folded her other hand around his and pressed, looking into his eyes. "I'd know you anywhere," she whispered. She dropped his hand and swiped at her eyes. "I'm sorry, son. We have so much to talk about, if you're willing."

His eyes were equally as damp as he sniffed. "Thank you, Corrine." He smiled through the emotion. "I'd like that."

Josie stood. "I'm not settling for a handshake, young man." She stretched out her arms and pulled him in for a quick hug. "You've just doubled my number of grandchildren and I couldn't be happier." She sat again.

"Me too." He cleared his throat and gave me a little wave. "Hi, Robbie."

"Marcus, this is Abe O'Neill, my significant other."

Abe stood and shook hands.

Corrine shook herself. "Well, now, everybody set yourselves down. Can I get you a beer or a glass of wine, Marcus?"

"No, ma'am, but thank you. A glass of water will be fine."

"Mom," Danna remonstrated. "I told you he follows Islam. No alcohol." She made a place for Marcus between her and Josie on the couch.

"I'm sorry I'm late." Marcus frowned and blinked. "A detective wanted to ask me some questions about Toni."

Octavia.

"Really?" Danna asked. The tiny silver ring in her eyebrow rose.

"I mean, Toni and I knew each other from the karate dojo." Marcus pursed his lips. "I didn't hang out with her or anything."

"So why did Detective Slade call you in?" I asked.

He stared at me as if wondering how I knew Octavia, but didn't ask. "Apparently some guy here in South Lick is slandering Muslims." His fists clenched in his lap exactly like they had in the restaurant when Geller mentioned Marcus's hat. "And I'm the closest target."

Chapter Eighteen

While the others talked over drinks and appetizers, my brain was going overtime. I'd be willing to bet the slander spreader was William Geller. He couldn't have evidence of Marcus killing Toni. Could he? I gazed at the tall young man, who, despite his dark coloring, really did look a lot like Corrine. He seemed so gentle, so intelligent. Maybe Phil could ask around at IU, see if they had any mutual friends. I thought. I didn't know anyone from the Friends Meeting in Bloomington, but surely there was contact between those Quakers and the ones in Indianapolis.

Corrine came in from the kitchen and announced, "Soup's on, gang. Come and eat."

We followed her into a surprisingly formal dining room. The wallpaper was a muted shade of red with a brocade pattern. She'd set the table with a white linen cloth, good china, crystal glasses, and cloth napkins under real silver. Chunks of crusty bread rested in a cloth-lined basket. A glass-fronted hutch set into the corner held more fine dishes and stemmed glasses, plus a few small framed pictures. The look was quite a contrast to the comfy country-decor appearance of the kitchen and den, the only other rooms I'd been in.

"Corrine, this is lovely," I said.

She threw back her head and laughed. "You sound surprised, Robbie."

"Mom, you know how different the dining room looks from the rest of the house," Danna said.

"That it is." Corrine smiled proudly. "My mama there taught me well. A woman needs a touch of elegance on a regular basis. This is my version."

Josie smiled and bobbed her head. "And you do it up nicely, Corrie."

Corrie? I'd never heard anyone use a nickname with Corrine. It must be her childhood moniker.

"Thank you. Now set yourselves down." She directed us to particular seats. "Dannie, help me serve it up."

Another nickname. Josie, Corrie, Dannie. I fit right in. Pretty soon they'd be calling Marcus Markie, I expected.

A minute later steaming shallow bowls of beef stew sat in front of each of us, redolent with carrots, pearl onions, and bite-sized potatoes. Josie poured red wine all around except for Marcus and raised her glass.

"To family," she said.

Marcus raised his glass of water. I echoed the toast along with the others and took a sip of a full-bodied red.

"Corrine, this stew is really tasty," Abe said.

"Thanks. It's pretty dang basic, but there's nothing

wrong with basic, even if you're eating off the good dishes." She smiled.

"Marcus, I hear you're in grad school," Josie said. "What are you studying?"

"Library science, ma'am. I've always been interested in information, and databases are like candy to me. I minored in computer science in college."

"So much of librarians' work these days involves the Internet, doesn't it?" Abe asked.

"It does," Marcus agreed.

"I'm a retired software engineer." Josie gazed at her grandson. "And now I have a consulting company doing the same. I'd say you came by that interest honestly, young man."

Marcus's eyes widened. "That's, uh, stunning."

"And he loves to cook, Josie, exactly like me," Danna added.

"Corrine, what did you do before you were elected mayor?" I asked. I realized I didn't know much about her life before I moved to South Lick. I knew she had her own bluegrass band and she liked to go hunting. And she'd said she'd waitressed as a much younger woman, a fact she'd revealed when she helped out at Pans 'N Pancakes once during a crunch.

"A little of this, a little of that. I can tell you the math thing skipped a generation. Even in high school algebra my eyes would glaze over."

Josie cleared her throat. "Getting your law degree isn't a little bit of anything, darling."

"You're a lawyer?" I asked. How hadn't I known that? I glanced at Abe, who gave a little nod. He clearly was aware. "Do you have your own practice?"

"I did. I'm pretty busy with the town now." She sipped her wine. "Tell us about your family, Marcus."

He proceeded to relate that he had an older sister, also adopted, and twin younger brothers his mom had given birth to. He told us about his Quaker parents.

"I've always admired the Society of Friends," Abe said. "Their idea that God is in each of us really makes sense."

"I agree," Marcus said. "And it leads to our values of equality, integrity, and nonviolence."

Our. It sounded like he still identified with the faith of his upbringing. Then I remembered Danna had mentioned that he drew from both Quakerism and Islam in his life.

"Do you mind talking about why you converted to Islam?" Corrine asked.

"Not at all. I visited the mosque in Bloomington two years ago with a friend. I can't explain it, but I felt the presence of God there more strongly than I ever had in the Friends meeting I grew up in. I began to read and thought the values of Islam—put in a modern context, of course—made a lot of sense."

"Did your parents push back on your decision at all?" Josie asked.

He laughed softly. "My grandfather asked Mom when I was going to join ISIS, but other than that, no. They raised us to make our own decisions."

Danna gazed at Corrine with fondness. "Just like this lady here did."

Corrine tossed her head. "To my regret at times."

"How do your parents feel about you connecting with your birth family?" Abe asked.

This was turning into a Grill Marcus fest, but he didn't seem to mind.

"I think Mom is a little nervous, but they were both supportive when I told them I'd found you all."

"If she ever wants to meet me, I'd be thrilled," Corrine said. "You tell her that for me."

"I will," he said.

"Marcus," I began. "Can you tell me a little more about what Octavia asked you at the station?"

Danna frowned at me. It was probably bad form to ask a question like that at such a joyous dinner, but it was out now. And I really wanted to know.

"She wanted to know how I knew Toni. How I got along with her. Where I was this morning. Stuff like that. Apparently some nutso dude hates Muslims. I don't even know him." He shook his head.

"Toni and you ate together, what was it, yesterday?" I asked. Marcus hadn't been very happy about Toni taking a place at his table, either.

"Yeah, but that was like the most social time I've ever spent with her," Marcus said. "She actually wasn't very friendly to me."

Danna was giving me a look, so I didn't pursue the subject. But I'd bet Octavia was going to. What if Toni and Marcus had had a publicly witnessed argument? They might have had other dealings Marcus wasn't letting on to. And if he had been alone during the time the police thought Toni was murdered, he might well be asked back for more questioning.

We moved beyond Grill Marcus to other, lighter topics as we ate. Corrine downed the rest of her wine and opened another bottle. "Anyone?" She offered it around and poured for those who wanted it, but her hand shook a little. Danna cleared the stew bowls after we'd finished the main course, then tossed a green salad with a homemade vinaigrette and served it.

After Corrine ate her greens, she stood. "Marcus, I have something for you. This is hard, but I need to do it." She went to the hutch and drew out a framed picture and an envelope the same size. "This is your birth father."

Danna gaped. Josie nodded knowingly. Corrine handed the picture and envelope to Marcus. He was seated across from me, but I glimpsed a dark-skinned man with a rakish smile.

Marcus gave a long look at the picture, then stood and hugged Corrine. "Thank you." His voice was full of emotion.

"You always said the guy in that photo was an old friend, Mom." Danna's voice brimmed with reproach. "You could have told me."

"I'm sorry, sweetheart. I couldn't." She touched Danna's hand, then gazed at Marcus again. "His name was Charles Morton. He was a jazz musician, and a darn talented one."

Marcus's eyes widened. "I played jazz trumpet in high school. Still do when I get a chance."

"Genes," Abe murmured.

"Where is he now?" Marcus asked softly.

"I'm sorry to say he died in a plane crash before you were born. What with me being a foolish young thing—I hadn't even gone to college yet—and him being gone, I didn't feel I could give you a good life.

That's why I gave you up. But I never forgot you. Not once." She took back the envelope and drew out a copy of the picture of Marcus's birth father as well as a baby picture. "I made you a copy. And this is you at two days old. The last time I saw you."

Chapter Nineteen

I was beating the pancake batter when Marcus followed Danna into the restaurant the next morning at six-thirty.

"Hope you don't mind, Robbie. Marcus spent the night at our house. Mom had to clear out early for a Rotary meeting, so I told him to come with me and get breakfast here."

"No problem," I said. "Good morning to both of you." The three of them, plus Josie, had a lot of getting to know each other to catch up on. Abe and I had gone home last night after a piece of chocolate cake, leaving the family still sitting around the table.

"Thank you," Marcus said. Despite his hair being damp, he again wore his Islamic cap. "Can I help with anything?"

The man was polite, I had to give him that. "No, we're a pretty well-greased machine by now, but thanks."

Danna pointed him to a chair, slipped into an apron, and scrubbed her hands. "Do we have a breakfast special?" She poured coffee for her and Marcus and took him a mug.

"Ugh," I said. "I forgot to plan one. Mocha muffins?"

"Yum," Danna said.

"You could do peppermint mocha pretty easily," Marcus piped up.

I stared at him. "That's kind of brilliant. We have a whole box of candy canes and peppermint flavoring, and of course we always have cocoa powder and chocolate chips. Let's do it." It was a perfect offering for heading into the Christmas season. If the muffins were popular, we could easily repeat the special weekly. I got a little tired of coming up with both breakfast and lunch specials every day.

"Want to crush?" Danna asked Marcus.

"Bring it." He rose and came over to the sink to wash his hands. "I totally crush crushing."

Danna beamed at him.

"Breakfast is on the house, but you'll have to wait until we open," I said.

"No worries. I don't have class until nine." He smiled. "And thank you."

Danna handed him the box of candy canes, a rolling pin, and the waxed paper dispenser. She flipped to the page in our recipe binder with the mocha muffin recipe in its plastic sleeve and went to work. I continued with morning prep. I poured the pancake batter into the plastic pitcher we used to pour it out from. I washed the mixer bowl, attached the whisk, and set to work cracking eggs into the bowl.

"That was a great dinner last night, Danna," I said. "Please thank your mom for me."

"I will. I'm glad you and Abe could be there." To Marcus she added, "They're really like family to me."

"I could tell." He finished breaking up the canes onto a sheet of waxed paper, laid another sheet on top, and went to work with the rolling pin, crunching away.

"You can grind those in the food processor if you want," I told him. "It might go faster."

"I'm good, thanks. I kind of like the Zen of it."

I itched to ask him more about his interview with Octavia but restrained myself. Even with three of us, we had to focus on getting ready.

By the time I turned the sign on the door to OPEN at seven, the first batch of muffins were in the oven, two pans of biscuits sat ready in the warmer, and sausages and bacon were ready to serve. Buck came in so fast it was like he'd been leaning on the door. Marcus had finished his task and sat bent over his phone at the table closest to the grill.

"Good morning, Buck," I said.

"Hey there, Robbie." He hovered near the coat-rack until I greeted the half dozen people who'd also been waiting.

I invited them to sit anywhere and did the same with my B&B guests, who were making an early morning of it.

Buck lowered his voice. "Sorry about Octavia yesterday. She shouldn'ta hauled poor Shirley out of here like she did. She's feeling under considerable pressure with Toni's death smack dab on top of finding her twin's bones."

"I'm sure she is. Anyway, I told Octavia what she did was unacceptable. I mean, I know you have to question people." I couldn't help myself from glancing toward Marcus. "But there has to be a better way to ask them to come in."

"I know. Thing is, the chief thinks this case is hotter than a goat's butt in a pepper patch."

"Geez, Buck." I squeezed my eyes shut for a moment. "Did you have to put that image in my mind so early in the morning?"

He chuckled. "Sorry. Phrases like that slip right out of my mouth like a greased porker . . . oh, you don't want to hear that one, neither."

"No, I don't think I do." I smiled. "So, you've determined those were Kristina's remains?"

"Yep. Indeedy they were. The old dental records trick worked for us."

"That's progress, at least. Now, you look hungry— for a change. Your favorite table's waiting for you." It occurred to me that Buck might know why Shirley didn't leave town. I'd ask him later if I got a chance.

Before he could head to his table, the door pushed open again, this time letting in William Geller and two other men. All three had blue medical scrubs showing below their winter coats. It must be surgery day in Columbus, at least for these doctors.

"Mornin', Geller," Buck said. "Gentlemen."

William said, "Good morning, Lieutenant, Miss Jordan."

"There are plenty of tables open." I gestured toward the restaurant. "I'll be by in a minute to take your orders."

"Go ahead," Geller said to his companions. "I need a word with the officer." He had dark patches under his eyes and his skin was pale, but his voice was strong and his posture erect.

The others moved on toward a four-top near the kitchen area. I probably should have gotten moving, too, except I wanted to hear this.

Geller looked at me like he expected me to go. When I didn't, he said, "Bird, update me on the progress you and your people have made on my wife's remains and her sister's murder."

"Don't got much to say." Buck cocked his head and lifted a bony shoulder in a fake-helpless gesture. "As I told you yesterday afternoon, I'm not in charge of either investigation. You're going to have to take and nail down Detective Slade for that."

"Fine." Geller nearly spat out the word and turned on his heel.

Danna gave me a frantic look. Customers needed coffee and wanted to order.

"Huh." Buck shook his head as he watched him go. "Man needs a little patience and some manners, too."

I agreed but didn't say so. "I have to get to work, Buck." I made a beeline for the coffeepot. I ran into trouble, instead.

Geller stood glaring down at Marcus. "How are you walking around free?" he asked in a loud voice. "I told them a known terrorist was in town, a man who hated my sister-in-law."

"What? Who?" Marcus slammed his hands on the table and stood. "What are you talking about?"

"Lieutenant," Geller called over to Buck, pointing at Marcus with a shaking finger. "This, this, Arab needs to be locked up."

"You're crazy, man." Marcus narrowed his eyes and shook his head, his color high.

Danna rushed to Marcus. "He's not an Arab. He's an American like you. He didn't do anything wrong!"

Bashir, whose skin was the same shade as Turner's, narrowed his eyes at Geller.

"It was his type who flew those planes." Geller's mouth turned down. "How can you let him walk free, Lieutenant? Who knows what else he and his kind are plotting?"

Marcus leaned into Geller's space and glared. "I'm not *plotting* anything. Are you?"

Everyone in the restaurant stared. I took a deep breath and prepared to go do something to restore the peace. I wasn't sure what, but I had a whole thirty seconds to figure it out.

Instead, Buck ambled over to the two. "Doctor Geller, Mr. Vandemere, let's all y'all relax, now. Doc, why don't you go set yourself down with your friends and have a nice breakfast. This young fella here ain't charged with no crime."

Whew. Leave it to Buck to defuse.

"I'm not eating in the same room as this filth." Geller turned his irate gaze on me. "And I'm never coming back."

He stumped out, leaving his fellow doctors. One looked bewildered, but the other raised his eyebrows and nodded once, as if Geller's behavior didn't surprise him. Marcus sank into his chair again. He set his forehead in his hand, staring at the table, breathing hard. Based on what Phil had said about Geller, his reaction to Marcus could be a combination of racism and anti-Islam sentiments. Marcus hadn't exactly been a peacemaker, himself.

I raised my voice and mustered a smile. "Sorry for the disturbance, everyone. I'll be right by to get your orders."

A buzz of conversation arose. Danna sniffed the air and whirled, rescuing a nearly burnt rasher of bacon. The B&B couple, who sat at the table next to Marcus, whispered to each other with worried looks on their faces.

Buck approached Marcus.

"I might should have a word with you while you're here, Vandemere, if you don't mind." He kept his voice gentle.

Marcus gazed up, the look of fury still on his face. "He's the one who accused me of murder, isn't he? The reason the detective called me in yesterday?"

"He is," Buck said. "Name's William Geller. Lost his sister in the nine-eleven attacks. Kinda been on the war path against Muslims ever since. Mind if I sit?"

Marcus flipped open his palms, as if he knew he didn't have a choice.

"Excuse me, sir?" Tanesha said to Buck. "You're an officer of the law, correct?"

"That I am, ma'am. Lieutenant Bird, at your service."

"We practice the faith of Islam. Are we safe here?" she asked.

Her head wasn't covered, and her husband didn't wear a cap like Marcus did, but there had to be variations in how people expressed the tenets of their religion.

"Yes, ma'am. South Lick is a safe community. Don't you worry about a thing now."

"And we have the best police department in the county," I added. Plus a county detective or two. Octavia wasn't my favorite person, but I had to admit she was good at what she did, and so was Buck. I hoped they would be in this case, too.

Chapter Twenty

The rest of the morning proceeded with a lot more calm, although the bits of conversation I picked up here and there often included either Toni's name or Geller's. Buck had eaten at Marcus's table, but I'd seen the occasional chuckle, so it looked more like a get-to-know-you meal than an interrogation. Both had left apparently peaceably. I knew in Buck's case that could be misleading. His intelligent brain was always at work behind his country hick, aw-shucks manner.

A number of people also asked me about the sign I'd added to the door for tonight's Bible and Brew event.

"Samuel MacDonald is organizing it, but it's open to the public," I responded. "Bring your own brew and your own Bible. There will be a small cover charge to get in. It's from six-thirty to nine-thirty and that's pretty much all I know." We didn't have a brew-pub in South Lick and, as I didn't have a liquor license, Indiana allowed customers to bring their own. Samuel had commissioned me to make up a few hot appetizers, too. He'd wanted to pay me for my time and I'd told him no way. It was always good to have bodies in the store, so to speak, especially at this time of year. I imagined holiday shopping would be part of the evening. Maybe we should call it Bible, Brew, and Browse for Baubles. Or cookware, as the case may be. "We'll have munchies, too."

"So folks are going to talk Jesus over beer tonight?" one middle-aged man asked. "Sound like my kind of evening. I'll be back for it." He glanced at his wife across the table. "What do you say, hon? Sound like fun?"

"You know I don't drink beer, sweetheart. You go on ahead and BYOB. I'll put up my feet at home and read a good mystery with a cup of doctored tea."

He rolled his eyes at her, but in a fond way.

Samuel and Adele came in at a little before eleven. It was our lull period before the lunch rush. We were sitting taking a break, at least Danna and I were. Turner was prepping his spiced Indian roasted potatoes for a lunch special. Danna frowned at her phone at the next table.

I waved at my aunt and her main squeeze. "Come on over." I popped in my last bite of sausage and drained a glass of milk.

Adele and Samuel sat across from me. "Is everything set for tonight, Robbie?" he asked.

"Yes, and a number of breakfast customers seemed excited about Bible and Brew."

"Good," he said. "Thank you for agreeing to host it. I heard about a group in Fort Wayne putting on an event like this, and it piqued my interest. Of course, they're doing theirs at a brewery. For ours, bringing bottles will work just as well. What are you planning to serve for food?"

"I'm going to do mini pizzas, Buffalo chicken wings, and little meatballs. Plus bowls of pretzels. That'll be enough, right?" I'd be working all afternoon getting the apps ready, but that was okay. The weather, while not raining—or snowing—today, was cold and miserable. I might be able to fit in a quick half hour spin on the exercise cycle in my apartment if I worked fast.

"Perfect," Adele said.

"Are you going to be able to come?" I asked her.

She stroked Samuel's weathered, age-spotted hand. "I don't care too much about the Good Book, as this man well knows. But I want to keep my sweetheart company and figgered you might could use a helper. So, yes, I'll be here for the duration."

"You're right, it'll be a lot easier with two of us." And it would. I hadn't even thought of asking for help. "Thanks, Adele."

"We'll come early and assist in the setup, too," Samuel said.

"I'd appreciate that."

"Quite the commotion in town lately, wouldn't you say?" Samuel observed.

I bobbed my head in agreement. "Plus this morning, William Geller accused Marcus of being a terrorist and murdering Toni."

"He did not." Adele stared at me.

"He sure did," Danna piped up. "It was awful. Luckily, he stormed out and said he wouldn't be back. Fine with me."

"Me too, actually," I said. "He was pretty outrageous."

"He was." Adele regarded Danna. "Did your mom get a chance to meet her boy yet?"

Danna stood and stretched her arms toward the ceiling. "She sure did, and Josie did, too. Last night. It's kind of mind-boggling, you know?"

"You have a lot to take in all of a whipstitch," Samuel said.

Adele agreed. "It's quite the afterclap, hon."

"Afterclap?" I asked. I could usually figure out Adele and Buck's jargon, but not this one.

"You know, something new that happens after you think a matter is closed, all buttoned up," my aunt explained.

Having a birth son, brother, grandson show up twenty-five years later definitely qualified as an afterclap.

"Adele, Danna and I were talking about Shirley Csik, what was it, yesterday?" I looked to Danna for confirmation.

"Right," Danna said.

"Do you know if there's some reason she stays in South Lick?" I asked, looking at both Adele and Samuel.

"Other than that it's God's prettiest pocket in the whole world?" Samuel asked. "Or at least in Indiana."

"Yes, other than that," I said. "I mean, working a retail job in a gift shop? Seems like she could do better."

"And she's a super-talented soccer player," Danna added.

Adele and Samuel exchanged a glance.

Danna picked up on it. "You two know something."

Samuel opened his mouth to speak, but Adele beat

him to it. "Her big brother Zeke is incarcerated at the Brown County jail," she said. "He's not too bright—"

"What we used to call slow," Samuel chimed in.

"Exactly." Adele nodded. "It's a pretty sad story. He was working at the market, but he upped and stole a car a couple few years ago and they nabbed him. He had a prior, too, so he got six years. Anyhoo, Shirley sticks around for her brother. He only gets a one-hour visit every week, and that girl is there regular as clockwork."

"Where are their parents?" I asked.

"Their daddy's in federal prison up in Terre Haute, and the mother died of cancer when the kids were teenagers," Samuel said. "Shirley's all Zeke's got, and vice versa, purt' nearly."

"What a sad story." I shook my head.

"So that's why she doesn't move to Chicago to play pro soccer." Danna rested her chin on her palm, looking pensive. "I guess if I was all the family Marcus had, I wouldn't move away from where he was, either. Especially if he needed me."

"Family counts for a lot," Samuel said.

Adele winked at me. For a couple of years after Mom died, she was all the family I'd had, or so I'd thought.

The bell jangled. "Speaking of family." Adele pointed to Phil, who once again was backing in with arms full of desserts.

I hurried over to help him. "Thanks, my friend. Do you have time to join us?"

"Sure." He slid the brownies onto the counter and lifted the cover on a wide shallow box. "Made something special to kick off the season."

"Gingerbread men!" My smile split my face at all

the brown grinning figures. "Thanks, man. That was a lot of work."

"It's okay. I Netflixed and iced."

Turner snorted.

"Check out the second layer," Phil instructed.

I lifted a layer of waxed paper. "And women. As it should be. These are going to go fast."

"It was fun. Dude, those potatoes smell like heaven," Phil told Turner.

"They pretty much are." He slid a pan into the hot oven. "But you'll have to wait a half hour to taste them."

I followed Phil as he sauntered over to the table in an easy athletic gait that always reminded me of a certain African-American president we'd had not too long ago. Phil's ears stuck out the same way, too. He gave Adele a kiss on the cheek and hugged his grandfather before sitting.

Danna shoved her phone in her pocket and stood. "Can I fix you all lunch before we get busy?"

"A hamburger, please," Samuel said. "Do you have any of the peppermint muffins left?"

"I'm pretty sure we do. One of those, too?"

"Yes, dear," he said.

"Bowl of soup, hon, and some of them taters when they're done." Adele smiled at Danna.

"I'll help myself, Dan, but thanks." Phil looked at Samuel. "You looking forward to tonight?"

"I am, son. In this holy season, we can all use a little more focus on the sacred instead of the profane."

Adele rolled her eyes. "By profane, he means shopping, not swearing."

When Danna disappeared into the restroom, I murmured to Phil, "She introduced Marcus to Josie and Corrine last night. Well, reintroduced him to Corrine."

"How'd it go?" Phil asked.

"Very smoothly," I said. "Joyously, you could say. But I wanted to ask if you know anybody in library science at IU, which is where he's in grad school, or any Quakers in Bloomington."

"Why?" Phil asked. "To see if he's an honest, up-standing citizen?"

"Pretty much."

"Is he a Quaker?" Adele asked.

I bobbed my head. "He was raised in the Society of Friends, yes. But he's also a convert to Islam."

"As so many brothers and sisters are," Samuel added.

"Interesting," Phil said.

"Phil, you said he might be the guy from karate. I know he does practice it. He said so when he ate lunch with Toni the day before she died."

"Does he have curly gold hair and a beard like this?" Phil traced the line of his jaw and chin. "Taller than six foot?"

"That's him."

Phil drew his brows together. "He's got a pretty quick temper. I saw him way overreact one time to a dude who bumped into him accidentally."

Marcus had reacted strongly to Geller, too. But who wouldn't, at being treated like the doctor had treated him?

Danna emerged from the ladies' room.

"I'll see what I can find out," Phil said softly. "Don't worry, Robbie. He's probably cool. Lots of people fly off the stick when they shouldn't. It doesn't make them bad."

Or murderous.

"But I'll ask around," Phil continued. "To be sure."

Greeted by the delectable aromas of frying beef and potatoes roasting in cumin and cardamom, a half dozen white-haired women pushed through the door.

"Oh my stars and nightgown," one exclaimed with a big smile, holding her hand to her heart. "Would you smell that, girls? I think I've died and went to heaven."

I stood. Investigations notwithstanding, I had a store to run. "Welcome to Pans 'N Pancakes, ladies."

Chapter Twenty-One

By three-thirty I was cooking with gas, as Adele said. Which was also literally true, since my kitchen was fueled by natural gas. I'd let Birdy into the store to keep me company, since I felt like I'd been ignoring the little guy the last few days. Right now he was weaving around my feet, purring and hoping for more bits of falling pizza cheese to snack on. I'd started my operatic favorites playlist going on my new wireless speaker, which had great sound for such a small object. And since I was the only human here, I cranked it up so the gorgeous arias soared in the quiet store.

We'd had a busy lunch rush, but nothing the three of us couldn't handle. Blessedly there had been no more wild accusations leveled or diners hauled away for questioning. Buck had come in, eaten, and left without either of us talking about murder. My helpers had made short work of the cleanup and left early with my blessing. I wanted to get to the bank, but they were open until six today.

Now I worked steadily spreading dozens of three-inch mini–pita bread rounds with a dollop of sauce and a sprinkling of my grated mozzarella-Romano blend. For toppings I scattered on sliced olives, minced green peppers, or slivered pepperoni. I'd laid out the pitas on rimmed baking sheets, and when I was finished I stretched plastic wrap over the pans and set them in the walk-in, ready to blast with a hot oven right before or during the event.

Luckily I had lots of large shallow pans. Next, I set to work on the Buffalo wings. I pulled two pans of quick-roasted chicken tenders and wingettes out of the oven and dumped them into a big bowl of my homemade Buffalo sauce. I let them sit and cool in it as I scrubbed the pans. And thought.

I supposed I'd been rude to Octavia yesterday, which I regretted. I knew she was only doing her job. I hadn't seen her again since she left with Shirley, who hadn't been back in, either. My brain meandered on to Jamie Franklin. He'd been suspicious about Toni's motivation for marrying his dad in the first place. Adele had said Toni and Tug had loved each other, though. And Jamie had sounded extremely bitter about Toni's inheritance. He must also hate her for squandering what he felt should have been his, both the money and his childhood home. What had he called her? *Evil.* That was it. Maybe he felt strongly enough about her to kill her.

Or maybe Octavia had evidence that Shirley had done the deed, and that was why the detective had insisted on taking her into the station for fingerprinting. I'd been too busy to even check news. Shirley, living in the same house, must have had a way to get into the other side.

Then there was the whole question of the skeleton

in the attic. I mused on that as I used tongs to array the coated pieces of chicken back in the shallow pans. I would warm them later on, too. Smelling made my stomach growl, so I used a fork to grab one tender and popped it in my mouth. *Sheer yum.* I covered the pans and stashed them in the cooler. I still had to make the blue cheese dipping sauce, but that was easy to whip up with sour cream, mayo, and blue cheese.

I emerged from the walk-in with arms full of ground beef and a carton of eggs. Meatballs were fun to make, and easy. I smooshed together the meat, a few eggs, bread crumbs, and seasonings like oregano, salt, and pepper. I threw in a dash of soy sauce and another of hot sauce and called it mixed, then perched on a stool to roll out Ping-Pong ball–sized spheres, laying them on a wire rack on yet another rimmed baking sheet.

Birdy butted my foot with his head and whined about not getting any raw meat. But he didn't try to jump up on the counter and help himself. He could have a treat.

"Okay, buddy." I rolled an extra-small meatball and set it in a little dish on the floor for him.

Could anyone other than William have killed Kristina and left her in the attic? Sure. The doctor worked half an hour away in Columbus. She could have been attacked in her own home and dragged up there. But by whom? Or maybe she hated her life and killed herself in the attic. Or had fallen and hit her head with fatal consequences. I wondered if they'd found her purse or anything else with her to provide a clue.

I frowned at the finished pan of meatballs. I had too many things to heat up at the last moment to bake these, then, too. The oven was still hot from the chicken, so in went the meatballs and on went the timer. They would be fine served at room temperature with toothpicks. Everything I was going to serve was finger food by design.

Too bad a murder—or two—didn't have such a neat solution.

Chapter Twenty-Two

Nashville sure knew how to decorate for the holidays. At five o'clock, dark was coming on fast, but the white lights twinkling everywhere upped the Wonderland quotient. Lampposts were swathed in greens and red ribbons, and store windows featured all manner of country holiday scenes. Carols floated on the air next to Santa's workshop, where a sign advertised that he welcomed young visitors every Saturday afternoon until Christmas.

After I'd finished my appetizer prep, I'd decided to not only hit the bank but also drive over and pay Shirley a visit in her gift shop. I hadn't quite come up with an excuse yet, but I was curious about her relationship with Toni as well as about how her visit with Octavia had gone yesterday.

Except the artsy county seat had a gift shop on nearly every block, it seemed, and I didn't know where she worked. I parked and made my rounds past fudge shops, restaurants, art galleries, and women's clothing boutiques. I hit pay dirt when I peeked my head into the Covered Bridge Bazaar—which had a working train set circling through a tiny Nashville in the window—and spied Shirley behind the counter. I wove through shelves of country-themed gifts. Carved wooden signs with cute sayings. A bin of rainbow-hued saltwater taffy. Silk scarves painted with scenes of covered bridges. Flour sack dishtowels stenciled with whimsical grinning vegetables. Crocks of handmade wooden utensils and much more. I appeared to be the only shopper.

"Let me know if I can help you with anything," Shirley called.

"Thanks." It didn't seem like she'd recognized me, but I was half hidden behind the shelves.

I paused in front of a display of T-shirts emblazoned with pictures of dogs. Flipping through, I found a green shirt with an adorable black Labrador. It would be a perfect gift for Sean, and they had a men's medium.

I took it to the counter. Shirley stood at the end with her back to me, straightening a rack of magnets. Her thick hair was loose on her shoulders, and she wore a long green sweater over leggings with low black boots.

She glanced over. "Oh, Robbie. I didn't realize that was you."

"Hi, Shirley. This is a great store."

She gestured with one hand. "It's kind of kitschy, but hey, it's a job." She looked at the shirt. "Aren't those fun?"

"I know a teenager who has a black Lab. He's going to love it."

"Let me ring it up for you." Shirley went around to face me over the counter. "Is this for Sean O'Neill?"

"Exactly. How do you know him?"

She gave me the side eye. "Because I live in South Lick? I grew up with Abe, so of course I know Sean. He's a good kid." She folded the shirt and rolled it into a neat sausage, tying it with red ribbon. "He mows our lawn in the summer months."

Interesting. Toni must have hired him. I pasted a mental sticky note into my brain to ask Sean about her and Shirley.

"That'll be fourteen ninety-five," Shirley said.

I handed her my credit card. "Hey, sorry about the detective yesterday." I shook my head. "She shouldn't have extracted you from the restaurant like that."

"It's not your fault." Shirley didn't meet my gaze as she handed back my card with the slip and a pen. "I don't mind being fingerprinted, but I agree Detective Slade wasn't the smoothest player."

"Did she question you, too?" I signed the slip.

"She sure as heck did." She handed me a small handled bag imprinted with the store's covered bridge logo, green and red tissue paper artfully sticking out. "How long had I known Toni, what kind of landlady was she, did I hear anything, the works." The corners of her mouth turned down.

"It's their job to ask questions." I tried to look sympathetic.

"Including where I was the night before and morning of the day she died. What do they think, *I* killed her? I didn't like her, and she was a crappy landlady. But, you know, if everybody killed their rotten rental owners, well, that's not much of a solution."

I laughed softly. "No, it certainly isn't. In what ways wasn't Toni a good person to rent from?"

"There was like zero maintenance on my side. Every time I asked her to fix a drawer that broke, a hole in a screen, or whatever, she always said she'd get to it, but she never did."

"Are you going to be able to keep living there?" I asked.

"I have no idea. I suppose it'll be up to Clive. He was her husband, so I'd think he's got to be her heir. But I haven't heard a thing about if he wants to be a landlord, is going to sell the place, or what."

"I hope you can stay. If you want to, that is."

"I need to live close by the—" She caught herself.

By the prison? Why didn't she want people to know about her brother? Shame? A need for privacy? Or maybe some other motive was involved.

"I need to live in the area. This job doesn't pay much, and my low rent almost made up for all the problems." She rubbed the back of one hand with the other, staring at them with a frown. She looked up at me. "This morning when I woke up? I realized there was something I didn't tell the detective. That is, I hadn't remembered I'd seen it until today."

I waited without speaking.

"Sometime that night," Shirley went on, "or in the early morning hours, I got up to use the bathroom. I glanced out the back window, and I could swear I saw someone sneaking away from the house."

Toni's murderer. I grew quiet. Time seemed to slow. The spiced scent from a cinnamon candle pricked my nose. A tinny din of Christmas music lilted in from outside. My feet radiated warmth in my fur-lined boots. How could she have conveniently forgotten this sighting when she was talking to Octavia? On the other hand, why tell me about it if she had anything to hide?

"Did you see anything about the person?" I asked softly. "Height? Gait? And why do you say he or she was sneaking?"

She reached out and straightened a display of covered bridge magnets, pondering my question. "The person was tall, wore pants. He—or she—wore a watch cap and a dark coat, but I didn't get a good enough look to tell if it was a man or a woman. I only saw him from behind. You know how much folks bundle up in the cold weather. I said he was sneaking because his head was kind of hunched into his shoulders."

"Did you see him walking?" A tall person, indeed. Like Marcus, Jamie, and William, for instance?

"Not really. He'd stopped on the front walk moving away from Toni's door. When he started to glance back at the house, I leaned away from the window. By the time I looked back, he was disappearing around the corner."

So she hadn't seen if he had a limp like William Geller's. A pity. She hadn't seen the person exiting the house. "Are you going to tell Buck or Octavia what you saw?"

A group of white-haired ladies bustled in with a clatter of chatter, oohing and aahing over the products for sale. I took a second look. One was the "oh my stars and nightgown" woman who'd eaten at my place earlier. I smiled to myself. Somebody should compile colorful local sayings—like that one and the phrases that came out of Buck's and Adele's mouths—into a book.

Shirley called out a welcome to the women.

"I won't take up any more of your time, Shirley," I said. "Thanks for the shirt." I slid around the shoppers and made my way out. A tall figure in the dark. And she hadn't answered me about telling the authorities. Something seemed fishy about her suddenly remembering the shadowy figure. If Shirley herself had killed Toni, this story could be a ruse to shift the blame onto any number of tall people. Or she might have simply seen a person passing on the sidewalk. I could certainly remedy the lack of reporting. It was Octavia's job to follow up on the alibi part.

Chapter Twenty-Three

I shouldn't have been surprised at how popular Bible and Brew would be, but I was. My restaurant was full of adults sipping, nibbling, conversing, and consulting their holy books. I saw Bibles bound in black leather and some paperback New Testaments. One woman about my age was even looking at hers on a Kindle. The types of brews people carried in varied, too, from Bud, PBR, and Strohs to the finest microbrews the region had to offer.

I'd decided to request a cover charge instead of running a bunch of tabs for appetizers. Samuel had been fine with the plan, and nobody had balked at the amount. The fee would also pay for the cost of washing all the small plates we were going through and beer glasses for those who requested them. And it would take care of the cost of light and heat at a time of day I usually didn't have to use either in the restaurant.

By eight o'clock, both Adele and I had been running our butts off for an hour. At first she'd sat at a table near the door taking the covers while I drew pans out of the oven or the warmer and slid fresh ones in. Now that newcomers had dwindled, we were busy keeping the food refreshed. Every table had a bowl of pretzels and one of peanuts, but mostly the biblical locals were restocking their plates at the long table where I'd set the meatballs, pizza-ettes, and Buffalo bits with the dipping sauce. Almost all of which we were going to run out of soon. At least we didn't really have to wait tables unless someone left, in which case we had empty plates to pick up. I'd had to mop up after a beer got knocked over, too.

Jamie Franklin was talking intently at a four-top with another man. I'd greeted Jamie when he came in but hadn't been near him since. I moseyed over with a bag each of peanuts and pretzels. Had he been the tall figure Shirley claimed to have seen? I'd sent a text to Octavia as soon as I'd gotten home from Nashville. She could follow up with Toni's tenant.

"Need a refill?" I asked, proffering the bags.

Jamie glanced up and did a double take. "Hi, Robbie." He looked back at the bowls, frowning.

His companion, an older guy with a shaved head and ski-jump eyebrows, shook his head. "I think we're set. Them wings sure were good, though." He smiled through a graying beard reaching halfway to the second button on his shirt and gestured to a plate piled high with red-stained wing bones.

"Thank you," I said.

"Robbie," Jamie began. He took a cloth bag off the back of the chair where he'd hung it. "I'd, uh . . ." His voice trailed off and his gaze went to the door.

I looked in that direction too, to see Clive Colton slip in. Toni had died only yesterday. Maybe he'd come to find solace in talking about the Bible. Jamie waved him over. *Interesting.* Jamie hadn't liked Toni, but her husband was okay with him? Apparently.

As Clive made his way to the table, receiving what looked like condolences on his way, Jamie murmured to me, "I need to talk with you before I leave. I have something—"

And then Clive was at the table. Jamie clapped his mouth shut and hung the bag back over the corner of the chair back.

"Evening, Clive," I said. "And welcome." He'd clearly been grieving from the look of the dragging lines in his broad face, but I thought it was a good sign he wanted to be here for the comfort of friends and faith.

He handed me the cover charge, which we'd clearly posted at the entrance. Adele and I had figured an honor system would be fine with this crowd after the first hour.

"Thanks for doing this, Ms. Jordan." Clive set a six-pack of Rooftop IPA on the table.

"You're welcome, but please call me Robbie. I'm so sorry for your loss."

He thanked me with watery eyes. As I moved away, the three men joined hands and bowed their heads, lips moving in silent prayer. I was dying to find out what was in the bag that Jamie wanted to show me. I clearly was going to have to wait.

I passed Samuel laughing with several others.

"Of course you can read it that way," he said. "But in this verse"—he pointed to his open Bible—"the message seems to be exactly the opposite. Wouldn't you agree, Robbie?"

I held up both hands—which held a bag each—and smiled. "I'm not getting involved in what the Bible says. You can work it out among yourselves. But I will get involved with your snacks." I topped up the peanuts and refilled the empty pretzel bowl.

"Thank you, hon," said a woman sitting next to Samuel.

I headed to the appetizer table. "How's it going?" I asked Adele.

"These five are the last meatballs. The wings and tenders are finished, and there's just one more pan of pizzas in the oven."

"Did you get any?"

"Indeed I did." She took a swig from an open bottle of Strohs at the end of the table. "I helped myself to an assortment right at the start."

"Good." I'd had a few bites before we opened, too.

"What in tarnation is Clive Colton doing here?" She lifted her chin to point at him. "One day after losing his wife. It's just not right."

"I wondered that, too. Grabbing some Christian comfort, I guess."

"You might could have a point there, Roberta." When the timer dinged, she hurried over to take out the little rounds.

I busied myself tidying up the table. I took the empty Buffalo tray to the sink as Adele transferred the little pizzas to a serving platter.

"Maybe I'll take Clive a plate, since he came late." I loaded up a plate with two pizzas and three meatballs.

"That's a sweet gesture. I doubt he's eaten today."

When I set it down in front of Clive, I said, "We're

almost out of the hot appetizers. I thought you might want something to eat."

"That is surely a nice thing for you to offer, Ms. Robbie."

"My pleasure."

"I'm Clive." He blinked at the plate. "My dear late wife, she wasn't supposed to eat things like this. No, indeed she wasn't."

I tilted my head, about to ask why.

Jamie piped up. "She'd had a cardiac condition for a long time."

Ah. Also, curious. Shirley had said Toni was super healthy. She must not have known about the problem with Toni's heart.

Clive went on. "Beltonia took medicine for it and all, but Doc wanted her to avoid red meat and cheese and such. And she tried real hard to follow his advice. Guess that's what you might call ironic," which he pronounced EYE-ronic, "that I eat all this crap and I'm alive and kicking. She was working on staying healthy and look what happened to her. Gone. Permanently and irrevocably gone." He popped a meatball into his mouth.

I hoped he didn't actually think my cooking was crap, but, whatever.

Jamie stood. "Excuse me for a minute," he said to his companions. He grabbed the cloth bag and cleared his throat. "Robbie, can we talk somewhere more private?"

I glanced around. Nothing and nobody seemed urgently in need of me. "Sure. We can go over to my office area in the far corner there." I half perched on my desk when we got there. "What's up?"

"I . . ." He squeezed his eyes shut for a moment, then opened them. "I have had this bag for ten years." He extended the handles of an IGA reusable grocery bag to me.

I gazed at him. This was about Kristina. It had to be. The bag was heavy in my hand.

"Kristina had kept a daily journal for years." Jamie's voice quavered. "She told me she had become frightened of her husband. She wanted me to keep these safe for her."

Wow. "After she disappeared, did you read them?"

"No. She made me promise not to, and I didn't. But now, knowing she's dead? What's the point? And if that monster of a husband killed her, I want him brought to justice."

"You mean William Geller."

"Yes." He swallowed. "I still haven't looked at them, but I know you're honest, Robbie, and that you and Buck are friends. And you have caught killers before."

"Not really, I haven't." I'd kind of gotten involved in more than one homicide case, sure. All I'd tried to do was help the police, though.

"Will you hand them over for me?" Jamie pressed.

"Wait a sec." This didn't make sense. "Why don't you give them to Buck yourself? Or to the detective investigating the remains?" I saw him wince at the word. I didn't blame him. I'd had the same reaction when a friend of my mom's had been murdered in Santa Barbara earlier in the year. I should have softened the word somehow. "The detective's name is Octavia Slade."

"I, I don't know." He squinted out of one eye. "You could say you found them somewhere?"

"I can't do that, Jamie." I peered at him. He hadn't sounded stupid before, and he was at least forty, but *geez*. "I don't understand why you don't want to turn the journals over to the authorities." I glanced into the bag. Nearly a dozen hardcover notebooks lined up like sad mourners in a funeral procession. I tried to return the bag to him, but he backed up a step and shook his head.

"All right, I'll give Buck the journals," I said. "But I'm warning you, either he or the detective is going to want to ask you questions about them, how you got them, and what's in them." A lot of questions.

Jamie's shoulders slumped in relief. He pumped my hand, saying thank you three times over, and headed back to his friends, his beer, and his Bible. As for me, by the time tonight's affair was over and we'd cleaned up, it would be way, way too late to call Buck. It couldn't hurt for me to take a peek at what the mysterious and now dead Kristina had written. Nobody would know. My conscience gave me a teensy bit of pushback, but I told it to shut up and go away. A quick read couldn't hurt. That was my position, and I was sticking to it.

Chapter Twenty-Four

The event wound down at about nine, and Adele and Samuel insisted on sticking around to clean up. Before they left, he reserved the first Friday in January for a repeat performance.

"I thought it went really well," he said. "How about you, Robbie?"

"I couldn't agree more." I'd cleared a surprising amount of money from the cover charge, plus quite a few people had also topped up the tips jar. "And if the next one draws even more folks, I can hire Danna or Turner to help so you both can enjoy yourselves."

Samuel beamed, but behind him Adele rolled her eyes. "We'll count those eggs when they hatch, Roberta." She stepped forward and bussed my cheek. "Right now I got to get two sets of old bones home."

"Thank you for your help, favorite aunt. Good night, Samuel."

"God bless." He kissed my cheek, too.

I made myself stay in the clean restaurant for another half hour doing high-speed breakfast prep.

Otherwise tomorrow morning would kill us. So to speak.

Back in my apartment, I answered a sweet good-night text from Abe with a similar message and a big YES for dinner together at his place tomorrow. Then, yawning and wearing PJs, a fleece, and slippers, I settled in at ten on the couch in my apartment with Birdy, a bourbon, and a book. A handwritten book penned by a woman a decade dead.

My thin blue cleaning gloves felt odd holding a glass of whiskey, but I'd pulled on a new pair before I'd extracted the first journal from the bag. I didn't want any trace of me on the cover or pages, just in case. I sipped and set down the glass, enjoying the warmth traveling through me as I opened the cover to the first page. It began:

Worst Thanksgiving of my life. Which might not last much longer if I don't get out of here.

I blew out a breath. The poor woman. I peered at the date. Sunday, December 1. Ten years ago this week. I took another sip and stroked my kitty with my foot before reading on.

W found my cash stash and came at me with the pry bar. I think he bruised the bone on my thigh before I got the bathroom door closed and locked. He only hits me where it won't show.

I shuddered.

J wants me to come to him. I don't think he's prepared for what W will do if I leave. We need, I don't know, new identities. Passports. Somewhere we can escape to where he'll never, ever find us.

Kristina hadn't gotten away in time. And Jamie, out of loyalty, hadn't read the journals, or so he said.

He must not have, because if he had, William would have been investigated while his wife's death was still fresh. I really needed to get these to Octavia or Buck, and soon. I read on.

At least tomorrow is Monday. He'll be away all day. I can get to my safe deposit box, the one he doesn't know about, and hide the money he didn't find. I wish I could talk to my sister, but that's a no-go.

A secret safe deposit box. Where could the key be? Did Jamie know about it? Maybe he had the key. Or maybe . . . I took out all the other journals and flipped through to see if she'd taped the key anywhere. No luck. I also didn't see any cryptic notes about a bank or a box number.

I yawned again. In the last book, a phrase caught my eye as I was closing it. I opened it again but couldn't find the page. Had it been the word "attic"? Why? Maybe she'd had a premonition or a dream about danger in an attic. I gave up when I couldn't find it, and stored all the books neatly in the bag again. I couldn't stay up another minute, even though I realized this would be the last chance I'd have to peruse them. Unless I didn't turn them over promptly tomorrow, and that would be neither cool nor appropriate. I wanted whoever had killed both twins to be caught and prosecuted. Soon. The journals had to be able to help the investigation somehow.

Chapter Twenty-Five

"Are you all right, Robbie?" a ruddy-cheeked Danna asked when she came to work in the morning. She tied on an apron and peered at my face.

"I'm fine. But I didn't sleep very well." Images of Geller going after Kristina with a pry bar had alternated with nightmares of him coming after me with a foot-long syringe. "I'd finally fallen into a solid sleep when my five-thirty alarm went off." My eyelids still felt like they were lined with sandpaper.

"That's no fun," she said.

"Yeah. Looks like it's cold out there."

"It totally is. Clear and frigid. It's actually great ice-skating weather, you know, when the pond freezes hard but the ice hasn't gotten messed up with snow. Isaac and I are going to go this afternoon."

"Have fun." I was still a Californian in that regard and didn't get the allure of going out on frozen water in super-cold weather to make your feet even colder by skating. "Make sure the ice is solid." The first time I'd stepped onto a frozen lake I'd been terrified I would fall through, even though it was posted by the town as safe to go out on.

"Yes, Mother." Danna rolled her eyes but smiled as she did. She busied herself checking and restocking the condiment caddies.

"Hey, falling through the ice is a valid concern."

"Robbie, it's fine. You're such a West Coaster."

"What can I do? At home the only place people ice-skate is indoors. And even that never appealed to me." I smiled and shrugged. "Anyway, I thought of a breakfast special. How about creamy cheesy Christmas grits? We do our usual recipe but sprinkle minced red and green peppers on top to make it look festive." Our creamy cheesy grits—the perfect comfort food—was always popular in cold weather.

"I like it." She gave me two thumbs up. "And it looks like you're way ahead on pepper prep." She pointed to the two piles on the cutting board in front of me. "I'll go write it on the board."

I scraped my mincings into two containers and set them to the side, then commenced cracking eggs into the dry pancake mix.

When she came back, Danna said, "For lunch we can do a split pea soup, but add in fresh frozen peas and minced tomatoes at the end so the peas stay bright green."

"Good idea. We have that frozen ham stock, and remember, we made it up already seasoned with sautéed onion and garlic." I hoped the stock would defrost in time. If she started heating it now, it should, and split peas didn't take long to cook. Adele had given us a couple of big ham bones last month, so I'd simmered them in an aromatic stock for a few hours and saved it for a late-fall soup. It sure already felt like winter out there even though by the calendar we still had two and a half weeks until the season's official start. "Can you get the stock heating?"

"Sure." Danna brought out two gallon-containers from the freezer and ran them under hot water to loosen the frozen stock. She slid the frozen chunks into our biggest pot and set it to simmer on a back burner. "How was the beer party last night?"

"It went well." I switched on the mixer to beat the pancake batter and started cracking eggs. "More people showed than I expected, and Adele and Samuel helped clean up." I glanced at my desk where I'd set the bag of journals. I'd texted Octavia this morning that I had something pertaining to Kristina's remains she might be interested in. I'd realized she was the person who should have them, not Buck. And adulting was all about doing the hard things, the things you don't really want to but know you have to, wasn't it? Octavia was the last person I wanted to see. She was going to want to read those journals, though, and they were in my possession.

"Cool."

"We'll try it one more time with only Adele helping me, but if January's crowd is even bigger, I'm going to ask you or Turner to work, if you will. For extra pay, of course."

"Sounds good to me." She squinted one eye. "Did people really talk about the Bible while they drank beer?"

I laughed. "Believe it or not, they did." I caught

sight of the clock. "Yikes. Five minutes. We ready?" I stirred the grits.

Danna glanced around. "Looks like it. I'll take first shift cooking."

"Perfect." I took a last sip of coffee and set my mug in the sink before heading to the door. Unlock, flip sign to OPEN, grab handle and pull. All things I did every morning but Monday. What I'd never been greeted with before was Octavia standing at the head of the line of hungry diners. And she looked peeved instead of peckish.

"Good morning, Octavia. Please come in. Good morning, everyone." I stood back and let a half dozen locals file in after the detective, who stood to the side rather than taking a table.

After they had passed, she said, "You have something for me?"

"Yes." I considered asking her to wait until I'd poured coffee and taken orders, but that could snowball into an hour of helping customers. Better to get this over with quickly. I led her to the desk and handed her the bag.

"What's this?" She took it, frowning.

"It contains Kristina Geller's personal journals. Last night Jamie Franklin brought in the bag and gave it to me. I told him he should take it to the station and turn it in, himself, but he was reluctant and asked me to. I'm not sure why."

"I assume he had read the journals?"

"He said he hadn't." But had he?

"Did you, while they were in your possession?" Octavia asked.

Truth or lie? I chose the high road. "I glanced at one. It was from exactly ten years ago. Kristina mentioned being beaten by her husband and hiding money so she could escape with Jamie."

She folded her arms, still holding the bag. "Interesting. You know, of course, you were tampering with evidence and had no business reading these."

"I didn't tamper with anything. I even wore gloves when I handled the book." I kept my voice level. I wasn't going to grovel and apologize for reading Kristina's desperate words. I wasn't the one who had sat on the journals for a full decade. Let her grill Jamie about that.

"Be that as it may. Are you quite sure the deceased wasn't writing a novel?"

A novel?

"The words you read could be pure fantasy," Octavia went on.

In the restaurant, a man waved at me, and an older woman pointed to her coffee mug. Her empty coffee mug.

"Octavia, I have no idea. I'm going to go ahead and let you figure that out. Right now I have a restaurant to run. If you'll excuse me."

She cleared her throat. "I'd like to eat while I'm here."

"You are welcome to sit anywhere you'd like." I hurried off to wait on customers who weren't going to give me a hard time about doing my civic duty and Jamie's dirty work in one fell swoop.

Chapter Twenty-Six

Buck set the bell to jangling twenty minutes later as I was loading my arms with food. He headed straight for Octavia's table. *Darn.* I'd wanted to intercept him and see if he knew anything new.

Octavia had ordered a small bowl of grits, two scrambled, and a bowl of fruit salad. Her meal, being behind all the other orders, was only now ready. I set it down in front of her and greeted Buck. Octavia hadn't taken out Kristina's journals, not that I could tell, anyway.

"Mornin', Robbie. Shoo-ee, it's as cold out there as . . ." He glanced at Octavia. "As a well-digger's belt buckle in Antarctica." He pulled off his watch cap and slid out of a police-issue winter coat.

I poured his coffee. "What can I get you to eat, Buck?"

"This cold gives me a hunger." He gazed mournfully at Octavia's grits. "How about a double-regular helping of them pretty grits? That tiny itty-bitty bowl she's got wouldn't satisfy my left baby toe. Plus one of them Kitchen Sink omelets y'all are so good at. With sausage and a side of flapjacks, please."

"You got it." I scribbled on my order pad, smiling.

Octavia slid her hand over her bowl. "Don't even consider taking my grits as an appetizer, Bird." She gave a half smile. "They're absolutely delicious, Robbie. You've outdone yourself."

I was so surprised at both her smile and the compliment, I almost uttered one of Buck's regular phrases, "Well, butter my butt and call me a biscuit." I restrained myself. "Thank you. It's a popular dish when the weather is like this."

"Sticks to your ribs better than about anything," Buck agreed. "Like a burr on a burro's rear end."

I shook my head. At least he didn't say "butt."

"Say, Detective, whatcha got in that there bag?" He pointed at the cloth bag on the chair between them.

Octavia lifted her chin in my direction. "Ask her."

I reprised for him what I'd told her about the journals, including where I'd gotten them and what I'd read.

"Welp, that's purty interesting," Buck said. "I can't imagine young Franklin didn't read them, though. Doncha think? Sit on his sweetheart's private words for ten whole years? Unlikely."

I'd wondered the same thing.

"The part about Kristina claiming Doctor Geller was beating her is what interests me," Octavia said. "Bird, we'll need to send someone to area hospitals and find out if she'd been treated for her injuries."

"Yes, ma'am. We can do that. Carl mighta found

evidence on her bones, too." Buck's stomach let out a hungry noise. He gave me a wistful look.

"I'll put your order in right now, Lieutenant." I headed in Danna's direction smiling. Never get between a tall hungry man and his breakfast. I handed Danna Buck's order. "His usual modest breakfast."

"As if. Anyway, I'm on it, but there are a few orders ahead of him."

We were nearly full, only a half hour after I'd turned the sign. The door opened, letting in Josie with a rush of cold air. I waved, and she bobbed her head in acknowledgment but didn't smile. *Uh-oh.* I made my way to her.

"Good morning, Josie. We still have a couple tables open."

She greeted me. "Thanks." Her dark hair had remarkably little gray in it for a seventy-year-old, but the frown she wore as she gazed in Danna's direction accentuated the lines in her face.

"Is something wrong?" I asked in a murmur.

"I might have learned something about young Marcus that's troubling me. I'm not sure whether to tell Danna yet or not."

Related to what Phil said about Marcus being quick to anger, maybe, and to how I'd seen Marcus react to Geller? The bell on the door jangled behind her and a party of four lean women about my age bustled in, all clad in running gear. They'd had an early start. They smelled of fresh air, and their flushed cheeks indicated this was the end of their run and not the start. All wore headbands with lights on them, as well as reflective pants and flashing red lights on armbands, necessities for a predawn jog.

"Good morning," I said to them. "Josie, go grab that open two-top. I'll stop by and get your order. If you want to tell me what you found out, I'll listen."

She nodded and made for the small table with a quick detour to the grill to give her granddaughter a kiss.

"Breakfast?" I asked the runners.

"Please. We earned it," the shortest one said.

"We just did our weekly long run," a taller one said, pulling off her watch cap.

"We're training for the Boston Marathon," the first added.

"We all qualified last month in Indy," Taller said. "Fifteen hilly miles is some workout, but we have to keep at it if we're going to make it over Heartbreak Hill."

"I know those hills." I smiled. "I'm a cyclist. Sometimes it seems like the whole ride is uphill. When's the race?"

"It's in April, on what they call Patriot's Day back East."

"Good luck," I said. "You can take that last open table and I'll be right over to take your order."

I grabbed the coffeepot and aimed myself for Josie, but had to top up a few mugs on the way. Buck and Octavia were conversing with intense looks on their faces, making me wish I was a fly on the table, or better, a tiny surveillance drone. Buck was sometimes forthcoming with me about cases. Octavia, not so much.

"Thanks, Robbie," Josie said after I filled her mug, looking up from a tablet device on the table.

"What can I get you to eat?"

"The grits sound good. Can I get a small bowl?"

"Of course."

"And one fried egg, over easy, with bacon and wheat toast, please." Her frown carved little canyons between her eyebrows and she blinked, as if it helped her think.

I waited for a moment to see if she'd offer up her information. She looked back at her tablet, instead, so I stopped by the runners' table and jotted down what they wanted, then took the orders to Danna.

"What's up with my grandma?" Danna asked. "She looks worried about something."

"She does. I don't know what it's about. I have her breakfast order, though. Want to swap? I'll cook and you handle the front. Maybe she'll tell you." And maybe Buck would stop by and tell me what he knew after Octavia left, too.

"Sure." She traded her greasy apron for a fresh one and loaded up her arms with the orders that were ready. She pointed to the grill. "These are for those two couples. Buck's is up next."

"Got it." I poured out three disks of pancake batter, slid on a couple of sausages, and added a handful of chopped onions, mushrooms, and peppers to sauté for his omelet. The Everything-and-the-Kitchen-Sink omelet had veggies, crumbled bacon, and grated cheddar, and was a popular menu item among the hearty-eater crowd. I checked the runners' orders, too.

When I glanced up, Octavia was headed out the

door, a black beret on her head and bag of journals in her hand. *Good.* With any luck, I would get a chance to chat with Buck. I ladled out a round of beaten egg and flipped everything else. A minute later I dinged the bell, but Danna didn't hurry over. She stood in front of Josie with her arms folded, shaking her head. That didn't look good at all.

Chapter Twenty-Seven

By the time Turner breezed in at eight, Danna was nearly sprinting trying to keep up. Ten people waited for tables. Everybody wanted to go out for breakfast on a Saturday morning, apparently. I hadn't had a chance to ask Danna what Josie knew.

"Hey, Turner. How are you this morning?" I asked.

"I'm glad to be inside where it's warm. We're having a real cold snap out there. But I'm here and ready to rock and roll." He slid an apron over his head.

"Good, because that's what this place is doing today. Start with busing, okay?"

"Yes, boss." He glanced at Danna, who stood taking a couple's order without her usual relaxed, happy face on. "What's eating her?"

"I don't know. I think Josie told her something Danna didn't want to hear."

"Huh. Maybe I can worm it out of her." He grabbed a tray and a damp rag and headed for a recently vacated table.

I worked steadily through the orders. When Danna

arrived to deliver them, she didn't make eye contact as she loaded up and turned to go.

"Danna, what's going on?" I asked softly.

"I can't talk about it right now." She shot a look in Josie's direction and strode away.

All righty, then.

Tanesha and Bashir emerged from the stairs to the rooms above. They stood as if not sure about something. She looked intently at him, saying something, but they were too far away for me to hear what. He shook his head, hard. First argument of the brand-new marriage, perhaps? She tucked her arm through his—not a serious disagreement, apparently—and they headed toward me.

"Good morning." I smiled at them. "I hope you're enjoying your stay."

"We are, thanks." Bashir's voice was soft. "But my wife has a question for you."

"Of course." I flipped three pancakes and poured out a disk of eggs. "Excuse me if I keep working."

"No worries," he said.

"Robbie, are you sure we're not going to be harassed for our faith here?" Tanesha asked. "This is such a, you know, mostly all-white town, and you have like fifteen Christian churches. After what that man said yesterday, well, I'm worried."

Bashir laid his hand on her back with a light touch. "It's that we've had trouble before. At home in Minneapolis, we live among others of our faith and we garb ourselves accordingly. But when we venture into certain areas, we encounter gentlemen like the one who stormed out of here because he didn't like that young man. You know, who make false accusations simply because of our faith, which is a peace-loving one."

"That guy was no gentleman, honey," she protested.

"I agree," I said. "His behavior was uncalled for."

Her husband went on. "So we thought we'd go incognito down here. My grandmother was from French Lick, and I've always wanted to come back to where I spent some of my happiest childhood days."

"But we didn't want anyone to hassle us." Tanesha leaned into him. "I think we should go home early. But if you think we're safe, Robbie, we'll stay until Tuesday as planned."

I considered this as I plated up the pancake order, added three links, and rang the bell. "I can't guarantee your safety. But I will say that kind of slur is basically unheard of in South Lick. Of course, there are ignorant types everywhere. But as I mentioned yesterday, we have an excellent police force and we really are a peaceable community." If you didn't count a half dozen murders.

"Thanks," Bashir said. "Come on, sweetheart, let's eat and talk it over."

Tanesha thanked me, too, and followed him to a two-top across the room.

Buck moseyed over. "Figgered you needed my table. Sure was a good breakfast, Robbie." He handed me too much money, as usual.

"Thanks. Glad you liked it." I carefully turned an order of two over easy and lowered my voice. "Any news on either of the cases?"

He turned his back to the restaurant and leaned

an elbow on the counter. "Not much. Only been two days, you know, for poor Beltonia."

And ten years for her sister. "Can you at least tell me how Toni died?"

"Octavia's people are still working on that. Autopsy's scheduled for this afternoon, I do believe. Kind of frustrating, between me and you. I saw her corpse after the cleaning lady called us," Buck said. "She had this look of panic on her face. It was the oddest thing."

"Panic. But why?" I smelled something overdone and turned my focus onto the grill. I saved the bacon, turned a few pancakes, and slid the eggs onto a plate.

"Autopsy can answer that. There are drugs, though, that can make you stop breathing. Anybody would panic at that feeling."

I shivered, remembering something from my dreams. Was it a giant syringe? The memory faded away, as dream memories do.

"Anyhoo," Buck went on, "the other odd thing was that the woman wasn't wearing nothing but her birthday suit. In December, can you believe it? She had a puffy quilt on the bed, but it wasn't covering her." He shook his head. "Who goes and gets herself in bed alone in the altogether? You know, buck naked, so to speak."

"Huh. Maybe she liked the feeling of being naked between the sheets." I wasn't going to get personal and tell him I enjoyed that feeling, myself, in the summertime. He and I were friends, but not that good of friends. I dished up the pancakes and bacon, buttered two slices of toast, and dinged the Ready bell.

"Leastwise she had the heat on," he continued. "It wasn't that cold in the bedroom. Sure would like to know what killed her, though. And more important-like, who."

"Why does Octavia think it was murder and not a heart attack?" I asked. "Somebody told me Toni had cardiac issues." Who had it been?

"Is that so?" Buck cocked his head.

The source came to me. "It was Jamie Franklin, last night at Bible and Brew."

Danna arrived and grabbed the finished plates.

"Thanks, Danna," I said.

She inclined her chin without speaking.

Turner slid past her and deposited dirty dishes in the sink. "You were right, Robbie," he said. "It's super busy this morning."

"I'll say," I agreed.

"Shoot," Buck said. "I wanted to go to that there Bible party last night, but duty came first. No drinking for me during a murder investigation."

I smiled. "Samuel and I are going to do it again next month. We'd love to have you. Anyway, Clive said Toni took medication for her heart."

"I'll check with the good detective, see if she's aware of that. I best be getting to work, now. You take care, Robbie."

"Thanks, Buck. You too."

He pulled his black cap down over his ears.

"And Buck?" I added. "Good luck."

Chapter Twenty-Eight

Danna was still frowning two hours later. Only a few of the tables were occupied. I'd taken a quick pit stop and then munched a grilled sandwich with a discarded broken fried egg I'd topped with cheddar.

"Danna, why don't you take your break?"

"I will." She threw her apron in the box and headed for the office corner, already thumbing her phone.

I slid on a clean apron and watched her go. I sidled up to Turner, who had come back from delivering an order. I kept my voice low. "Did she talk to you about what's bugging her?"

"She did not." Now he was frowning, too. "We have to find out, Robbie."

"Agreed."

He headed off to take money from a customer. I dished up the last two breakfast orders and dinged the bell. The ham stock was simmering by now, so I measured out enough dried split peas for the pot and dumped them in. We'd add the fresh frozen peas at the last minute. Danna started back from the corner but paused, frowning at her phone. She caught sight of me as I waved at her and walked slowly toward the kitchen area.

"Split peas are in," I told her.

"Okay."

"I want you to tell me what's going on." I kept my voice calm and encouraging. I hoped. "It looked like Josie told you something that made you unhappy."

Danna took a deep breath, giving one nod as she let it out.

Okay, I could pull teeth with the best of them. "What did you learn?"

She turned away, but I touched her arm.

"Danna, tell me. Was it something about your mom? About the murder? About Marcus? Come on, girl, dish."

She faced me again, eyes flashing. "All right, I'll tell you. My own grandma—Marcus's grandmother, too, mind you—said he's had serious anger management problems. That he was accused of assault as a minor. I don't believe it. Not. A. Word." She punctuated the last three words with vehemence I rarely heard from her.

Assault? That didn't sound good, but the story corroborated what Phil had told me. What kind of assault? I wondered how Josie had found out, but then again, she was an expert in all things digital. She'd apparently done the digging I'd been meaning to and hadn't gotten around to.

"She said he had to go to some group to learn how to deal with his temper."

"Did she mean a therapy group?" I asked. From what I'd seen, he could use something like that.

"I guess. Court-mandated. Robbie, the worst part is I think Josie doesn't trust him. Or maybe doesn't even believe he's my brother. I mean, what's up with that? Even Mom recognized him!" She shook her head, hard.

Turner brought a load of dishes. Danna turned to the stove, grabbing a long-handled wooden spoon, and stirred the soup. Turner tilted his head toward her. I raised a finger in a *wait* gesture.

I thought about the right thing to say. "Dan, you know Josie loves you. She's looking out for you. I'm sure everything's fine. If Marcus has been in an anger therapy group for some years, then he's working on his issues, and that's a good thing." I caught Turner making his mouth into an O of surprise.

"I guess." Danna stirred with more vigor than necessary.

"And the accusations from William Geller are simply that, a bunch of hot air. I haven't heard that Octavia is suspecting Marcus of anything, have you?"

She shook her head, her back still toward us.

"So there you have it. Are you going to see him again soon?"

Finally Danna faced us. "Isaac and I are going into Bloomington to hang out with him tonight. I want them to get to know each other."

"You'll fix it up with your grandma, Danna." Turner gave her shoulder a gentle fist bump. "She needs to get to know Marcus, too. I liked him a lot when he was in here. The dude is cool. She'll come around. Grandmas are like that."

I'd never known my mom's and Adele's mother.

I'd met Roberto's mother when I visited him in Italy, but she had a bit of dementia. She'd been sweet to me, though. She gave me a big smile and kept looking between her son—my father—and me with a sage gaze, over and over. I'd simply squeezed her age-spotted parchment-skin hand and smiled back.

Right now, though, I was thinking I'd like to have a one-on-one chat with Josie Dunn sometime very soon. What if Marcus was a powder keg waiting to ignite? I shuddered at the thought of the unstable young men who had caused so much grief with their assault weapons in recent years. Schools, places of worship, theaters, even clubs—nowhere seemed safe or off-limits. I'd do anything to protect Danna, my customers, our community from that kind of mass slaughter.

"Whatever." Danna gave her body a shake. "I don't want to talk about it anymore. Robbie, should we top the soup with crumbled bacon when we serve it?"

"Why not? It's already made with ham stock, so vegetarians won't want to eat it, anyway. Do we have enough bacon?"

Danna leaned down and checked the under-counter fridge. "Yeah. I'll start cooking it now."

"Maybe we should divvy up what's in the big pot into smaller ones, so we can add the frozen peas like two quarts at a time," Turner suggested.

"Good idea. Otherwise they'll overcook. But let's just do one saucepan at a time."

"Right," he said. "Good idea."

I surveyed the restaurant. "Turner, take your break now while you can."

"Will do."

I headed over to two middle-aged couples at a four-top. They looked about finished with their meal. "Can I get you folks something else?"

"I'm fixing to do me some shopping," one of the women said.

"Sounds good." I smiled. "Would you like me to hold your check and combine the amounts if you find something you'd like to buy?"

"The meal is on me," said the man sitting opposite her.

"Thanks, hon," the first woman said. To me she added, "No, thanks. I'm not going to make my brother-in-law here pay for my shopping habit." She guffawed.

Her husband rolled his eyes. I handed the other man the ticket for the four of them. I turned when the doorbell jangled, and my eyes widened to see Jamie Franklin. *Good.* One more person I wanted to have a little talk with.

I gave him a wave. "Sit anywhere, Jamie," I called.

But he didn't budge, shaking his head slowly.

I made my way over to him. "Are you here to eat?"

"Did you hand over the journals?" His eyes bore dark pockets beneath them, as if he hadn't slept all night.

"Yes," I said. "You asked me to, remember?"

"I know."

"Are you all right?" I asked in a low voice.

"I worried all night about what might have been in them." His voice shook.

I knew part of what they contained, but I wasn't going to tell him I'd leafed through the books. "Tell me something. Did Kristina have an issue with attics, by chance? Had she had a bad experience in one, or . . ." I let my voice trail off. I was sure I'd seen the word "attic" on the pages.

"How did you know?" he asked in surprise.

"I didn't. I'm simply curious." And if she died in one, she might have been terrified.

"She hated attics, every aspect of them. Low eaves with the business end of nails sticking through. Spiders and cobwebs. Low light and uneven floorboards. But the worst thing was, *Toni* had locked her in the attic of their house as a child." He narrowed his eyes as he spat out the name. "Kristina would never have gone up into her own attic voluntarily."

Chapter Twenty-Nine

Jamie left without eating, and I texted Octavia what he'd said. Which, combined with the journals, probably meant she was going to bring him in for questioning, but that was her business. I'd done my due diligence. Poor Kristina, terrified of attics and apparently dying in her own, unless she'd been killed elsewhere and deposited there. Why would Toni have locked her in an attic when they were children, though? I thought twins were usually closer than that. Maybe Toni had had a mean streak her whole life. Marcus had mentioned she hadn't been very nice to him. She'd also kicked her second husband out of the house, and didn't seem to have gotten along with stepson Jamie. Could Toni have killed Kristina, as horrifying as that thought was?

I flashed on what Shirley had told me yesterday, about Sean mowing the lawn for Toni. I texted him, asking him to come by if he had a minute to chat during the day. He might know something about Toni, or about Shirley, for that matter.

The lunch rush started way early, with the restaurant filling up well before eleven-thirty. The three of us took orders, flipped, served, bused, and started over. At about twelve-thirty Sean ambled in, with Buck close behind him. I wiped my hands on a towel and hurried over to them.

"Welcome, gentlemen. Are you here together?"

Sean shook his head but smiled. "He happened to come in right behind me." Sean's cheeks were rosy, and he wore a hoodie in place of a winter coat. At least he had on gloves.

"But we both agreed we're awfully dang hungry," Buck added.

"Did you ride your bike here?" I asked Sean.

"Yeah, but it's almost too cold to. Brrr." He hugged himself.

"You might want to wear a warmer coat, son," Buck said.

"It is cold today. I've switched to my indoor cycle," I said, "even though I miss riding outdoors. It's not worth getting frozen." Come to think of it, I hadn't even ridden indoors in a few days. I hoped I could squeeze in a cardio workout this afternoon after we closed. I often rode with my good friend Lou, but she had spent the whole semester doing her doctoral research at Johns Hopkins Hospital in Baltimore, so we hadn't ridden together since August.

"I know what you mean," Sean agreed. "But since I can't drive yet, my choices are, like, to ride, walk, or beg for someone to drive me."

"I remember those days," I said. Except being a bike-riding adolescent in Santa Barbara hadn't included freezing my tush off.

"I know Buck's here for lunch," I said. "Are you going to eat, too, Sean?"

"Please. It smells super awesome in here."

"You can say that again," Buck said. "We can share a table, right, O'Neill?"

"Sure," Sean said. He knew Buck well enough not to be uncomfortable eating alone with a grown-up, and a local cop, at that.

I smiled at the pair of beanpoles as two women rose from their table across the room, and no one was waiting for a two-top. "Go snag that table." I pointed. "I'll be right over to clear it." I might get to witness that eat-off, after all.

"Thanks," Sean said. "You said you wanted to ask me something?"

"I do. I'll stop by when I get a minute." I headed back to the kitchen. Danna was already on her way to clear the table, and Turner had just rung the Ready bell. I loaded up lunch for four and delivered it. On my way to Buck and Sean I was waylaid by a half dozen customers ready to order, wanting their checks, pointing at empty coffee mugs. I back got to the two-top as soon as I could.

"We have a hearty split pea soup on special, guys," I said.

Buck pointed to Sean. "Let the lad order first."

"I love pea soup." Sean looked up from his phone. "Gramps makes a mean one. Is it with a ham bone?"

"We made the stock that way, yes," I said. "And we've added crumbled bacon on top."

"Yes, please, and a double cheeseburger."

"I'll have the same," Buck said. "Double dessert, too. You, O'Neill?"

"Of course!" Sean grinned.

"Coming right up." I glanced around. Turner was signaling that food was ready, and Danna was busy cleaning. The place was chock full and buzzing with conversation and the clink of flatware on porcelain. I spied a customer at the cash register holding three pieces of cookware. Lunchtime on the first shopping Saturday before Christmas? This was not a good time to ask Sean about Toni or to fill Buck in about Kristina and attics. "I'll be back."

After I handed Turner the order, I headed first to the cash register, ringing up a lethal-looking curved chopper and the aged wooden bowl it fit perfectly in. I thanked the customer.

"Merry Christmas, Miss." He smiled. "Or the happy holiday of your choice. I ain't picky."

"Thank you. I'm not either."

"Last time I checked, Christmas was a holiday. Might's well not offend no one, that's what I say." He ambled toward the door.

I wished everyone had such an accepting view of the season. I wondered how Marcus reacted when people wished him a Merry Christmas. He'd seemed pretty secure in his beliefs when William had suggested he remove his cap and Marcus had refused.

I returned to Sean and Buck with their orders ten minutes later. "Enjoy." The restaurant had calmed down a little. I leaned in a bit. "Sean, I hear you mow Toni Franklin's lawn in the summers."

He nodded around a mouthful of burger. I was

glad he swallowed before speaking. Buck noticed the nod and went on high alert.

"I do," Sean said. "I mean, I did. I shovel the walks, too. She hired somebody to plow the driveway, but I do the small stuff." He shook his head. "It's really awful, what happened to her."

"I know." I reflected on how, in my youth, murder was not happening around me.

Buck broke in. "Where'd you hear about young O'Neill's employment, Robbie?"

"Shirley Csik told me." When he narrowed his eyes at me, I held up a hand. "I was Christmas shopping in Nashville yesterday. I happened across the store where she works, and . . ." *Oops.* I couldn't say I'd bought a gift for Sean with him sitting right there. Wait, of course I could. I didn't have to say what it was. "And Sean came up in conversation."

The boy blushed. "I'm not even going to ask."

"Don't worry, Sean," I said. "I was buying your Christmas present, that's all, and she said she knew you. She told me you mowed for the duplex, which is cool."

"Ms. Csik is a super-nice lady," Sean said. "Always gives me cookies and a coke when I'm done."

"How did Toni treat you?" I asked. "I mean, was she nice, too?"

He rubbed his nose. "Not nice, exactly. I mean, she paid me, but she wasn't usually around when I mowed, so I would have to go back to get my money. She would just, like, hand it to me without smiling. Never told me I did a good job or anything."

Buck set down his half-demolished burger and

studied Sean. "Don't suppose you was around that property on Thursday morning."

"Of course not, Lieutenant." He looked at Buck like he was nuts. "I was at school. And we haven't had snow yet this winter. Nothing to shovel."

"Did you ever happen to see or hear Toni argue with Shirley?" I asked.

Sean examined the stamped tin ceiling for a moment, as if it helped him think. "There was one time, I think in September, and Ms. Franklin was actually home. I'd turned off the mower to empty the bag or add gas or something. The windows were open and the two of them were pretty much having it out."

Buck grew quiet. I knew that meant he was paying close attention, but he let me lead the conversation.

"What were they disagreeing about?" I kept my voice low.

"Ms. Csik was super mad about the condition of her apartment," Sean said. "Ms. Franklin had had dudes in doing work on her half for a couple of weeks, but I guess she never fixed stuff or improved the other apartment."

"That doesn't sound fair." I wanted to ask a million questions but decided to wait for the story to unfold, instead, even though I could get called away any minute now.

"Yeah." Sean shook his head. "Ms. Franklin kept telling her—"

Danna waving at me caught my attention.

Turner passed by with an armful of dishes. "Sorry, but we need you, Robbie." He pointed to the cash register, where a small line of shoppers had formed.

"Gotcha." I stood. "Sorry, guys. Sean, tell Buck all about what you heard, okay?"

"Okay."

I headed to my customers and my livelihood. What had Toni kept telling Shirley? I hoped Sean would finish the story. And that Buck would tell me.

Chapter Thirty

I didn't get back to Buck's table for another twenty minutes. Sean had left, and things weren't exactly calm, but business was down to a dull roar instead of a literal feeding frenzy. Buck's table contained only the slightest traces of their lunches. A smear of soup sat in Sean's bowl, an orphaned scrap of lettuce rested on Buck's plate, and not a speck of abandoned brownie crumb remained on either dessert plate. They both qualified to be high-ranking officers of the Clean Plate Club.

"Told young O'Neill I'd cover his lunch." Buck pointed to where Sean had sat. "He said he had to go do something for his grandma and to tell you good-bye. You was too busy to interrupt."

"Thanks." I stacked the dirty dishes. "Did he finish telling you about Toni and Shirley's fight?"

"Yep. He heared Toni say if Shirley didn't like the cheap rent, she could move out. That Toni had lots of people asking to rent the place."

"And? That was it?"

"Hold on to your team of wild horses, there,

Robbie. No, that wadn't it. Shirley told her landlady she'd take her to court about all the bits and bobs what didn't work in the apartment. And that's not all the two of 'em said, neither."

I clasped my hands behind my back so I wouldn't reach out and shake his slow-talking shoulders.

He finally continued. "Toni upped and declared in that case she'd broadcast Shirley's secret from the rooftops."

Secret? "What secret? Her brother being in prison? That's not really a secret around here, from what I can tell."

"You'd be right about that. I don't rightly know what Shirley's hiding."

"Wow." Maybe Adele would know.

"Way I figure it, we're all hiding something, ain't we?" He tilted his head and leaned back in his chair.

I blinked. Was he implying I was hiding something? Or maybe that he was. I glanced around the restaurant, which wasn't crazy busy at the moment. I wasn't done talking with him. I could take another minute or two. "Buck, I wanted to tell you something Jamie Franklin told me this morning. He said Kristina was terrified of attics. That Toni had locked her in theirs when they were young girls. So whoever killed Kristina must have coerced her up to the attic."

"Or killed her somewheres else and dragged her body there." He drummed his long, bony fingers on the table. "Thank you. I'll pass that tidbit on to Octavia. Who, by the way, spent the morning with her nose in them journals you gave her."

"I already texted her about it earlier, after Jamie

mentioned it." I studied him. "Here's something else. What do you know about Toni's husband's death?"

"Tug Franklin." Buck nodded slowly. "At the time of his demise, back three years, we investigated the circumstances pretty careful. Jamie had a lawyer who pushed us to do so. Sure Tug was old and kinda cuckoo, but he passed on sudden-like. We was looking into the possibility of smothering. You heared Toni inherited all his considerable funds, I suppose."

"Yes. And that she blew through them so seriously she had to sell the house."

"That's true. Welp, Coroner Carl, he couldn't find nothing suspicious, neither did the autopsy. Seems old Franklin's heart just upped and stopped."

"Certain drugs or poisons can mimic a heart attack, can't they?" I leaned forward.

"Robbie, all's I can tell you is that we didn't find nothing."

"All right. What about now? Do you think the same person killed both twins? Or are there two murderers wandering around out there." A shudder ran through me and I hugged myself.

"I surely can't say, but I'd best get back to it." He unfolded his extra-long self and handed me enough money for both orders and then some. "You take care now, Robbie. I don't want to hear you been doing none of your amateur sleuthing. That can be a dangerous proposition in times like these."

I stowed the money in my pocket, finished clearing the table, and loaded up my arms. "Yes, sir. I hope this business gets solved soon. I'd hate to see anyone else be killed."

"You and me both, hon." He ambled away.

I carried the dishes to the sink. As I rinsed a sinkful and loaded the dishwasher, all I thought about was secrets. Shirley's mysterious one. Toni's saga of cruelty to her twin. Jamie sitting on those journals for a full decade, and his hatred of Toni. Kristina and Jamie's affair they kept secret from William—or had they? Marcus's apparently volatile temper. The now-revealed secret of his birth. And Buck seemed to imply he was hiding something, too. Was I? I didn't think so.

Danna finished loading two plates, hit the bell, and stepped back from the grill. "I have to take a quick break, Robbie."

"Go. I'll take over there."

She whipped off her apron and walked at a brisk clip to the restroom. I turned off the water, wiped my hands, and picked up both spatulas, which by now felt like extensions of my arms. Three tickets still hung from the carousel. I frowned at one. It included a breakfast order of grits with three links and two scrambled, but we'd run out of grits and nobody had erased it from the board. The lunch order from the other person at table five wanted pea soup. I checked the pot. Exactly one bowl left. *Whew.*

Turner arrived to pick up the ready order.

"Can you please erase all the specials?" I asked him. "We're out."

He checked the big wall clock. "A little over an hour until we close. Not worth making more, I guess. I'll wipe the board after I deliver these."

I thanked him. I'd laid on two meat patties and

turned the sausages when Phil blew in. He strode to the grill.

"Hey, Phil." I took a closer look at his uncharacteristic frown. "What's up?"

He glanced around. "Where's Danna?"

Uh-oh. This had to be about Marcus. "She's in the bathroom."

"I asked around about her new brother. A woman in the music department attends the Quaker church and she knows him." He shook his head. "It's not good, Robbie."

"What's not good?"

The door to the store opened. Two dozen women trouped in, chatting and laughing. My feet ached, we were an hour from closing, and a tour bus had deposited its excited hungry contents in my establishment. Danna emerged from the restroom, saw them, and hurried toward us.

Phil shook his head. "Shoot. I'll have to tell you later." He plastered on a bright face. "Hi, Danna."

"Yo, Phil." She gave him a fist bump. "You eating?"

"No. I wanted to stop in to say hi. Looks like you guys have your hands full."

"Looks like it," she agreed. "Catch you around."

I wanted to mouth "Text me" at him but Danna was looking at both of us.

"See you, Robbie." Phil made a What can you do? gesture and headed for the door.

"You good here?" Danna donned a clean apron and grabbed an order pad.

"Yeah. We're out of specials, though." I pointed to the now-empty board.

"Do we need to put in an order for tomorrow?"

"I'll check. We have until three if I put a rush on it." I watched her head toward the newcomers. Too bad I was a responsible business owner. What I really wanted to do was run after Phil and find out what he'd learned. Instead, I focused on finishing the current orders before twenty more flooded in.

Chapter Thirty-One

I locked the door after Danna and Turner left for the day at three o'clock and collapsed into a chair. The three of us had managed to feed and satisfy the big group and still get them out of the place by closing time. We'd pushed to clean up and reset the tables for tomorrow in a record half hour, but now I was totally bushed. Danna had also reminded me to put in the order in the nick of time. We hadn't had a minute to talk about specials, though.

I knew I should get busy prepping for the next day's breakfast, since I would be at Abe's tonight. That could wait a few minutes. I trudged into my apartment, cracked open a beer, poured it into a pint glass, and tucked my feet up onto the couch. Birdy coiled himself to leap onto the arm, commencing a thorough wash when he got there.

After a long drink of cold hoppiness, I set down the glass and stood. I paced the small area of my living room with a million questions nagging my brain. I could address one of them. I pulled out my phone and hit Phil's number, but then glared at the phone when he didn't pick up.

"Phil, it's Robbie. Please text or call me with whatever you learned about Marcus. Thanks." I jabbed the Off button. So that was a dead end for now. I was also itching to know if Octavia had made progress in finding who caused either death. Wondering how the twins died. Perplexed by why Toni had treated her tenant so badly. Curious about how I could learn more from Jamie. Considering if Clive had told the truth about how much he loved Toni. I ended up pondering William Geller. If what Kristina had written was true, this apparently upstanding medical doctor had been so cruel to his wife she'd been plotting a secret getaway.

It reminded me of the death a year ago and another abused wife who had taken steps to extricate herself. At least I didn't fear abuse from my Abe. He'd never been anything but kind to me and to all he met. He'd been shocked and disgusted last year at hearing about the treatment the woman had had to endure, as had his father.

My eyes widened. It was Saturday afternoon, when the Nashville Santa would be in his workshop hearing children's wish lists. Adele had said William Geller volunteered at the workshop. Maybe I could swing by there and have a little chat with him. I gazed with longing at my exercise bike in the corner. I knew I needed a heart-rate-lifting, mind-clearing hard ride. Right now? I needed to clear some of this mystery first. I promised myself a good ride tomorrow afternoon, and a double one on Monday, my day off.

My phone dinged. I glanced at it to see the notification that the delivery was here. Today's response was record quick. They must have put extra people on for the holidays. I carried my beer into the store, letting Birdy dash ahead of me. Visiting Nashville would have to wait a bit.

By the time I had the perishables—meats, milk, eggs, fruit, peppers, lettuce, and more—put away, I'd kind of gotten my second wind. Might as well get my prep done now while I was in here. As I measured out baking powder, salt, and brown sugar, I thought back to what Jamie had said about Toni earlier in the week, before she'd been found dead. He'd called her evil. I mixed the dry ingredients into the whole wheat flour. "Evil" was a strong word expressing an extreme sentiment. Could his anger at her marrying his father apparently for money have boiled over into murder this week? He'd clearly loved Toni's twin and knew about Toni's being mean to her, so that might have factored in. But why ten years after he'd lost Kristina?

I dumped the dry mix into a big plastic container and secured the lid. Kristina seemed to be a focal point in this mess. Who would have known her well, besides her lover and her husband? The two likely suspects would be Corrine and Adele. Both ladies knew everything about everyone. Before I started on the biscuit mix, I dusted off my hands and jabbed Adele's number.

I was again greeted with a voice-mail greeting instead of an actual person. I sighed and asked her to call me when she could. Corrine, on the other hand, picked up right away.

"How's it shaking there, Robbie?"

"Good. I was going to head over to Nashville in a couple minutes, and I have something I want to ask you about. Need to do any shopping?"

"Do I ever! Haven't bought one thing yet, hon, and now I'm thinking I'd best pick up a gift for my boy, too."

"Nashville's the place to do it."

"You are correct about that. I've got to be over there for a dinner at six, anyway. Meet you in half an hour?"

"Perfect."

Chapter Thirty-Two

I hung back from the hubbub at Santa's workshop where Corrine and I had agreed to meet. A naturally round-bellied man with his own snowy white beard sat in a big easy chair in front of the evergreen-bedecked wooden structure, his red suit and black boots true to legend except for the pipe. Excited children wearing rosy cheeks and red sweaters lined up to sit on Santa's lap. Most looked delighted, but one little boy clung to the back of his mother's coat with tear stains on his face. She juggled a baby in one arm and leaned down to pat his head, murmuring reassurances. Why was she so determined to get in a visit with Santa? The four-year-old didn't want to be here, and surely the baby didn't care.

When I became a parent, no way was I forcing my kid to sit on some booming-voiced stranger's lap if he or she didn't want to. Prioritizing a holiday photograph over your child's needs would not be in my mothering tool kit. I guessed I was jumping the gun a bit. Abe hadn't even proposed, although we had started talking about a future together. I couldn't imagine anyone else I wanted to spend mine with.

William Geller, clad in a black wool coat and green scarf, sat at a table taking money and swiping credit cards. A poster on a stand read, PURCHASE PROFESSIONAL SANTA PHOTOGRAPHS, TEN DOLLARS EACH. FUNDS TO BENEFIT SICK CHILDREN CHARITY. The logo on the bottom was for a Hoosier medical professions association. I would have thought the booth would be subsidized by the Nashville Rotary or Chamber of Commerce. And maybe it was, but the photo franchise was given to the doctors' charity.

I frowned. He was way too busy to make casual conversation with. I shivered and pulled my scarf closer around my neck. Even though the workshop was in a courtyard between shops and all the lights and illuminated shop windows looked warm and welcoming, the temperature was dropping as fast as the sun.

A hand clapped me on the back. "Quite the festive scene, ain't it?" Corrine asked. She was clad in a red wool coat, with black stretch pants tucked into red fur-topped heeled boots. Corrine, true to form. "Santa's coming to South Lick tomorrow evening when we light the tree. You'll be there? Down at the gazebo."

"Of course."

"Shall we get shopping?" she asked.

"Sure, but first, what do you know about William Geller there?" I pointed my chin at him. "And did you know Kristina well?"

"Funny you should ask. That detective was over the house inquiring about the same thing this very afternoon."

"Octavia?"

"The same. The twins was five years older than me, so I didn't know them real good when we was coming up. Funny how two eggs in the same batch can come out so different."

That was one way to refer to twins.

"Kristina never really stuck up for herself," Corrine went on. "She was smart, but way too sweet for my tastes."

I must have made a sound, because she glanced over.

"Nothing wrong with sweet, okay?" Corrine pointed at her chest. "It's that I've always been the more rambunctious type. Toni could be sorta abrasive, but she had herself some spunk and definitely had opinions on near about everything. She went after what she wanted. Usually got it, too. I like that in a gal. Sure is a shame she got herself killed."

A woman in a puffy white coat bustled up to William and conferred. He stood, ceding the seat to her in an apparent shift change.

"Let's go say hi to the doc." I pointed.

Corrine gave me the side eye. "This a friendly meet and greet or a interrogation?"

I smiled, lifting a shoulder. "A little of both?"

"I like it." She followed me to intercept the good doctor.

"Howdy there, Doc." Corrine stuck out her red-gloved hand. "Merry Christmas."

He started and narrowed his eyes for a brief second. Summoning a smile, he shook and said, "If it isn't Madam Mayor. And Ms. Jordan." He narrowed his eyes again at me.

I waited for him to dredge up the business with Marcus being a terrorist, and his own threat to never set foot in my store again.

"Welcome to Christmas in Nashville," he added.

Whew. "Hello, Doctor Geller." I smiled. "You're part of the group running the workshop?"

"We provide the photography part of it. We used to raise a lot of money to support children in the hospital and their families. Now everybody takes their own pictures with their phones." He spread his hands. "What can you do?"

"I didn't get a chance yesterday to express my condolences on your sister-in-law's death," I said.

"Thank you. Not that the police are making any progress on finding who murdered her. They certainly haven't arrested that terrorist I told them about."

Marcus a terrorist. *As if.*

"Have they said how Beltonia died?" Corrine asked.

Bingo. I'd been about to ask the same question.

"They aren't telling me anything, more's the pity. I don't even know why they thought she was murdered and didn't simply have a cardiac event. She'd had issues with her heart for years. Congenital."

"Did your late wife have the same problem?" I asked.

"No." He shook his head. "They weren't identical twins. Her heart was fine. I mean, her cardiac health." His mouth twisted as if he'd tasted week-old catfish, probably thinking of Kristina's heart in the sense of love instead of a muscle.

"How do you think your late wife's remains got into the attic, Doctor?" I asked.

Corrine glanced at me as if she'd been about to inquire exactly that. We were quite the team.

"Like I told the detective, I don't have the foggiest." Geller folded his arms on his chest. "I thought she left me. She just disappeared."

I tilted my head. "I heard she was afraid of attics."

"She was. Some silly thing that happened when she was a child." He jutted out his chin and squinted at me. "Where did you hear that about her, anyway?"

Uh-oh. I didn't want to out Jamie.

Corrine batted away his suspicions. "Everybody who growed up here knew it."

Saved by the bell, or the mayor, as the case may be. Sort of. Geller still stared at me as if he didn't think I should have known that about his wife.

I smiled brightly. "We'd better get to our shopping, Corrine. Nice talking with you."

He didn't say a word or smile in return.

"Merry Christmas, Doc." Corrine gave him a little wave, took my elbow, and steered us away.

I glanced back after we'd walked a few steps. His gaze at me was icier than the wind.

Chapter Thirty-Three

"The doc wasn't over the moon with us asking him questions, there, was he?" Corrine asked as we strolled past a group of high school carolers holding forth in front of a church.

"He sure wasn't. Did you really know Kristina was afraid of attics?"

"No, but I picked up a teensy touch of panic from you, hon." She gently elbowed me. "We girls gotta support each other."

I laughed. "Thank you."

"Where'd you learn she was ascared, anyhow?"

"Jamie Franklin told me Toni locked Kristina in an attic when they were kids. And it freaked Kristina out for the rest of her life. He said she never would have gone up there voluntarily."

"Don't that take the Pillsbury Bake-Off–winning cake, though. So that's why she hated attics. I never knew that part of the story." Corrine whistled. "Them two was carrying on, did you know? Jamie and Kristina."

"I gathered as much." I spoke slowly. "Do you think Doctor Geller knew?"

"Shoot, he musta. Everybody else in town did."

Interesting. "Why did she stay with her husband?"

"I told you she was the sweet, accepting type. She never liked to rock the boat. Plus, Jamie don't make much money, and Geller, he was rolling in it being the big-cheese doctor and all whatnot. I think the lovebirds was fixing to leave, though, right abouts the time she went missing."

In fact, they were about to escape, according to her journal.

"Now, by rights she shouldn't have strayed like she did," Corrine continued. "And young Franklin had no business messing with a married woman. You shoulda heard the gossip around town. I'm not sure how them two walked around with their heads up."

"But Geller never confronted them?"

"Not that I ever saw."

We passed a brightly lit flag and banner store. "Corrine, I haven't talked with you since that lovely dinner with Marcus. I know Danna is thrilled he found your family. How are you feeling about it?"

She moseyed in silence for a moment. "I'm glad, of course. It sure brings up a boatload of old emotions I haven't had to deal with in a quarter century."

"I can guess. I'm sure it's not easy. How's Josie doing with him being in contact?"

"Ma's happy I sorta kinda have him back, however that shakes out. She was real supportive of my decision when I got myself pregnant. She'd offered to help me raise the child, but I knew it would have put a big old burden on her shoulders, and I was mostly all growed up by then. I knew he'd have a good full life adopted by two parents who wanted him, and it sounds like he did."

A good full life plus an issue with his temper, but I didn't need to bring that up with Corrine.

She pointed at a swingy rainbow-colored dress in the window of a women's clothing shop. "Ooh, would ya get a gander of that piece of pretty? Wouldn't it be perfect on my girl?"

"It would." The garment was exactly Danna's style. We entered into warm, fragrant air, and it wasn't from scented candles, thank goodness. "Something smells great."

Corrine pointed at a round table. The staff was offering hot mulled wine and gingerbread women cookies, so we both accepted a half cupful and a sweet. As I sipped and munched, I lingered over an array of locally made earrings, finally picking out a dangling silver pair perfect for Adele. Corrine bought the dress and a scarf to match. Once we emerged onto the sidewalk with our purchases in tissue-paper-stuffed bags, a woman down the block hailed Corrine.

"Why, if it ain't my old girlfriend from law school!" Corrine waved back. "Robbie, you want I should introduce you two?"

"Thanks, but I need to look for one more thing and then head home. Have a fun visit."

"You take care, now." She lowered her voice. "I wouldn't go anywhere alone with Doc Geller in the near future, if you get my drift."

"Girl Scout's honor." I held up my right hand with the first three fingers glued together, thumb folded over pinky.

She headed for her friend and I moved along, wondering what perfect gift I could find for Abe. Instead I found myself in front of the Covered Bridge Bazaar where I'd visited Shirley earlier this week. Or maybe it had been only yesterday. I doubted Abe would want any country-cute items but headed in, anyway. I could always look at stocking stuffers and maybe have a chat with Shirley, too.

This store had a table of cheese and crackers out for the taking, as well as little paper cups of cider and white wine, but the buzz of my taste of mulled wine was still with me. I moved past. Shirley didn't seem to be here, though. An older woman came out from behind the counter.

"Merry Christmas." She smiled. "Help yourself to refreshments."

"Thanks, but I'm good. Could you tell me if Shirley Csik is working tonight?"

The smile slid off the woman's face. "No, but I'm the proprietor. Can I help you find something?"

"I'll just poke around. I own a country store and restaurant in South Lick, myself." The shop appeared to be empty except for us.

"Pans 'N Pancakes? Your reputation precedes you, Ms. Jordan." She stuck out her hand and introduced herself.

I shook. "Nice to meet you."

"Shirley was supposed to be in today but didn't show."

I blinked. "That's too bad. She didn't call in sick?"

"She did not. Weekends from now until Christmas

are our busiest times." The set of her mouth reflected her displeasure.

Did she know about Shirley being questioned in Toni's death? "It's sad about her landlady's death, isn't it?"

The shopkeeper shook her head with her lips pressed together, then glanced around and lowered her voice. "Shirley isn't too broken up about it. I can tell you, that woman treated her badly, and Shirley hated her for it."

"Do you know in what ways?" I picked up a carved wooden ornament of a covered bridge and turned it in my fingers, keeping my tone casual.

"Toni Franklin was a b— a witch of the highest order. Why, Shirley's apartment was literally falling down around her and the skinflint owner didn't lift a dang finger to fix things, may she rest in peace."

"Why didn't Shirley find somewhere else to live?" I asked.

"Can't find cheaper rent than she had. And Shirley, bless her heart, funnels most of her money to her poor addled brother in prison."

"I'd heard something about that. What a shame. I wonder if she'll have to move now."

"She said she has no idea what's going to happen to the place."

A group of gawky teen boys slouched into the store, pausing at the refreshments table. "Only the cider, boys," she called to them. "Excuse me. Gotta keep an eye on these rascals."

I walked out after having purchased the ornament a few minutes later. Abe's mom, who collected ornaments like others collected signed baseballs or first-edition books, would love it. Unfortunately, I hadn't really collected any new information except that the intensity of Shirley's feelings toward Toni were more extreme than I'd heard. And that the whole town had known of Kristina and Jamie's attraction to one another.

Chapter Thirty-Four

I'd parked at the end of a side street. Returning to my car alone, now after sunset, I wished I'd opted for the well-lit public lot, instead. This narrow residential way wasn't equipped with streetlights, and the modest homes lining it hadn't opted for festive Christmas lights, either. One house had five junked cars on the property, three slumping on the front lawn and two on the gravel driveway. A dim light in a listing garage illuminated a broken window, but the house itself was dark.

Shivering—and not only from the cold—I hurried to my little Prius parked along the edge of a dark and abandoned park at the street's terminus. Eerie woods lay beyond. The lights and cheer of the Nashville Christmas Shop Local evening seemed a hundred miles and years away.

I held my keys in my left hand but felt for my phone in my right coat pocket. I was about to pull it out and hit the flashlight icon when a crack sounded from nearby. I squeezed my eyes shut, waiting for the sting of a fired round at the same time as my heart raced faster than a twin-turbo-charged IndyCar. When no pain came, I broke into a sprint. The noise could have merely been a squirrel burrowing for one last acorn to add to the winter stash. I wasn't taking any chances. I thought I heard another noise close behind me between the thuds of my own footsteps.

The toe of my boot caught on a crack. I cried out as I went flying. I grasped at air. My gloved hands encountered the side of my car and slid down, but the vehicle broke my momentum. I scrambled up and hit the Unlock button on the key fob. I'd never inserted a key and driven away so fast in my life, pulling a tire-squealing U-turn.

I reached a streetlight and paused at the stop sign long enough to lock the doors and fasten my seat belt. Had someone really been after me? Or was it the fear of the unapprehended killer—or two—walking around that had spooked me? I blew out a breath.

The shortcut back to South Lick wound along a dark country lane. I opted for the slightly longer state route. Between the towns, cars came toward me and sped past regularly, but I seemed to be the only vehicle driving in this direction. Now calmed down, I laughed out loud at how jittery I'd been, but sobered when I realized my nerves came out of experience. Bad guys had pursued me before. It was only prudent to be careful and not do stupid things while alone like park on a street that would be dark after sunset. My defense, that I hadn't thought about such things while a winter sun shone, was a weak one.

A car had come up behind me while I was musing about danger. An intense white light nearly blinded me when I checked my side mirror. What was with people and their super-strong headlights? I was happy with my small energy-efficient car. Big honking SUVs and pickup trucks ruled the road around here, and because they were bigger vehicles, their lights shined straight into my eyes. This driver had flipped on the high beams, too. I scrunched down and forward to avoid getting night blindness from the rearview mirror.

My hands turned cold as they gripped the wheel tighter than they had to. What if the person who had chased me was now tailing me? I let out an obscenity that would have turned Adele's cheeks red and caused her to scold me up one side and down the other. Were there any ditches on my side of the road to worry about? I pressed down on the accelerator. The headlights followed suit. My heart kept pace. How far did I have to go? Half a mile? A quarter mile? Let me get there safely. Or spy a South Lick police car.

The bright lights of the grocery store parking lot at the edge of town had never looked so welcoming. I slowed and swerved in. My tail blessedly drove past with only a loud blare of the horn. I hovered in the no-parking zone near the market's door for a moment, surveying both of the lot's entrances. No big vehicles pulled in and searched for me. As far as I could tell, I'd once again let my fears override my confidence.

I exhaled and pointed the Prius toward home three blocks away. The sooner Octavia caught Toni's killer, the sooner I could toss this tension in the trash.

Chapter Thirty-Five

Breakfast prep completed and personal hygiene achieved, I made it over to Abe's by seven that evening without a single blinding, tailgating pursuer. I walked into a cottage redolent with smells of seafood, fresh bread, and chocolate. I'd tucked black stretch pants into my turquoise cowboy boots and my tunic length sweater was in the same hue. I loved the feeling of my hair loose on my shoulders, and I knew Abe did, too.

I spied him at the stove. His Hoosier cottage featured a wide arched passageway from the living room into a dining room. He'd taken down the wall beyond, so the kitchen was now open to the other rooms. He liked to cook for others and had said it didn't make sense to do it in isolation.

"I think I just arrived in heaven." I bestowed a kiss on his newly bearded cheek. I rubbed the soft curly growth with my hand. "I like this beard thing, you know."

"Good. It's easier, and actually warmer for the winter." He finished stirring a big blue pot of deliciousness and set the lid on. "And if this is heaven, I get more of a kiss than that."

I threw my arms around his neck and obliged, with the kiss lasting way longer than it ever could in public. "Mmmm," I murmured, my cheeks suddenly hot. My stomach burbled its empty status of its own accord.

He gave me a fond, crinkly-eye look. "Mmm is right, but I know not to get in the way of Robbie Jordan and her dinner." He nudged me toward the refrigerator. "If you can pop the cork on the pinot grigio in there, I'll serve up the grub."

Two minutes later we sat at right angles to each other. He'd set two wide bowls on brightly colored placemats. The bowls brimmed with a tomato-based seafood stew. A basket of warm crusty bread was calling my name, and a wooden salad bowl stood full and ready for later. I lifted my wineglass.

"To my very most favorite chef," I said.

"And to mine."

We clinked and sipped. I tasted the thick, rich stew, savoring it on my tongue, then poked around in the bowl.

"Absolutely to die for, Abe. The trinity, plus carrots. Fish and shrimp. A hint of hot. Fresh dill. And . . . and what? The flavor is incredible."

"Thanks, and you're almost there. Haddock, salmon, and catfish, because they all add their own flavors. A few drops of habanero sauce. What I think you picked up on is a couple tablespoons of the basil pesto I made and froze last summer."

I pointed at him. "That's it. What a combo." I buttered a hunk of bread. "Smells like you made this, too."

He cast his eyes to the ceiling. "Can I plead the Fifth?"

"What, is it from Buddy's Breads?" A new artisanal bakery had opened in South Lick recently. "I promise not to tell."

"Hey, I warmed it all by myself. That should count for something."

The chewy, crusty loaf was nearly as perfect as the soup. I smiled around my mouthful. We proceeded to update each other on our days as we ate and drank. I didn't mention murder once, and left telling him about my fears that I'd been pursued for another time.

"Dessert on the couch?" he asked forty-five minutes later.

"If I can waddle that far." I helped clear and rinse until Abe told me to go relax.

Snuggled on the couch side by side, our feet up on a homemade wooden coffee table, we nibbled at ramekins full of a deep, rich chocolate mousse topped with a dollop of whipped cream. After I finished, I stroked my left palm.

"Something wrong with your hand?" Abe asked. He took it and bestowed a kiss on the palm.

"I think it's a little bruised."

"Flip too many burgers today?"

"No. But I had a bit of a scare before I came over. Two scares, actually." I related what had happened— or what I thought had happened—as I'd walked to my car.

"The public lot is well lit, you know, sugar," he said gently.

"I know. I was trying to save a buck, because the free lots were full. Silly of me. And then, as I drove back to South Lick, it felt like a car was after me, too. High beams, riding my bumper even when I sped up, the works. At least I took the state route and not the back roads."

"Did you see what kind of vehicle it was?" He slung his arm around me and squeezed my shoulder. "I hope whoever it was didn't follow you home."

"No to both. I pulled into the market parking lot and the car kept on going. It was dark out, and I was rattled, so all I know is the vehicle was big and had bright lights."

"Did you learn anything new today about the investigations?"

I yawned. "It was a pretty full day. I heard a lot, but not necessarily from the police." I stared at the dark night above the café curtains Abe had pulled shut. "Abe, do you know Clive Colton?"

"Not well, but I know him. He's worked on construction sites where I've run a new service from the street before. Always seemed like a good guy, although I'm not sure how good a plumber he is. Why?"

"Naturally Buck and Octavia wanted to question him, as the husband of a homicide victim. He seemed really broken up when Buck broke the news about Toni to him on Thursday. He said he adored her. But then last night he showed up at Bible and Brew. It seemed early for a grieving spouse to be out and about."

"You think he might have been putting on an act? That he already knew she was dead?"

"I don't know. It's all so muddled. Things get that way when people's feelings and motives are involved."

He held up a finger. "Here's one thing I do know.

I've heard Colton was in bad shape financially. I'm not sure if he's a gambler, manages his own accounts poorly, or maybe, like Shirley Csik, plows his money into supporting someone."

I widened my eyes. "Thus wanting Toni's inheritance. If he inherits."

"She was pretty sharp. I doubt she died without a will somewhere."

"Yeah, but what does it say? I also don't know anything about alibis for folks like Clive, William Geller, Jamie Franklin, or even Shirley, Toni's tenant. I don't know anything, really, except a lot of people didn't like Toni at all."

"That's a fact. What were you doing in Nashville, by the way?"

"I went for a little Christmas spirit after we closed the store."

"While I was here slaving over a hot stove for you?" He gave me a mock frown.

"Hey, how do you know I wasn't shopping for you? Anyway, Corrine met me there, and we talked to Geller. Can you believe he volunteers at the Santa's workshop?"

"With the medical group, yes." This time Abe really did frown. "Robbie Jordan, did you go there in order to interrogate the doctor?"

"No. Well, a little. Don't you be acting like Octavia, now." I cleared my throat. "I saw him near Santa, so we said hi. He mentioned Toni's heart condition, and I asked if Kristina had the same thing. He said they were fraternal twins, and that Kristina's heart had been healthy." I drummed my fingers on my knee.

"Penny for your thoughts, hon?"

"I would really like to know how Toni died. Clive said she was taking a heart medication. What if someone poisoned her with a drug that interacted—badly—with the one she already took?" Someone like Clive, even.

Chapter Thirty-Six

I'd never been more grateful for our practice of opening the restaurant an hour later on Sundays. Even though Abe and I had made an early—and delightful—night of it, and I'd scooted home at six-thirty this morning to shower and change into work clothes, I still felt as bleary-eyed as Danna looked when she dragged in at seven.

"Yo," I called. "Coffee's ready."

She sniffed the air. "That smells good," she mumbled. "Still, I think I'm ready to turn over the early shift to somebody else on Sundays."

"Same here. I'll ask Turner today."

"Nooo, you won't." She shook her head slowly. "He's got that thing for his grandpa. It's only the two of us on shift today."

"Shoot." I squeezed my eyes shut. How could I have forgotten? The week before Thanksgiving, Turner's mom's father had finally succumbed to a long-standing illness. Today had been the soonest they could assemble the far-flung family for a memorial gathering. If Danna and I thought we were tired now, we were going to be totally exhausted by the end of a day operating minus one employee. I cracked another egg into the pancake mix, but it slipped and pieces of shell fell into the batter. I swore as I began picking them out.

"Language, language, Robbie," Danna said in a wry tone as she dried her hands and slid on an apron.

I laughed. "Yes, Mother."

"We'll be all right. And let's forget about specials for today."

I tapped the counter. "We could. Or we could throw dried cranberries in the pancake mix. We have a couple big bags of them."

"Excellent idea. I'll put it on the board."

"You'd better eat something while you can, too."

"Yeah. Soon as I get the caddies out."

We bustled about in our well-practiced routines until we were as ready as we were going to be at a quarter to eight. Danna whipped up a big cheese omelet that we scarfed down while standing.

She swallowed a bite. "Marcus told me something interesting. It makes Doctor Geller calling him an Arab even more screwy. My bro said in some places, there's animosity between the Arab mosques and the African-American ones. Isn't that strange?"

"Sure. But you know by now how strange people can be. Everybody wants their own group to be the correct one, and they look down on outsiders. It doesn't make sense, but lots of people are like that." I drained my coffee. "Do Muslims have that kind of rivalry in Bloomington?"

"I don't know. There's only one Islamic Center

there, but Marcus said there are like seventeen in Indy." She popped in her last forkful of omelet.

"Indianapolis has that many Muslims?"

"Yeah." She pointed at the clock.

When I pulled open the door, a mini-horde faced me. I groaned, but silently, at the sight of twenty eager couples. Forty hungry senior-citizen diners, that is. All. At. Once. On a day when we were shorthanded. And the new light of dawn revealed snow starting to fall, too. *Wonderful.* I'd have to shovel the walk and clear the steps sometime soon.

"Well, good morning, everyone. Come on in out of the snow." I stepped back to let them troop in.

"We're up for the day from Evansville," one of the men said.

The woman with him smiled at me. "Some of us are the Silver Singers. We're giving a Christmas concert this afternoon in Bloomington and decided to make a shopping day of it. We've heard so much about your restaurant, we just had to start here."

"I'm glad you did. Sit anywhere you'd like."

"Thanks," she said. "I'm going to start my shopping right here, too."

I was about to head for the coffeepot when Clive followed the last senior in. Exactly the man I wanted to talk to—or one of them—except I wasn't going to have time for that, not with all these enthusiastic customers. His hair was shower-damp, and today he'd dressed not in the work clothes I'd seen him in previously but in a crisp pale blue shirt, a maroon sweater, and dark slacks with polished shoes. Off to church, perhaps. He certainly wouldn't have been Shirley's tall shadowy figure, not with his squat thick build and big blocky head. He'd claimed to have loved Toni deeply. Murderers claimed a lot of false things, however, I'd learned over the years. I greeted him.

"Morning, Robbie."

"Breakfast before church, Clive?"

"Yes, ma'am, that's why I'm here."

"Where do you attend services?"

"Over to the Quaker Meeting in Bloomington. I sure do love the quiet. Sometimes the whole dang hour is silent."

"You must know Marcus Vandemere, then. Tall guy, a little younger than me?"

"Yes." Clive frowned. "I don't know him well, and he seems to be practicing Islam, as well. Boy's got quite the temper on him."

Marcus's anger seemed to be noticed by everyone. "Did Toni attend with you?"

He wagged his head back and forth. "She did not. Said the stillness made her nervous. She liked to get things done, not sit around waiting for God."

I glanced at the restaurant. "I've got to get busy, Clive. Look, there's a small table over there you can snag. Coffee?"

"Yes, please."

The next forty-five minutes were the definition of busy for Danna and me. By the time we got everyone served, the first tables were ready for their checks. Clive ordered a big breakfast and read a Bible while he ate. After he was finished, I laid his ticket on the table.

"Whenever you're ready." I smiled.

He pulled out a small wallet. After he opened it, he looked up with something I couldn't decipher written on his face. "Robbie, I'm afraid I forgot to go to the bank yesterday. I seem to be plum out of cash."

"We take credit, of course." Was that shame or wiliness on his face?

"I'm not good with credit cards. Had to cut them up a couple years ago. I ran up too much debt. Don't supposed I could give you an IOU?" He gave me a look that was half frown and half hopeful.

I sighed inwardly. This was a bad precedent, but what could I do? He'd already eaten the food. A lot of it. "Of course." I scribbled TO BE PAID on the check. "I'll put your ticket in the cash register. Stop back any time we're open to pay." Only two days ago I'd said I could open a tab for Buck, but that was different. He was in here at least once a day and overpaid every single time.

"I thank you." Clive stood, giving a last swipe to his mouth with the napkin.

The bell jangled, bringing Octavia into the store. Clive turned toward the door, then froze.

"That woman is bad news," he muttered.

"What do you mean?"

"Believe me, she's bad news."

Chapter Thirty-Seven

It turned out the detective was here to talk with me, not with Clive. After he saw her, he aimed himself for the door. Octavia glanced at the new widower as he passed but didn't speak to him. Instead, she beckoned to me.

I made a T with my hands. I had to bus, clean, and reset Clive's table before I took time to speak with her. I was waylaid by other diners wanting to pay, two tables whose orders were ready, and a woman needing to pay for an armful of gifts from the store section. I needed another pair of feet and hands each, and soon. Danna was a two-handed fast-moving miracle at the grill, bless her heart.

By the time I reached a displeased-looking Octavia, Buck had joined her. Two more parties pushed through the door after him, dusting snow off their shoulders and stamping it off their feet. I swore silently. I needed to get out there and clear the steps at the very least. The porch's wide overhang usually kept it mostly snow free unless it was blowing a lot.

"I need to speak with you, Robbie," Octavia said.

"Good morning, Octavia, Buck. I'm sorry, but we're swamped and are missing one employee. You can have that two-top I just cleared if you want to eat." I pointed.

Buck nodded with enthusiasm. Octavia opened her mouth to object, but I held up a hand to forestall her.

"Otherwise you can wait on the bench, or you can come back. I have a business to run."

"Fine." Octavia let out a noisy breath. "We'll eat."

It didn't sound like it was fine, but Buck nearly skipped to the table. I seated the other two parties, grabbed the coffeepot, and poured for the newcomers before ending up where Buck and Octavia sat. As I filled Octavia's mug, she spoke in a quiet voice.

"Thank you for the information you texted me on Friday about Shirley Csik. Would you happen to know her whereabouts?"

I frowned. "I know where she lives and works, if that's what you mean."

"No, it ain't," Buck said. "Ms. Csik is missing, plain and simple."

"Missing?"

"She doesn't appear to be at home," Octavia said. "She doesn't answer her phone. Her car is gone. She did not report to her workplace yesterday."

Right. What the gift shop owner had told me. "And she hasn't turned up in a hospital? Maybe she had an accident."

"Not in Indiana, she hasn't."

Danna hit the Ready bell twice. "Let me take your orders real quick. I'll be back to talk when I can." I hurried to Danna thirty seconds later with Buck's usual Breakfast of Giants order and Octavia's oatmeal with a banana. I stuck the ticket on the carousel. As I loaded up the orders, I murmured to Danna, "Shirley is missing. What was that soccer team in Chicago you mentioned?"

"The Red Stars? Why, do you think she went up there for a tryout or something?"

"I have no idea. But it was a thought." I carried the orders over to a big table of six, but my brain was focused on Shirley. Was she on the run? I couldn't think of a reason unless she'd killed Toni and decided to make a break for it. But why now and not right after she did it? Or had someone hurt her? Abducted her? Her absence could be as simple as an unscheduled trip out of town to pursue a professional soccer career. Early December seemed like a funny time to hold tryouts for an outdoor sport, but I didn't know a thing about sports in general and soccer in particular. And if a tryout was the case, why not tell the gift shop owner she couldn't make it in? The same as a few days ago, I had another uneasy feeling, this time about Shirley being gone and unaccounted for.

By the time Buck's and Octavia's orders were ready, business had calmed down a little. Buck poured on the syrup and tore into his cranberry pancakes so fast I thought they would catch on fire.

"Did you know Shirley is an accomplished soccer player?" I asked, glancing from Buck to Octavia. "Abe told me she was captain of the team in high school, and Danna said Shirley coached her team when she was a kid. You might want to call a women's pro team called the Red Stars in Chicago. She could have driven up there for tryouts."

Octavia cocked her head and regarded me. "Good information gathering, Robbie. Thank you."

Whoa. A compliment from the taciturn, all-business detective. "You're welcome."

She tapped into her phone. "We'll check that out."

"Are you thinking Shirley might have killed Toni and is trying to evade being charged?" I asked in a soft voice.

"Unfortunately, our investigation is still in progress," Octavia said. "Ms. Csik certainly is a person of interest. We asked her, along with the others, not to leave the county."

Buck swallowed a mouthful. "We want to find the woman and there's no two ways about it."

"Did you get to question her about what she told me? About seeing a tall person outside the house that night?"

"We did not have that opportunity, no."

I stuck my hands in my apron pocket. "Could she be tending to her brother? The one in prison?"

Octavia pressed her eyes shut for a moment. Opening them, she said, "I won't even ask how you know about that. Bird, can I assume you have already checked on the brother's status?"

"As a matter of fact, I have not," he said. "I'm sorry to say it did not occur to me. I'll get one of my people on it ASAP."

Still, if the brother was sick, why wouldn't Shirley return home in between visits? Why wouldn't the police be able to find her? That didn't seem like a plausible scenario for her disappearance. A customer caught my eye. She waved her check and some money in the air. I signaled I'd be right there but flashed on what Clive had said.

"One more quick thing. Clive Colton was in earlier. He apparently has a lot of trouble handling his personal finances. He didn't have cash for his breakfast, and said he no longer carried credit cards because of a bunch of debt he'd run up. It might be something to consider."

Octavia sliced the banana onto her oatmeal and topped up the dish with the whole milk she'd requested. A dainty bite later, she swallowed. "Thank you for helping us. Now I have a few matters of business to discuss with the lieutenant, if you don't mind."

I was dismissed. *All righty, then.* Buck cast his gaze briefly to the ceiling and then winked at me. I hid my grin and turned away. But his good humor didn't completely dispel my unsettled feeling about Shirley. In lieu of prayer, which wasn't my thing, I sent out my intention into the universe that she be all right. I crossed my fingers for good measure.

After I took the waving woman's money—five twenty-five for two over easy with bacon and rye toast, plus a dollar tip—I donned my coat, winter hat, and gloves before heading outside. I had an arrangement with a plow guy to come and clear my driveway and the parking area in front when it snowed. It was up to me to get the white stuff off the sidewalk and walkway as well as the steps. The last thing I needed was for a customer to slip on a freshly snow-covered surface.

Chapter Thirty-Eight

Danna and I barely got our usual midmorning lull. The pre-church crowd was followed closely by the Sunday morning athletes, who drifted in in Spandex and breathable jackets. After them came the early-service church folks and the midmorning brunchers. It went on from there. My helper and I each took quick bathroom breaks before diving back in. I also grabbed a moment to text Abe.

> Shirley C is missing. Text or come in, K? I have questions. OOXX, R

Abe had gone to school with her. He might know someone, something, that could lead to the missing woman.

He wrote back.

> Sure. Be there in a bit. Plus community party at 5, right?

He meant the annual South Lick gathering to celebrate the lighting of the municipal tree, complete with a visit from Santa riding in an antique fire truck. It was always a cheery event, and I didn't have to lift a finger to prepare for it other than putting on warm clothes.

You bet.

I'd opened the door to check the snow again—not that I had time to shovel right now—when William Geller approached the store. He must have forgotten his pledge never to enter my store again. He was accompanied by a woman and two teenagers the same size, twins, perhaps. They were nearly as tall as the woman, but the boys slouched and hid their faces behind floppy long hair. Family, maybe? Or perhaps this was his girlfriend and her children. Geller took one more drag on the lit cigarette he held and stubbed it out on the ground with his toe.

Great. I had a butts bucket filled with sand on the porch for exactly that purpose.

I greeted them and ushered them in. I glanced around to see that a four-top had opened up. "Follow me."

"Thank you, Ms. Jordan," Geller said. "This is my sister and my nephews visiting from Fort Wayne for the day."

I smiled. "Welcome to South Lick."

The woman thanked me, and the teens ignored my greeting. Were they here to help Geller make burial arrangements for his wife and sister-in-law, maybe? The latter would be up to Clive, come to think of it. I could have asked him this morning what his plans were for a funeral or memorial service, but it hadn't crossed my mind.

At the table, Geller sat first.

The woman said, "You sit there, Jimmy." She gestured to the seat to Geller's left.

"Mom," the boy complained in his best teen sullen.

"You know Uncle Bill's a lefty like you. That way you won't bump elbows when you eat." Shaking her head, she gave me a *What can you do?* look.

I left them to work out their family interactions and bustled about tending to diners. I was clearing a table near Geller and company when a woman wearing a well-sprayed white coiffure walked up to him.

"Doctor Geller, I just need to shake your hand." Her voice was shrill and loud. "You were the best anesthesiologist I ever did have when I was in last year to get my lady plumbin' taken out. Previous ones, they did not treat me well. With whatever all you give me, I didn't feel a thing and wasn't sick after, either. I never got to thank you, and I want to do that right here and now." She stuck out a heavily be-ringed right hand.

The doctor stood and took her hand in both of his. "I want you to know I appreciate that, ma'am."

"You are most welcome. And let me express my condolences on the loss of your dear wife and her sister." She shook her head but the hair didn't budge. "It's a sadness and a pity, that's what it is."

By now everyone in the place was watching the two, even Danna. Geller's smile turned forced. He murmured his thanks and released her hand, sitting and facing his sister. The woman beamed down at them, but finally got the message that he had moved on. She set sail for the door, trailing way too much perfume in her wake.

I hurried over to Danna when she hit the bell.

"That man's in again." She gestured toward Geller with her eyes. "I'm glad Marcus isn't here."

"Or Phil, for that matter," I agreed. "On the other hand, a woman just complimented the doc on his skills with anesthesia, and he apparently has a sister and nephews who care about him. Nobody's all bad, Danna."

She didn't comment, instead pointing to a slew of plated meals. "Those are ready for that group of ladies at the big table, and these are for the couple in the back."

I loaded up and headed out, set down the meals, and returned for more. Buck was the next customer to come in. He'd inhaled a ginormous breakfast only two hours ago. Could he really be hungry enough for lunch already? He moseyed toward me, tugging off his cap. I pointed to the area in the back near the restrooms and met him there.

"Hey, Buck. You're hungry again?"

He wagged his head. "You know me, I can always eat. But no. I'm here to tell you Shirley's brother is status quo. Nobody over there's seen her or heard from her. Irregardless, it was a good idea you had, checking into him and all."

"Thanks. Sorry it didn't pan out. Abe said he'd stop by this morning. He went to school with Shirley. He might have an idea about some friend of hers or a favorite place she used to go." I scanned the restaurant and frowned. Where had Geller gone? The sister and nephews were where I'd seated him. Maybe he'd had a call and had gone between the shelves in the retail area to take it. I realized I'd never gotten back to take their orders. I'd tend to them once Geller got back to his seat.

"Welp, I want to thank you for lending your ideas to the case. You'd make a fine homicide detective if this restaurant thing doesn't work out."

"Thanks, but I'm happy cooking and stuff." I tilted my head and gazed up at him. "So, no real progress in either case?"

"Nope, more's the pity."

"That thing about Kristina hating attics is really bugging me, Buck."

"You and me both, hon, with Octavia looped in for good measure."

Behind us, the door to the men's room opened without a sound and Geller emerged.

"Excuse me, Lieutenant," he said.

Buck startled, but stepped aside. I got out of the way, too.

"Ms. Jordan, we'd like to place our order when you get a chance." Geller moved toward his relatives.

"I'll be right there," I called after him as I watched him go. *Huh.* The restroom doors always clicked. The lack of a noise made me think Geller might have started to open it but stopped when he heard Buck and me talking. Exactly how much of our conversation had he overheard?

Chapter Thirty-Nine

Lunch continued as packed as the morning had been. It turned out Buck hadn't come to eat, but he promised he'd be back in early afternoon for lunch. Geller and family had eaten, paid, and left, with him giving me an odd look before he walked out.

I was on the grill when a ruddy-cheeked Abe slipped in at a little after noon. Smelling of fresh air, he sauntered over to me after hanging up his jacket and his Greek captain's hat. He bussed my brow, which was hot from the grill and from the speed at which I was trying to move. I knew I looked frazzled, too.

"Things seem kind of busy here today, hon." He glanced around. "Where's Turner?"

"He had a family thing. Busy isn't the half of it." I gestured to the full sink and to customers waiting patiently and not so patiently for their meals, drinks, checks. "It's gonzo busy. I mean, it's totally crazy in here and we have four hours to go." We opened an hour later on Sundays but we also closed an hour later.

He grabbed a clean apron off the stack and slid it

over his head. "Tie it for me?" He turned his back. "I've never mastered making a bow behind my back."

"Sure, but what are you doing putting on an apron?"

"I happen to have a couple free hours, so I'm helping my best girl. How hard can it be to do dishes and clear tables?" He winked, picked up a tray, and headed for a table currently *sans* diners but *avec* piles of dirty dishes, silverware, and napkins.

"Thank you," I murmured, then flipped a beef patty in time to save it from the burnt pile. My man was also an excellent cook and personable to the general public. He could fill in for either of us. I caught sight of Danna high-fiving Abe on her way back to the kitchen.

"Nice job recruiting the boyfriend." She poked her thumb over her shoulder. "Want me to call Isaac, too? I should have offered. He's not a bad cook, either."

"I think we'll be fine with Abe. He said he has a few free hours, but thanks. Good to know you think Isaac might be willing to help out in a pinch."

Danna looked over my shoulder and pressed her lips into a line. I twisted to see Josie at the door looking in our direction.

"Aren't you going to go say hi to her?" I asked Danna.

"I guess." She trudged off, clearly still upset with her grandmother from yesterday's revelation about Marcus.

I finished four orders, plated them up, and hit the bell. Danna returned with a frown on her face.

"What?" I asked.

"She says she wants to talk to you."

I turned to look. Josie stood near the entrance, her

blue wool coat still buttoned, a purple beret at a slant on her silver hair. I waved her over.

"You don't know what it's about?" I asked Danna before Josie reached us.

"She wouldn't tell me," she muttered.

What had Josie learned? Was it something about Marcus, or about one of the murder victims? Abe arrived at the kitchen area at the same time as Josie. He stacked his trayful of bused items and started the water running into the sink. The woman of a recently seated couple waved a hand.

"Can you get that couple's order, please?" I asked Danna. If Josie didn't want to tell Danna what this was about, she wouldn't want her lurking and listening, either.

Danna gave one look at her grandma and headed away from the kitchen.

"Good," Josie said. "Robbie, I think you should read this article." She pulled a newspaper from her huge designer handbag and held it up, since I had a spatula in each hand. The paper was folded open to an article in today's *Brown County Democrat*. My eyes widened of their own accord when I saw the headline, AREA MAN SUSPECTED IN MURDER. The real shocker was the photograph of Marcus, a shot that revealed his *taqiya*. The byline was James Franklin.

I whipped my head to look at Josie. "He's not a suspect, not the last I heard. A person of interest, maybe, but Buck hasn't been talking about Marcus for the murders, believe me. He and Octavia have others they're looking into." At least I hoped they did.

She folded the newspaper the opposite way so the article and picture were hidden. Abe gave me a quizzical glance. I focused on my meat patties, buns in the toaster, and a cheese omelet. What did Jamie know? Was he reporting only on what the police had told him, or had he also been investigating on his own?

"Better not let Danna see that," I whispered out of the corner of my mouth when I spied her turning toward us, order slip in hand.

"I'll drop it on your desk," Josie whispered in return. She brightened when Danna arrived. "Well, I'm off, sweetheart," she said in a regular voice. "See you at the tree lighting?"

"I haven't decided if I'm going." Danna didn't return her grandmother's smile.

Josie walked off and Danna faced me, arms folded. "What did she tell you? Was that a newspaper she gave you?"

"Hang on a sec." I finished everything that was cooking and plated it before I responded. No sense burning perfectly good food, plus it gave me time to think. If I lied to cover Josie's rear end, all Danna had to do was pick up a newspaper. And if she didn't, her mother certainly would. I happened to know that Corrine read the *Democrat* cover to cover every week. If I pretended Josie didn't tell me anything, or said I didn't know why she'd come in, Danna would stop trusting me, which I did not want. If I told her, she might get mad at Josie, but they'd loved each other every day of Danna's life. They would work it out. And she had a right to know about a story naming her half brother.

"Josie brought in the paper, the latest *Democrat*." I

laid a hand on Danna's arm. "There's an article saying Marcus is a suspect in Toni's murder."

She opened her mouth in outrage, nostrils flared.

"Hey," I said. "I haven't read it yet. Josie knew you'd be upset and she didn't want me to tell you. But I figure you deserve to know. You're as much an adult as she is."

"At least somebody treats me like one."

"I haven't heard Buck say anything about Marcus in relation to Toni's murder. I don't know what Octavia is thinking."

"Who's the liar who wrote the article?" She slid fists to hips.

The bell on the door jangled yet again. Jamie trudged in, covered with snow. I sucked in a breath. I'd been ignoring the snow, but that hadn't made it stop falling. I needed to get back out to shovel again, and soon.

I pointed to him and waited for her to look that way. "The byline read James Franklin."

Chapter Forty

Danna still glared at Jamie, but he hadn't noticed. She looked like she was about to go over there and confront him. Yes, she was an adult, but she was a relatively young one with heightened passions. Right now it was time for me to exercise my best management skills.

"Danna, please take over on the grill. The last three tickets you brought over need filling. I'll deliver these."

"But I need to talk with Jamie. He's totally wrong." She couldn't wrest her gaze away from him. "Saying something like that about Marcus is so not fair."

Jamie, on the other hand, had perched on the waiting bench and was leafing through a magazine, apparently unaware of our mini-drama.

I moved in front of Danna and pulled up to my full five foot three. "Danna?" I pointed to my face to get her attention. "Right now you need to cook. We have a full house and then some. Okay?"

She focused on me and took a deep breath. "You're

the boss, boss." She read the first ticket and went to work.

Abe cleared his throat. "Robbie, the dishwasher is full. Where's the detergent? And is the machine quiet enough to run while customers are eating?"

"Thank you. I totally owe you." I pulled out a dishwasher pod from under the sink and handed it to him. "We need to run it, and it is pretty quiet. Use the express setting or we'll run out of dishes before we close."

"You got it. But I can always hand-wash plates and mugs, if it comes to that."

"Of course." I grabbed the waiting plates and headed for the hungry diners who had ordered them. I tended to a few others, then approached Jamie.

"Did you want to eat, Jamie?" I asked.

He glanced up from under his Neanderthal-worthy brow. "Yes, ma'am, I do. Do you happen to have a free table?"

I surveyed the restaurant. Abe was clearing the two-top of a couple who had paid me a few minutes ago. "Yes. But first, can I ask you where you got the information you based your article about Marcus Vandemere on? I'm afraid I haven't had time to read it yet, but I saw the headline and the photo."

He stood, looming over me. "Here and there. I'm a journalist, Robbie. I can't reveal my sources."

"Was one of them the police?"

He gazed at the corner of the room. "Of course I integrate the information from the department's press releases and press conferences."

They'd held a press conference? I wasn't aware of

one, but then, I hadn't exactly had time to sit down and watch the news, either on TV or my tablet.

"Have you been talking with William Geller?" I asked.

His chiseled lip curled. "Why would I speak with that man? What he did to Kristina was criminal."

So much for that theory. "Marcus is my assistant's brother. She's pretty upset by your story."

He shot a glance at Danna for a moment, then flipped open one hand. "Names make news, what can I say?"

What about substantiating a claim before publishing it? I swallowed down my retort. "I'll show you to your table."

I seated him, got his order, and took it to Danna. Abe was elbows deep in suds at the sink. I clipped the order to the carousel.

"I asked him about his sources, Danna, and he wouldn't tell me. No spitting in his coleslaw, now." I waited for her to show her agreement before pointing to three plates. "Are those ready?"

"They need pickles," she said. "The jar ran out."

"I'll get another one from the cooler, then I need to go out and shovel."

Abe cleared his throat without turning around. "I shoveled on my way in."

I stared at him. "You did?"

"Yes, ma'am."

I wrapped my arm around his neck and planted a big wet kiss on his cheek, even though I had to stand on tiptoes to do it. "You're the best, you know?"

"My middle name is Aim-to-Please." His dimple deepened. "You can make it up to me later, baby," he said, his voice almost imperceptibly low—and very sexy.

My neck grew hot. I gave him one more squeeze and hied myself off to find the dills. I cooled down quickly in the walk-in, and as I did, I remembered I hadn't asked Abe about Shirley yet. I hauled out the gallon jar and set to slicing pickles lengthwise, adding them to the small metal bin we kept at the ready for this garnish. We could buy them pre-sliced, but it was more expensive. This way we had the ends and odd bits to use in our homemade relish.

Abe was off busing and wiping down tables again. I delivered the ready plates and returned to my slicing. Danna heaved a heavy sigh, assembled a cheeseburger, and slapped it onto a plate.

"Here's the liar's order." She shot a daggers glare in Jamie's direction. "And no, I didn't spit on it. Can't say I didn't want to."

"Thank you." His order was the last on the carousel. "We seem to be caught up for the moment. Why don't you take a quick break while you can?"

"Thanks." She tossed her apron in the bin and headed for the retail area, pulling out her phone as she went. I delivered Jamie's order. He thanked me without looking up from his own phone.

Back at the kitchen, I wiped down the grill and bit off half a slightly charred sausage.

"Is that lunch?" Abe asked.

"It's a start."

"You texted that you wanted to ask me something about Shirley. I'm here, and it looks like we have a reprieve. What's up?" He leaned an elbow on the counter. "Is she really missing?"

I swallowed. "According to Buck and Octavia, she is. You went to school with her. Is there a relative she might be visiting? Or did she have a favorite hideout anywhere?"

He frowned. "A hideout? Shirley was a pretty straight arrow in school. You know she was an athlete. I don't think she smoked pot, and she certainly wasn't part of the drinking party scene."

"Were you?" I asked with a smile.

"Once in a while. Not to destruction, and never while I had Dad's car. So if she had a hideout, I didn't know about it. She did talk about her grandfather some, her dad's father. They seemed very close. He was an immigrant from Hungary. I met him once. Short little guy with an accent straight out of a Dracula B-movie."

"I wonder if he's still alive."

"I don't know. He lived in Columbus."

"Indiana or Ohio?"

"The former."

Interesting. The town, full of buildings designed by famous architects, was only twenty-five miles to the east from here. And it was where Dr. William Geller practiced medicine. I closed Pans 'N Pancakes on Mondays and suspected a field trip to Columbus might be in my very near future. Did I need to tell Buck about Shirley's grandfather? Not yet. He might have died long ago. If I found Shirley, then I would communicate her whereabouts—or convince her to return.

Danna returned from her break. Three women signaled for their check. A family of five pushed through the door. It was back to business as usual.

Chapter Forty-One

"Man, Birdy," I said to my kitty at four o'clock. "What a day." I spooned out half a small can of what we called his treat as he purred, chirping and twining through my legs. I set it down and drew my own treat out of the apartment's fridge, a cold IPA. A moment later, pint glass and reading material in hand, I settled onto the couch with my feet up. After the first delicious sip, I set down the beer and picked up the newspaper Josie had brought. I wanted to search for Shirley's grandfather on the Internet, too.

I set down the paper a few minutes later. That was the most nebulous article I'd ever read.

"Indiana University graduate student Marcus Vandemere is being suspected of the recent homicide in South Lick. Sources say he had expressed animosity toward the victim and was a well-known antagonist in the community."

And more. It almost sounded like a gossip column, right down to the passive voice, "is being suspected." By whom? If it wasn't the police, who cared? And Jamie made a living as a journalist? Hard to believe. It was a

wonder he hadn't been sued for libel. I shot off a text
to Buck.

**Read the Democrat article about Marcus being
suspect. Did that info come from you or O?**

Somehow I didn't think Jamie had gotten it from
either of the officers. And Jamie hated Geller, so it
wouldn't have been the doctor's accusations that
fueled the words. I hit Send before picking up my
tablet. Birdy moseyed into the living room. He
paused near the couch and proceeded to bathe,
showing off his best foot-over-shoulder yoga pose.

First I searched the news for a police press conference, whether led by the South Lick department or
the Brown County sheriff's office. Zip. Where had
Jamie come up with saying Marcus was a suspect? As
far as I knew, that was a more official designation
than simply a person of interest.

I leaned back. I'd been successful at restraining
Danna from accosting Jamie. He'd paid and left without incident. After we'd closed and cleaned up,
Danna had said she was going to call Marcus as soon
as she got home. I would call him myself, but I didn't
have his number. Anyway, she could handle it. And if
she didn't show at the tree lighting in an hour, I
could text her about what she found out.

I checked the time. *Ugh.* Barely an hour until Abe
and Sean arrived at a quarter past five to walk to the
gazebo together. I took another sip of beer and slid
open a search window on the tablet. I typed, "Csik
Columbus Indiana." *Bingo.* A Tibor Csik appeared to
live in a retirement community there and in fact led
the historical fiction book group. I texted the address

to myself so I'd have it tomorrow. I could try to find a phone number and call ahead, but if Shirley was there, I didn't want to spook her.

Sipping my beer, I laid down the tablet, thinking about what Clive had said when he saw Octavia. Why would he say she was "bad news?" Because she'd questioned him, the husband of a homicide victim? As far as I knew, that was standard practice. Of course it would be a shock to be suspected of murder even while he grieved Toni's death. But if he was innocent, he didn't have anything to worry about.

The washing machine in my back hall started thumping its spin cycle. The load of store napkins, aprons, and dish clothes must be off-balance. I was going to have to try to remedy that. But tomorrow, not today. It was probably out of level, and most machines had adjustable feet.

The rhythmic thump knocked at my brain. Was there something I was forgetting about Toni's death? About Kristina's? I wished I had time to sketch out a crossword puzzle as I had in the past. Sheesh, I hadn't even worked on one all week, or cycled, either. Two things I could look forward to doing tomorrow on my day off.

Right now it was time to finish this beer, grab a handful of almonds, and change into my warm boots and red sweater before the menfolk showed up.

Chapter Forty-Two

The snow had stopped falling during the afternoon, and the town had sent out the little sidewalk snow plow to clear the walkways before the tree lighting. Everywhere except the roads and sidewalks was coated with five inches of fluffy white, making it truly look like a Hoosier Christmas. It wasn't a sight I'd ever seen growing up in Santa Barbara, of course, but children's holiday books had been full of snowy country lanes and white-bedecked trees. I walked with my arm tucked through Abe's along the final block to the town square, with Sean on his other side. We weren't alone. It appeared all of South Lick was converging on the tall conifer the fire department had erected the day before, a tree now perfectly decorated with soft-looking clumps of snow.

White lights festooned the gazebo and Christmas carols played from a speaker somewhere behind the buzz of excited conversation. The decorative red and gold bells hanging from the lampposts were festive, too.

"Robbie, Abe!" Adele called out from a few yards away, waving at us.

We made our way to stand beside her and Samuel. Phil was with them, accompanied by his redheaded girlfriend, hands clasped. I surveyed the crowd, but didn't spy Danna anywhere. She was probably still annoyed with Josie for trying to hide the article from her. I hadn't heard back from Buck about where Jamie had gotten his information. The lieutenant would no doubt be around here somewhere.

A girl about Sean's age came up to him and elbowed him in the arm. "We've been waiting for you, dude. Hi, Mr. O'Neill," she added to Abe. A red and green South American knitted cap with pointed earflaps and knitted tassels adorned her head, with two long blond braids stretching from it nearly to her waist. "We're all over there. Come on." She took his elbow.

Sean glanced at his dad.

"Six-thirty at the gazebo," Abe instructed. "Have fun."

After they hurried off together, Abe said, "Math team social, from what I can gather. And my boy has the biggest crush on that girl. He could do worse—she's team captain." He gazed fondly in the direction the youth had gone.

"And cute, too," I added.

"They're good kids, no doubt about it," Adele said.

Corrine, her red scarf flying, bounded onto a platform that had been set up near the gazebo. Red velvet ropes connected by stanchions delineated a path to two steps. A three-foot-high painted wooden gingerbread man sporting a garish grin—which bordered on a grimace—and a green elf's hat decorated each post at the start of the ropes. The steps led up to the platform, which had a big cushy armchair positioned in the middle of it lit by floodlights on stands. An aide handed the mayor a microphone.

"Hey, South Lick!" Corrine's voice blared. "How are all y'all tonight?"

A murmur of "hey" and "fine" arose.

"I can't HEAR you," Corrine pressed. "Merry Christmas!"

This time the crowd joined in unison, calling out the greeting. A little boy in a too-big Santa hat chimed in late, shouting "Mewwy Chwithmuth!" Everybody nearby laughed, and his dad hoisted him onto his shoulders.

"Now, for them who don't know who I am, I'm honored to serve as your mayor, but I know you're not here to see me. The man in red will be along in half a jiff, so sit tight."

I spied my Muslim B&B guests standing in silence across the way, not smiling. I felt bad for them. Jewish families lived in town, too. Corrine could have slanted the celebration in a more secular direction. Too late now. It was probably a good thing Danna hadn't brought Marcus. Beyond where Tanesha and Bashir stood, Buck strolled the periphery of the crowd, eyes alert.

I hadn't seen Geller or his relatives, or Jamie. Octavia didn't seem to be around, either. *Good.* The community didn't need a homicide investigator to butt her head into a happy occasion like this. The sound of a siren started up in the distance, and a bell clanged. I looked up at Abe in alarm. Another murder?

He smoothed back my hair. "Did you forget about Santa?" he asked softly.

Santa. Coming on an antique fire truck with a full escort of contemporary fire and police vehicles. I'd been at this very celebration a year ago. I shook my head, but a smile eluded me.

"I must be really spooked by what's been going on," I said. "I had a vision of a new disaster, a fresh tragedy." That woo-woo feeling of foreboding rose up again right along with the hairs on my arms.

The sirens grew closer. Children hopped up and down in excitement. Bunches of them now rode on parents' shoulders. Buck ambled into the center of the circle that surrounded the platform. He put his palms together, then spread them apart in an opening gesture with his hands to Corrine, who still held the mike.

"Santa Claus is almost here," she announced. "Please stand back and keep control of the young ones. Don't block the aisle. Santa's a big fella, remember, and he needs room. Everybody who wants one will get a turn to sit on his lap."

Buck and a deputy walked the inside perimeter of the circle, gently encouraging people to move back. Finally two statie cruisers appeared at a crawl, sirens wailing, escorting the vintage wagon to the square. The vehicle was resplendent with polished chrome and a big brass tank on the back, also brightly polished. Mrs. Claus was in the driver's seat, smiling and waving. Two green-clad elves perched on the back. Santa sat in the passenger seat, pulling the rope that clanged the bell. He waved his other white-gloved hand. "Merry Christmas!" The crowd roared their approval.

Jamie, with a green scarf wrapped around his neck, appeared out of nowhere and began snapping pictures of Santa with an actual camera, not a phone. To illustrate another freelance article for the *Democrat*, I expected. He'd better get his facts straight on this one.

Buck lent a hand to the portly Santa, who looked a lot like the Nashville one from the day before. Once off the high seat, Corrine led him along the roped-off aisle and up the steps to his chair, with Mrs. Santa and the elves following. Corrine handed Santa the mike.

"Have you all been good girls and boys?" he asked.

"Yes!" came a chorus of high-pitched voices.

"Who wants to see some lights?" he asked.

"We do!" was the resounding reply.

Jamie was now snapping photo after photo of the crowd. Had he gotten Marcus's permission to take the picture of him for the article? Somehow I doubted it. There must be parents in the gathering who didn't want their children's photos used, either.

The elves positioned themselves at the base of the steps, each holding a huge basket of small candy canes to give out. I didn't see an official picture taker, unlike in Nashville, but as Geller had mentioned, all the parents would be taking their own photographs, anyway.

Santa held up a hand. "Three. Two. One. Merry Christmas!" He dropped his arm.

The perfectly shaped conical tree, which had to be thirty feet tall, came to life with strings of lights stretching from top to bottom. Multicolored plastic globes dotting the branches were lit from the inside, and boxes wrapped in brightly hued plastic paper nestled under the tree. The lights glowed against the night sky. A chorus of oohs and aahs filled the air. Abe threw his arm around my shoulders and squeezed. I happily leaned into him, all thoughts of murder vanquished for the moment.

Corrine regained the microphone. "All righty, people. Children who want a visit with our special guest, please line up nicely. Parents, kindly don't leave their sides. The Chamber has generously provided refreshments under the tent, and the beer garden is open to those with appropriate identification. Have yourselves a fun old time, now, and enjoy a safe holiday season."

"Beer garden sounds fun," Abe said. "Shall we?" He included the oldsters as well as Phil and his girlfriend.

"We're headed to a party," Phil said. "Catch you later. Oh, and I'll bring in desserts Tuesday morning, Robbie."

"Thanks, and have fun," I said.

Adele pulled a Four Roses flask from her coat pocket. "Heck, I didn't know they was going to have a beer garden. Never did before. I brought this to add to my hot cider."

Samuel laughed fondly. "I think I'll stick to plain cider, my love."

"Beer sounds good to me," I told Abe. "And whatever the Chamber has for snacks. I just realized how hungry I am."

After Abe proffered his elbow, I threaded my arm through, and off we went. Before we got there, I saw Danna's signature rainbow-colored hat. She was talking intently to someone even taller, and it looked a lot like Marcus. I tugged Abe in that direction.

"Where are we . . ." He spied Danna, too. "Oh. But not for too long. I'm ready for that beer."

"Me too," I murmured, then, "Hey, Marcus. How did you like the tree lighting? Isn't it pretty?"

He nodded once without smiling. "It is. Danna insisted I come see it."

"Hey, man." Abe extended his hand to Marcus.

Marcus shook it, then stuck his hand back in his jacket pocket. "Listen, Danna, I need to get out of here. This place is toxic for me."

"Don't you want to confront him?" Danna said softly.

She must be talking about Jamie. A public confrontation was not going to go well.

"No. I told you I didn't. I still don't." He kept his voice low, too. "Didn't anyone ever teach you, when you were growing up, about turning the other cheek?"

Huh. It sounded like he was taking his anger management therapy to heart, a wise choice.

"Of course. It doesn't mean it's always the right thing to do." Danna's words were clipped, fast.

Abe nudged me and looked pointedly in the direction of the beer tent.

"Okay," I whispered, then spoke in a normal voice. "See you around, Marcus. Tuesday, Dan."

She gave a little wave without looking at us. We started to make our way through the crowd, which was thick. We'd only walked a couple of yards when I heard Danna's voice.

"Hey, don't do that," she yelled.

My heart sank. I whirled.

Jamie was walking up to Danna and Marcus, camera to his eye, his finger pressing the button repeatedly.

"Stop taking pictures, you liar," Danna shouted at Jamie. "That story was all fabrication. Nothing was true in it. You didn't even talk to the police."

He lowered the camera. "I have my sources."

"You don't have my permission to take my picture." She stepped toward him.

He stepped back, calmly raised his camera again, and snapped more pictures of her and Marcus.

"Stop it. Quit taking pictures." She grabbed at the device and got a fistful of strap, too.

The strap around Jamie's neck grew taut as he pulled back. He didn't let go.

I hurried back, Abe at my side.

"Let's chill, folks," Abe said. Nobody listened.

"Danna, leave it. It's his property." Marcus grasped her shoulders from behind to pull her back.

"Let go of my camera or I'll have you arrested," Jamie snarled.

"You're not publishing more dirt." She didn't release the camera or the strap. With one more tug, and Marcus's weight behind her, Jamie toppled forward onto Danna. They all went down. Danna cried out. Marcus's head hit the ground with a thud.

Chapter Forty-Three

Buck and the other deputy materialized. "What's going on here?" Buck asked.

Jamie rolled free and stood, dusting himself off, and his camera, too. "This girl attacked me."

Abe extended a hand to Danna, but she knelt, her face drawn in fear.

"He's unconscious!" She patted her brother's face. "Marcus, wake up."

"Ambulance," Buck said tersely to his deputy.

The deputy turned away and spoke into his radio. Jamie turned away, too, and took two steps toward the gazebo.

"Franklin, you're not going anywhere," Buck ordered. "You stay right here."

Jamie obliged, but folded his arms and tapped his fingers on his bicep with impatience.

Abe, a former Army medic, knelt on the other side of Marcus. He felt for a pulse in Marcus's neck. "Pulse is good." He listened to the younger man's breathing. "Respirations are, too." Abe pulled a penlight out of somewhere and shone it in one eye, then the other. Marcus's arm came up to shield his eyes.

"Quit it," he mumbled.

I let out a long exhale. Marcus was alive, conscious, and coherent. He was going to be fine. Danna sank back onto her rear end, raised her knees, and buried her head in them. A crowd encircled us, watching with the universal curiosity about all things morbid.

"Nothing to see here, people." Buck made a shooing gesture at them with both hands. "Young fella took a fall, and he's going to be fine. Move yourselves along, now."

Octavia walked up. "What's this about an altercation?" She kept her hands loose at her sides and her gaze on Jamie.

Marcus struggled to sit up.

Abe laid a gentle hand on his shoulder. "You rest there, young man. We're going to get that head checked out by the professionals."

Danna lifted her head. "First Mr. Franklin published a false and defamatory article about my brother, then he wouldn't stop taking pictures of us when I asked him to. I told him he didn't have my permission, but he kept taking them. So I grabbed his camera."

"She attacked me," Jamie said, glaring down at Danna.

"Is that so?" Octavia asked.

"Yes." He lifted his chin. "I was exercising the rights of a free press."

Corrine strode up as he was speaking. "What the hell you yapping about, Franklin? My girl wouldn't attack a flea."

The mayor had some learning to do about her

daughter. Or maybe those words were bravado about the person she loved most in the world.

Buck held up both hands. "We are not solving this here. Everybody kindly shut your pieholes. We'll resolve the dispute and level appropriate charges, if necessary. But not here and not now."

Two black-clad EMTs hurried up, bag in hand. Abe started to stand to get out of their way. I held out a hand to help him up, leaning back to counterbalance his weight.

One EMT knelt and started checking out Marcus. The other looked around at us. "Medical story, please?"

I stepped forward. They must specify "medical" so they didn't elicit finger-pointing and blame slinging. "Abe and I saw the whole thing. They all fell down, but Marcus hit his head."

Abe piped up. "He was out for maybe thirty seconds. Heart and respirations were good from the get-go. I light-checked his pupils, which were equal and responsive. He awoke and protested the light."

"Thanks, Abe." The woman smiled at him. Of course she knew him. Everybody did.

"I don't want to go to the hospital," Marcus said, his voice now stronger.

The EMT glanced at her partner. "We need to evaluate you for a while, and we'd rather do it in the emergency department. How old are you?"

"Twenty-six," Marcus said.

"He's passed cognitive clarity," the other EMT said.

The woman continued. "If you insist on refusing, we can stay here until you are cleared to leave."

"Yes, that's what I want." Marcus's voice seemed to grow deeper and more clear every time he spoke.

"You shouldn't drive tonight," she added.

"I've got it," Corrine said. "I'll take care of him."

Buck cleared his throat. "Imma need a statement from Danna and Franklin, at the very least." He looked at Abe and me. "And one or both of you two."

Abe murmured to me. "I'm going to have to meet Sean at six-thirty and take him back to his mom's. School night."

"I know." To Buck I said, "I'll do it. Do I need to go to the station?"

"Thanks, but no," Buck said. "I'll talk to you first so you don't have to hang around. The rest of y'all? Don't go anywhere."

He and Octavia exchanged a look. She moved closer to Jamie as if making sure he didn't make a dash for the exits, so to speak. *Interesting*.

Buck touched his eye and pointed to the deputy, who nodded. "Robbie, step over here, if you will, please?"

Abe checked his watch and came with us. "It isn't six-thirty yet."

We followed Buck a few yards away.

He pulled out a paper notebook and a pen. "Please tell me again what you witnessed."

I related what I'd seen. "To his credit, Marcus kept trying to get Danna to let go of the camera, to leave Jamie alone."

"Yes," Abe agreed. "He was doing his best to deescalate the situation. He advised Danna to turn the other cheek and urged her to let go of the device after she grabbed it."

"Marcus got behind her and had his hands on her shoulders," I continued. "She kept pulling at the camera. They all toppled over, and Marcus's head hit the ground hard."

Buck scrunched up his face. "I thought he did one of them Japanese sports. Don't they teach them to fall the right way?"

Abe smiled. "You're thinking of judo. Marcus was a karate-ka."

"A what?" Buck looked even more confused.

"He studied karate." Abe pronounced it ka-RAH-tay. "You know, the martial art."

I sometimes forgot Abe had lived in Japan while he was in the army.

"You mean karate?" Buck said the word like most Americans, kuh-RAH-dee.

"Yes."

"You got anything else, either of you?" Buck looked from Abe to me.

"I texted you about that article Jamie wrote, but I didn't see that you answered," I replied. "Did the police give him any information about Marcus?"

"No, we did not," Buck said. "I'm pretty dang curious about them sources of his."

I glanced over to where Octavia stood calmly regarding an increasingly impatient Jamie. "You and me both," I said. "Anyway, I think we told you all we know about what happened, right, Abe?"

"Yes."

Buck thanked us and said we were free to go, then ambled back to the others.

"Want Seanie and me to walk you home?" Abe asked, laying his hand gently on my cheek.

"I would like that, yes." I usually felt safe in South Lick. Tonight, a walk alone in the dark was about the last thing I wanted to do.

Chapter Forty-Four

Alone in my apartment with Birdy, I drew all the curtains and turned up the heat. I glared at the washing machine full of wet store laundry and vowed to hire a service in the spring. In the meantime, it wasn't going to dry or fold itself. My stomach rumbled along with the dryer after I started the machine. It was seven o'clock and way past dinnertime.

I grabbed a serving of lamb curry and rice from the freezer and nuked it in the microwave. Abe— bless his handsome heart—had sent me home with leftovers after a big dinner he'd prepared for us and another couple in October. I cooked so much in the restaurant, the last thing I needed to do was make a solo dinner from scratch on my day off.

A glass of red and a delicious meal later, I stared at the few remaining empty squares on yesterday's *New York Times* crossword, which I'd worked as I ate. Mustering up arcane answers like "Elis" for an ancient Greek land, "rhos" for density symbols, and "taro" as a bubble tea flavor, had kept murder out of my mind for a little while. What I really needed were the answers to the clues, "The reason Jamie wrote an unfounded article about Marcus," "Shirley cut out of town because . . . ," or "The cause of Clive being broke."

It was possible ye olde Internet could help me figure these out. I actually had time to dig deep, research-wise, as it was my one night not to do breakfast prep for the next day, and Abe was at home. I set my dishes in the sink and headed for my laptop.

A couple of minutes later I sat back. I'd found a British guitarist named Clive Colton, and a white-haired man by the same name in the States somewhere who'd won an Unsung Hero award. The man I was interested in was the South Lick Clive, who'd been in small-claims court for not paying a debt he owed. The plumber who'd been employed by four different contractors. The one who'd had his license revoked. *Ouch.* He must be singularly bad at his chosen occupation. And if he was a shoddy plumber, no wonder he had money woes. He'd have to work under the table for similarly unlicensed contractors.

Could he have faked his grief at Toni's death? Sure. He could have been planning for Toni's death all along so he would come into her money and the property she owned. I wondered if he knew for sure that he was her heir, or if he only assumed it. Surely Octavia would know the contents of Toni's will by now. After Clive had eaten—for free, as it turned out—this morning and spied Octavia, he'd said she was bad news. She must be keeping a close eye on him. I drummed my fingers on the desk. I so wished I could know how the investigation was really going. Who had alibis? What information had the detective and her team unearthed? I could wish until the cows came home. She'd never tell me.

I blew out a breath. It was time for a splash of Four Roses to help me in my search. Splash duly poured, I returned to my desk only to find Birdy happily ensconced on the laptop's keyboard. The screen displayed a message that made me laugh out loud:

Your search -wwwwwwwwwwwwweeeeddddddddddddcccc-cvvvxxxaaaaaaaaaaaggggggggttttttttttt- did not match any documents.

Suggestions:

-Make sure all words are spelled correctly.

-Try different keywords.

-Try more general keywords.

"Birdy, you silly cat. You have to spell the words correctly." A giggle slipped out as I lifted my research assistant onto the floor and cleared his paw-initiated search. I'd probably mined to the end of the Clive vein. How about Jamie Franklin's background? Was he really who he made himself out to be? Why was he going around taking pictures of someone like Danna who'd asked him to his face not to? That had to be an invasion of privacy and against some kind of law or ordinance.

But James Franklin was a much more common name than Clive Colton. Even adding "South Lick" to the search only got me some of the local news and feature articles with his byline. So much for that vein.

I didn't think a search would tell me the reason for Shirley's precipitous departure from town, either. Someone had mentioned a secret connected with her, though. Who had it been? I sipped the bourbon, then snapped my fingers. It was what Sean had told

Buck about the argument he'd overheard between Toni and Shirley. Sean had said Toni threatened to air Shirley's secret if Shirley went public about Toni's bad stewardship of the rental apartment.

My fingers got busy. Shirley Csik had a unique name, at least in the googlesphere. Shirley had apparently been enrolled at Purdue University and had been a scoring striker on the women's soccer team even as a first-year student. She must be as good as Danna had reported. I kept poking around. College news about her disappeared after her junior year. I couldn't find her in the graduating class or any other mentions. *Huh.* Maybe that was when her father went to prison? She might have had to come home and take care of her brother. Him being incarcerated wasn't a secret, though.

I kept searching. "Bingo," I said aloud, sitting back in the chair, gazing at a blog called The Brown Sleuth. A post from five years ago claimed the Sleuth learned Shirley had bribed a prison official to try to get her brother transferred to a different facility, but the official had refused to take her money. The Sleuth wondered why she hadn't been arrested on a felony.

Was this a gossip rag or a news source? I couldn't find a thing on the site acknowledging who the author was. And was the story true? Further searching yielded exactly zip. The dryer beeped that the load was done. As I transferred the laundry into a basket, I found a pair of colorful socks Adele had knitted me. I must have thrown them in the washer at some point instead of into my personal hamper. Adele might well know more than the Web about what had happened to soccer star Shirley.

"Hey, Adele," I said when she picked up. "Do you know what happened to Shirley Csik in college? She was a soccer whiz at Purdue, but she didn't play senior year and it looks like she probably didn't even graduate."

"Why are you asking, hon?" When I didn't respond right away, she went on. "Never mind, you probably got your detecting hat on."

She knew me way too well.

"It was this way. She was doing real well up to that college, but that was when her daddy went and killed a man. He always claimed it was accidental and all like that, but they give him life, anyway. So Shirley had to drop out and head home to look after Zeke."

"Thanks. I wondered if that was what had happened. Now, have you ever heard of a blog called The Brown Sleuth?"

"Of course I have, and it's a darned disgrace. Nobody knows who runs it, but the thing is nothing more than a gossip rag."

"It kind of seemed that way. I ran across a post saying Shirley tried to bribe a jail official a few years ago. Is that true? Did she?"

"That would be a crime in and of itself, doncha know?" Adele made a *tsking* noise. "I was mayor at the time, and I admit to hearing the same rumor. Nothing ever came of it, though. Hang on a sec, Roberta." She spoke away from the phone. "What's that, sugar buns?"

I smiled and shook my head at my aunt calling Samuel "sugar buns."

"Samuel says it was Toni who hushed up the whole affair about the bribery."

"Toni?" My voice rose. "I thought she and Shirley didn't get along."

"They sure as heck did not. I never was quite sure why she upped and did Shirley that favor."

Possibly to have power over her. Maybe Toni was about to go public, finally, about Shirley's brush with the law. But would Shirley have killed her for that?

Chapter Forty-Five

The next morning I slept in until seven, way late for this early riser. The sun wasn't up yet, but when I glanced out the back door, the sky was littered with celestial diamond dust, and a glowing Venus hovered above the eastern horizon. We wouldn't be getting any more snow for now.

I sat in my PJs, playing with Birdy and sipping my coffee. My gaze fell on the crossword puzzle I'd started to create last night. I'd sketched out clues like "William's motive for killing Kristina," "Toni's tenant," and "How Jamie felt about Toni." I'd added "Kristina's fear" and "Shirley's relationship to Toni."

But it hadn't clarified my thinking at all, so I'd switched to solving yesterday's *New York Times* puzzle, one that had nothing to do with murder. I'd even picked up a new word from the puzzle, "eldritch," which meant sinister or darkly ominous, according to the dictionary. Despite today's crisp, clear, predawn sky, the events of this week were definitely eldritch, as was my mood.

Yesterday after the tree lighting Jamie had seemed

a lot more sinister than he had earlier in the week. Marcus, if anything, had acted less so. Not that I'd witnessed him being hardly anything but quiet and humble, but the multiple reports of his temper problem had worried me. That, and him showing up unannounced and out of the blue to join Corrine and Danna's family. Or rejoin, in Corrine's case.

I knew one thing that would clear my mind and lift my spirits. I set my mug in the sink and went to change into biking clothes. There was nothing like a good hard ride to clear the cobwebs, both physical and mental. I had no schedule today other than to put in a food order and do breakfast prep sometime before tomorrow. A morning ride was always the right way to start a day.

Twenty minutes later I was sweating hard, pushing myself on the hardest program the cycle came with. As I pedaled down a virtual hill, the thinking brain came back to life, and I remembered I'd planned to head to Columbus to look for Shirley. Was her leaving town so abruptly the act of a guilty woman? Or had her grandfather fallen ill and she'd simply gone to his side? Most people would at least tell their employer what was going on, in that case.

I was hungry to find out what else was going on in the case, especially when it came to alibis. Octavia and company must have canvassed Toni's neighborhood. Had anyone corroborated what Shirley said she'd seen? Shirley, Jamie, and William all lived alone. So did Marcus, although for Danna's sake I hoped he wasn't involved. If any of the suspects had gone into Toni's side of the house, wouldn't someone have seen them?

Jamie. Octavia had been paying him close attention after she showed up at the town square yesterday. Maybe he was more of a suspect in Toni's murder than I'd thought. He had called her "trouble." Why? Because she'd questioned him? He might well have a secret I hadn't uncovered.

I shook my head and focused on the last ten minutes of my ride. No thinking, just pushing my muscles, including the most important one—my heart. After a five-minute slow pedal to cool down, I hopped off and wiped my face. Now I was hungry for food, and I'd earned it. I fixed a cardiac-healthy breakfast of homemade almond-laden granola, cut-up dried apricots, and a sliced banana, and sat down with my tablet to search for news.

Five minutes later I sat back in relief. Jamie had not submitted an article or photos of his altercation with Danna. *Good.* Maybe Corrine had pulled strings, maybe she hadn't. Either way, I was glad for Danna's sake. I hadn't even found anything in the police report column. I texted Danna.

Is Marcus okay?

I poked around a little more. The latest Middle East conflict was worsening. National news was way too depressing. The Pacers were losing. At least the IU basketball team was doing well, as always. And on the Cycling News site I saw an encouraging story from a DC-area bike advocacy group called WABA about the capital district implementing much-needed protected bike lanes. It wasn't all bad out there.

At a ding, I checked the incoming text.

Yes. No concussion. Me? Might be in trouble for
assault. Will call U later.

Poor Danna. I would think any reasonable magis-
trate would cancel out her grabbing his phone with
his taking photographs against her wishes.

I couldn't do anything about it. After I showered
and placed the supplies order for the restaurant, I'd
head out. Maybe I could make my own small contri-
bution to improving the news right here in South Lick.

Chapter Forty-Six

I timed my visit to Columbus for midmorning. It was when my weekly cleaning service came in to do the restaurant floors and restrooms. We kept up during the week, but I was finally doing well enough financially to hire people to really scrub down the place. You don't mess around when you're serving food to the public.

I also figured by ten o'clock an old man would be up, washed, and have eaten breakfast, but wouldn't be busy with lunch or a postprandial snooze. I'd forgotten how little time it took to drive to the small city, though, and I rolled into town at nine-thirty. If I was here long enough, I could even get a Gom sandwich at Zaharakos, a restaurant and museum in an historical building. The Gom was famous in the area—a spicy sloppy joe mix on thick grilled slices of white bread—and I hadn't indulged in one in a while.

It had been a couple of years since I'd visited. The retirement place was on the far side of town from where I entered. As I was earlier than I'd intended, I could park downtown and walk around a little, check

out the innovative buildings. I was sure I could find
a walking guide on my phone. On my way to the
Avenue of the Architects, though, I spied a big blue
H on a sign. *Huh.* I slowed, earning an uncharacter-
istically rude beep from the car behind. Hoosiers
rarely honked unless it was a friendly greeting on a
back road.

I turned at the next blue **H**. *Bingo.* I was looking at
Columbus Regional, the hospital where William
Geller dosed up patients with anesthesia. Could I
poke around and ask a few questions? Why not? The
downtown buildings weren't going anywhere.

After I pulled into a big parking lot, I circled until
I found an open spot. But I didn't get out of my car.
What excuse could I possibly give for asking questions
about a longtime anesthesiologist? And who would I
ask? Not the receptionist or the volunteer at the information desk. They wouldn't tell me anything about
his reputation. I narrowed my eyes at the sprawling
building. I needed to think creatively here.

I climbed out and locked the vehicle. Phone in
hand, I checked a map of the inside of the facility.
Bingo. Several minutes later I took a seat in the surgical waiting room near a worried-looking woman in
her fifties. Who better to ask than relatives of patients
currently under anesthesia? The woman was knitting
at a fast clip. Maybe it took her mind off of whoever
was under the knife.

I picked up a magazine but dropped it after a
moment. "I'm so worried," I confided in the woman.
"My aunt has been in there for a long time."

"My hubby has, too." She raced through another
row.

"Who does he have for anesthesia today?" I kept

my voice low. "My aunt has Doctor Geller but I don't feel that confident about him."

My neighbor set her knitting in her lap and drew her mouth into a wrinkly point. She glanced around before speaking. "I'm sorry to hear that, hon. We specifically asked not to have Geller."

"You did? Why?"

"Last time Hubs was in, that was who he had. My man complained of feeling pain during the procedure and was sicker than a dog after. He's got a lot of problems and has had a half dozen surgeries in the last two years, but Geller's the only anesthesiologist he's ever experienced problems with." She shook her head. "Never again."

"Gee, I hope my aunt comes through okay."

The woman patted my knee. "I'm sure she will, dear."

The television facing us was reporting on a horrific crash on Highway 80 north of here. We tsked and chatted for a few more minutes. I was about to leave when a door from the inside opened. All dozen people waiting in the room looked up expectantly. I blinked when I saw William Geller in scrubs and a blue surgical hat. He was about to speak to someone on his left but caught sight of me and strode in our direction, instead.

"Do you have a relative in surgery?" he asked me.

"Ah, no, I was keeping my friend here company."

Her mouth dropped open but I plowed on. I stood. "I'm sure he'll do fine," I said to her. "Call me once he's home and I'll bring over a meal." I risked a wink at her.

A smile spread over her broad face. "I'll surely do that, hon."

"See you around South Lick, Doctor," I said to him. I calmly walked out and didn't look back. But once I made it to the stairwell, I sank onto the top step. Was I too stupid to live, or what? If Geller was a killer, and if the woman hadn't gone along with my fib, he so would have had his hackles up about me. I blew out a breath. The luck of the Jordans had better hold until the killer was safely behind bars.

Chapter Forty-Seven

When I emerged from the hospital's revolving front door, I stopped short so fast the man who came through behind me nearly bumped into me.

"Might want to move away from the entrance before you stop next time, Miss," he said as he skirted me.

"I'm sorry." I stood still and stared as Octavia walked briskly toward me. What was she doing here? Unless . . .

"Robbie?" She looked as bewildered to see me there as I was her. "Are you well?"

"I'm fine. And you?"

She frowned. "I certainly hope you weren't here asking questions about Doctor Geller."

I mustered my most innocent face, or so I hoped. "Would I do that, Octavia?"

"You know you would."

"Is that who you're here to see?" I asked.

She hesitated, then spoke. "Yes. He called and said he has something to tell me."

"I don't suppose you'd let me tag along." When I saw her expression, I held up a hand. "Yeah, I didn't think so. But would you sit and talk with me for a

minute?" I assumed she'd refuse, but gestured to a
snow-free bench under the wide porch overhang.

"All right, but only for a minute."

I was gobsmacked, as they say, but I'd take it.

She followed me to the bench. "And only as thanks
for being so generous with the information you discover on your own. Not that I encourage you to pursue
said information, you understand." She perched on
the end.

"Got it." I took a seat at the other end, twisting to
face her. "Have you made any progress in Kristina's
death? Like, how did she die, do you know yet?"

"We're still working on that. I have an idea, but I
can't talk about it."

"Have you ruled out natural causes or death by sui-
cide?"

"I'm sorry, Robbie, I can't say, although as you co-
operatively passed along to us, she very likely would
not have gone into the attic of her own volition because of the fear she harbored. If she killed herself
or died at the hand of another, it would have had to
been elsewhere, and someone would have had to
transport her up there."

"What about the safe-deposit box she—" I swore
silently. Now she would know for sure I'd pored over
Kristina's diaries. *But wait.* I'd already admitted I'd
read one of the journals, or glanced at it anyway.

She gave me a hint of a smile. "The safe-deposit
box she mentioned in the diaries? We're still tracking
that down." She rummaged in her shoulder bag and
pulled out a deck of cards.

Cards?

"You're wondering why I'm showing you playing
cards while we're talking about murder."

"Something like that."

"These aren't playing cards, exactly. They're a deck of cold case cards. Our department got the idea from one in another state. It's to keep these unsolved cases salient in detectives' awareness." She extracted the deck from its box and flashed me the top card, which read KRISTINA GELLER. "When I heard about the remains in the burnt attic, I requested that I be assigned to this case. Anybody who can delete a card from the pack—solve the case—gets great satisfaction from doing so. And I fully intend to solve this one."

"Good. Speaking of Kristina, why were you watching Jamie Franklin so closely last night?"

The change in direction threw her for about three milliseconds. "He was well known to have intensely disliked his stepmother. He is still a person of interest in her death."

As I'd thought. "I still haven't heard how Toni died. Can you tell me that much?"

"We believe it was a toxin."

"She was poisoned?"

"The autopsy discovered several puncture sites. The lab is still running tests to discover the nature of the poison." She cocked her head. "Shut your mouth, Robbie. Winter flies will get in."

I closed my gape of astonishment, but my brain was still working hard. Who had access to drugs and syringes? Medical doctors, that's who. "So are you thinking William Geller killed her?"

Octavia gave me her *you know I can't tell you* look over the top of her glasses and stood.

"And what about Marcus Vandemere?" I asked, squeezing in one more inquiry before she left. "Is he really a suspect?"

She scoffed. "Not at this time. That's another issue I have with Mr. Franklin. Listen, I have to get going. Please don't share any of what we talked about."

"I won't." I watched her push through the turning door. I guessed pigs could fly, after all.

Chapter Forty-Eight

I drove away from the hospital with my mind working overtime. I made my way across town, following the GPS on my phone. I could look at the architecture on my way home. Or another time.

Riverwoods Retirement Residences stretched out long wings on either side of a three-story building in the middle. I hadn't realized what a big place it was going to be. The large analog clock behind the reception desk read ten-fifteen. A middle-aged woman with mousy hair and a big snaggle-toothed smile welcomed me.

"I'm looking for Tibor Csik, but I lost his room number."

"Mr. Csik is in East 136. Down that hall and take a left." She pointed a well-manicured hand. "If he's not there, check the solarium. Keep going along past his apartment to the end. We have singing there on Monday mornings and he loves to participate."

"His granddaughter said she might be here, too."

Her smile slid away. "Yes, she's visiting for a few days."

Bingo. Now for me to come up with an excuse for appearing unannounced.

The woman pressed her lips together as if she didn't approve. She leaned toward me, lowering her voice. "It's against policy, but Tibor is such a charmer he convinced the director to let Shirley sleep on his couch."

I thanked her and made my way toward 136. When I was two steps away, the door to the apartment opened. A wizened little man shorter than me emerged, wearing a tweed cap and a sweater vest over a pressed shirt and neatly knotted tie. He leaned on a red walker, the kind with the seat covering a storage pouch. Shirley followed him into the hall. Her eyes flew wide open.

"Robbie? What are you doing here?"

Tibor twisted his upper body as if it was hard to turn his head, but he couldn't get far enough to see me.

"I thought you might be here, and I wanted to see if you were okay," I said.

"Who is there, Shirley?" he asked, speaking with an accent.

I hid a smile. It was exactly how Abe had described his speech, like an actor in a bad Dracula movie.

"*Nagypapa*, this is Robbie Jordan, someone I know from South Lick. She owns that breakfast and lunch restaurant I've told you about."

"Come around here, young lady, so I can greet you properly."

I obliged, smiling and extending my hand.

The old man took it and kissed the back lightly, bowing his head a little. "*Enchanté*, my dear. I am Tibor Csik. You are welcome here." The old-world charm fit him perfectly.

"Thank you, Mr. Csik."

"You may call me Tibor. It's the modern way. Would you like to come and sing with the old folks?"

I glanced at a frowning Shirley.

"I'm sure Robbie is busy," she said. "I'll walk you down there and—"

He interrupted her. "*Edeskem*, I have been walking to the solarium by myself for nine years. You stay and converse with your friend. Offer her coffee, or a small glass of sherry. I will see you when I return for my dinner." He inclined his head slightly toward me again. "I hope you will come back, my dear."

"Thank you. I'd like to. And maybe Shirley can bring you to South Lick for lunch some time."

"That would be a treat. This old man likes to visit with pretty girls."

I stepped out of his way. We both watched him shuffle down the hallway until he reached an open door where notes from a piano began to float our way.

Shirley faced me, folding her arms across her chest. "I don't get why you're here. There's nothing wrong with me getting away and visiting with my grandfather for a few days. You barely even know me. What's going on?"

"In case you hadn't noticed, your landlady was murdered last week," I said. "Your boss said you just disappeared, that you didn't even tell her where you were going. And I heard it on good authority that you were asked not to leave Brown County."

She looked away, then back at me. "How did you know where I was?"

"I didn't. But Abe told me he thought your grandfather lived in Columbus. Since Tibor is your father's father and you share a last name, he wasn't really very hard to find."

She gave a slow nod, but her eyes narrowed. "Did the detective put you up to this? Do you work for her?"

"No, and no. Shirley, can't you see it looks suspicious to leave town like that?"

She stared at me, then turned to the apartment door as if she'd made a decision. "Come in and sit down. I'll tell you why I took off." She unlocked the door with a key hanging from a stretchy curly yellow band around her wrist.

I hesitated for a moment. Wasn't I here because she was a person of interest in a homicide investigation? I mentally shrugged. There were caregivers all over the place, and I was sure every room had an alarm button for the residents to push in case of emergency.

I followed her into a one-bedroom apartment with a postage-stamp kitchen. The sitting room was tidy but overwhelmed by dark wooden antique furniture. A violin case sat in a corner next to a music stand in front of a straight chair.

"Sit. My grandpa wasn't kidding when he offered sherry. He buys only the finest and is in the habit of taking a glass before his midday meal, what he calls dinner." She turned to a bottle sitting on a silver tray and poured into a small stemmed glass etched with flowers. "Want a taste? It's a little early, but I'm having some."

Why not? "Thank you, but not too much." I didn't have to do more than sip from the glass she handed me.

She poured herself a full measure and sat opposite

me next to an end table with a silver oval picture frame in a place of honor. "That's him and my grandmother back in Hungary."

"I wondered what his accent was." She handed me the picture. Both were dressed formally, and neither husband nor wife was smiling. I handed it back. "How long has he been in this country?"

"They were intellectuals and musicians and had to flee in the fifties. All he brought was his violin. I never knew my grandmother. She was so weakened by their escape she died giving birth to my dad." Shirley sipped her sherry. She turned the glass in her hand, staring at it.

"That's so sad," I murmured, also sipping. This was extraordinarily good sherry, as smooth as velvet going down with a remarkable and subtle flavor I couldn't even begin to identify. I waited for her to tell me why she'd made her own escape from South Lick.

She took a deep breath, then looked me full in the face. "My family has suffered horribly at the hands of police. Regular police, AVO—the Hungarian secret police—detectives, prison officials, you name it. They've ruined our lives for decades. Not only my grandparents. My father, too. *Nagypapa*—my grandpa—is a fine man, but he didn't know how to be a single father, and there wasn't any other family around. Daddy got in with some bad sorts in high school. After he got out of the service—and after my brother and I were born— he was convicted of murder. He's spending life in prison, over in Pekin, Illinois."

"I'm so sorry."

"And then there's my poor brother. He's never

been right mentally, and he stole a car. He's in prison for a felony and doesn't even understand why. He's bullied by guards and prisoners alike. When those two, the detective and the lieutenant, came asking me questions about my rotten landlady's death, it put me over the top. I couldn't stand Toni, but I didn't kill her, Robbie. I swear. I just had to get out of town."

"I understand." Pretty much what Abe had told me. At least the eldest Csik seemed to be clear and free of the criminal justice system. I wanted to ask her about what I'd discovered last night but decided not to. When I finally spoke I used a gentle tone. "You need to contact the detective or Buck, Shirley, and tell them what you told me. It'll help them understand. Buck is a really good guy, and Octavia is fair."

"Yeah, maybe. Or maybe they'll trump up charges and I'll really have to go underground." Her eyes turned hard as she traced the oval frame of a photograph taken in an Eastern Europe that no longer existed.

Chapter Forty-Nine

I stood outside the South Lick Provident Bank at eleven-thirty after depositing my considerable till from the last few days since I'd never gotten there on Saturday. It felt good to get the cash out of my safe and into an insured institution. After I'd left Shirley's, I felt I had no choice but to text Octavia that she was at Riverwoods. Shirley wouldn't like it, but I was sure Octavia would operate within the law and with justice. I'd never known her not to. And if I wanted her to keep telling me things, I would have to hold up my end of the limbo stick. I wasn't completely sure I believed Shirley's reason for leaving town, anyway.

I'd also skipped the walking tour of fabulous buildings in Columbus. Many of the older ones were on the National Historic Register and, unless a tornado hit, they would be there the next time I visited. I hadn't stayed for a Gom, either. I'd get one when I returned, for sure.

Now I glanced up and down South Lick's main street. The cloud-free sky of the early morning persisted, with temps in the thirties. Half of yesterday's snow had already melted, so sidewalks were wet. The place would turn into a skating rink when it went below freezing tonight, but that was life in southern Indiana. Thaw, freeze, thaw, freeze. Rinse and repeat.

At the click of high-heeled boots, I turned in the direction of City Hall to see Corrine busily making her way along the sidewalk.

"Robbie, hey there," she called. "Hold on up, would you?"

I waved back and waited. A text came in from Adele at the same time as Corrine's arrival. I shoved the phone back in my jacket pocket.

"How's Danna?" I asked her.

The mayor looked skyward for a moment, then back at me. "That girl's in a mess of trouble with me, but she seems to have evaded criminal charges. I'd heard a few rumblings here and there about her brother's temper. If anything, he was the calm one last night, from all reports, including yours."

"And Danna told me he didn't get a concussion, so that's good."

"Indeed it is." She glanced both ways and lowered her voice. "But I have me a piece of real news for you."

I waited, but she just looked bright-eyed at me. "So?" I made a rolling gesture with my hand.

"Heared on the scanner William Geller confessed to Detective Slade he found his wife dead on the floor. He was worried he'd get the blame, because everybody knew how unhappy they were. So he upped and carried her to the attic, bum leg and all."

"Seriously? Wow."

"Wow is exactly right. He plum left her there to rot. Can you even believe it?"

"I'm not sure I can, actually." That was a lot to take in. I didn't trust a man who would beat his spouse, not about anything, whether he was a member of the AMA or a stonecutter. "What if he's lying? And did he say how she died?"

"Said he couldn't tell. Mind you, all this wasn't on the scanner, but I got me on the horn with our buddy Buck and he filled me in on the details. The doc said he thought he saw Toni leaving the house as he approached." She wagged her head. "Killed her very own wombmate."

I held up an index finger. "Hang on, Corrine. You don't know she did. And Toni can't defend herself, either." I thought some more. "Did Octavia bring Geller in? It must be a crime not to report a body you find." If that was what happened. If he was able to carry a heavy weight to the attic, maybe he'd killed his wife himself—with all those drugs and syringes he had access to—and then toted her body to where it wouldn't be found.

"He convinced the detective to wait to interview him," Corrine said. "He was scheduled for surgeries all afternoon."

"Really? Why call Octavia during his workday, then?"

She gave me an amused frown. "You expect me to unravel the workings of the male brain? I resigned from that job a heck of a long time ago, hon."

I laughed. "I hear you."

The bell atop Our Lady of the Springs chimed

once for the half hour. "Holy chicken feed, I'm late for a meeting. Catch you later, Robbie."

I waved her on, then checked Adele's message.

News. Call me.

Adele was quite fond of her police scanner, and I had a sneaking suspicion I already knew the news. I started walking back to my store as I pressed her speed dial.

"Roberta," she began without saying hello. "Doc Geller confessed to dragging his poor wife to the attic."

Bingo. "Except he said she was already dead." *Oops.* I glanced around, but nobody seemed to have overheard me.

"Well, dangnation, how'd you come to hear that so quicklike?"

"Corrine told me a few minutes ago."

"It's something, isn't it?"

"Do you believe him?" I slowed at a bakery emitting the most delectable yeasty aroma of fresh-baked bread.

"For corn sake, dear, why wouldn't I?"

Because he's a murderer and he's hiding the truth, maybe? I wasn't going to say that in public, not even softly.

"Corrine also told me he said he saw the, uh, sister leaving the house right before he found his wife," I added.

"Toni," Adele said dramatically. "It was the sister in the hall with the . . . how'd Kristina die, anyway?"

"I asked Octavia that when I ran into her this morning. She wouldn't say." I sniffed the bread again.

"Adele, I have to run. It's my day off and I still have items on my to-do list."

"All righty, then. See you at the Chamber mixer at five-thirty?" she asked.

I groaned. "I forgot all about that." It was the annual holiday cocktail party for South Lick business owners. I was going to have to get somewhat dressed up and go be polite and respectable. "Are you going?"

"'Course. Free drinks and food? I may own a sheep farm and yarn business, but I'm an old lady, Roberta. We never turn down freebies." She chortled. "See you at Hoosier Hollow."

She had a point. I could grab a glass of wine at the restaurant, which was usually closed on Mondays. I'd make my dinner from the hot appetizers cooked up by the chef, a good friend of mine, and still get home at a reasonable hour to do breakfast prep. And a little networking never hurt.

"See you there," I agreed. "Love you."

"Love you, too."

I pulled open the bakery door. I was headed home, but who didn't have time for a warm loaf of yummy?

Chapter Fifty

Spreading a thick layer of Irish butter on a crusty, still-warm slice of an artisanal *bâtard* was pure pleasure. Taking a bite took me to the heavenly plane.

"So good," I mumbled around the mouthful at a few minutes after noon. Birdy gave me the slitted eyes from his half-alert pose on the kitchen chair next to mine. As I chewed, I cut a few slices of a Manchego cheese I'd picked up last week, laid a half dozen olives and cornichons on a small plate, and called it lunch. I swallowed the bread and munched on one of the tiny spicy pickles as I gazed at my not-so-successful crime-solving crossword on the table.

On a fresh sheet of paper I scribbled a list of questions:

-Significant that Geller is bad at his job?

-Toni murdered her sister? Or her husband?

-Kristina died of natural causes and Geller hauled her upstairs?

-Shirley staying away from police not because of family but because she's guilty of murder?

-Is her grandfather involved?

-Jamie lying about Marcus to hide his own guilt?

-Is Marcus really over his anger issues?

-Clive killed his wife for her money?

Unfortunately, answers from my brain weren't anywhere near as forthcoming. I sent a message to Abe in case he had time to talk, but he didn't answer. I finished my lunch and, after I buttered one more slice of bread, I headed into the restaurant, letting Birdy accompany me. When in doubt, cook. Having my hands busy often freed up my brain, and the order should be arriving soon, too. They were good about coming during the window I specified, and I knew I'd be back from Columbus by the afternoon.

Cold weather called for a hearty soup. Beef and barley sounded like exactly the ticket for tomorrow. I could use the big jars of beef stock I'd gotten from a Nashville butchery as the base. I chopped onions and celery, heated oil in the big pot, and set them to sauté. The sun, almost as low in the sky as it was going to get, shone in the eastern windows a little more brightly than it should because of the now white-covered ground.

Normally, cooking on a sunny day even in December would also brighten my mood. Not today. That list of questions nagged at me. I thought of Octavia, Buck, and other law-enforcement professionals whose job it was to solve crime. How much more not solving a case must nag at them. They were the ones responsible for keeping the peace and restoring justice, not me. It had been almost a week since the fire and nearly that long since Toni was killed. The lack of resolution had to be driving them more nuts than it was me.

I was on my way to the walk-in to find the barley and the stock when I froze. Was that a noise at the service door on the west side of the building? A while ago someone had picked the lock on that door and threatened me. I'd added a new, more secure lock. Any one of the people on my list could be trying to get in. I felt my pocket. No phone. Where was it?

Stealing a look at the front door, I let out a breath. Nobody there. I raced to my apartment and grabbed the phone off the table where I'd left it. The tension rushed out of me. The delivery person had sent a message.

Am outside your service door. You want this stuff or not?

I laughed, albeit weakly. I jabbed back a message.

B right there!

A moment later, I checked the service door's peephole to make sure the truck had the appropriate logo on it, then let in the woman standing outside. Her dark jacket bore the company logo. It was usually a man who brought the order. Whatever.

"Sorry about that," I said.

"No problem. Got a full schedule. Where do you want it?" She didn't waste words.

I showed her and helped unload the boxes. I signed for the delivery and thanked her.

"Should oughta add a doorbell out there." She left as tersely as she'd entered.

I didn't care about her gruffness, and she was right about a service doorbell. Anyway, a food delivery was a lot better than an intruder, any day.

Chapter Fifty-One

With my delivery stored and the barley simmering away in the soup, I was wiping down the stainless counter when a knock came from the front door. Jamie Franklin stood on my sun-splashed porch peering in through the glass in the top half. Did I want to talk to him? Not really. Could I sneak into my apartment? He saw me looking his way and waved. Too late now. Of course I could signal, "No," but if I talked with him, I might learn something. I patted my back pocket, feeling the reassurance of my phone. To be safe, I unlocked the door and stepped out on the porch, shutting the door behind me. No way was I inviting him inside.

I smiled. "Can I help you? I'm closed on Mondays."

"I know that." He didn't return my smile. "I hear you've been challenging my credentials. You've got a lot of nerve."

Whoa. "Um, what are you talking about?" And who had he heard that from?

"You know what I mean. Saying my articles are unfounded."

I folded my arms and lifted my chin. Sure it was cold out here, but I also wanted to signal my position. "You wrote that Marcus Vandemere was a suspect. The police say he's not. So, yeah, that was unfounded. False, actually."

"I had a credible source who said he was."

"Who was it?"

"A professional journalist doesn't reveal his sources."

"That's not good enough. You obviously didn't check the facts with the police. That's called libel, Jamie."

"Oh, so now you're a lawyer as well as a snoop?"

As if. I stared up at him. "Maybe you killed Toni yourself and you were trying to throw out a smoke-screen."

"Nice try." His laugh was harsh and his eyes burned. "Maybe you should butt out of what's not your business."

This was going nowhere. I had no interest in letting his ire escalate. "If you'll excuse me, this is my day off. Enjoy your afternoon." I swallowed and gripped the doorknob.

He glowered, but didn't make a move toward me. I slipped inside and tested the door to make sure it was shut tight, then flipped both locks. *Whew.* He could look in all he wanted. I was so out of here.

Back in my apartment, I set a timer so I wouldn't forget to turn off the soup. I sat on the couch stroking Birdy. Tall and glowering Jamie had felt threatening, but he hadn't made a move to harm me. And I hadn't learned anything new, either. I might as well see if I could.

"Sorry, buddy." I set Birdy on the cushion next to me, grabbed my laptop, and picked up the sheet of paper I'd scribbled my questions on earlier. I put my feet up again, staring at the one about Shirley's grandfather. Tibor Csik wouldn't be a common name. Searching him yielded a bantamweight boxer who won gold at the 1948 Olympics. But he'd also died in 1948. All the others I could find—who weren't dead—lived in Hungary, where it apparently wasn't an unusual moniker. So much for that line of digging.

Looking for details about Shirley didn't get me any further than her past soccer achievements. I already knew Clive was very nearly the Ungoogleable Man. What about this business of Toni murdering Tug? Buck had claimed there'd been no basis in the claim, that they had investigated and found no wrongdoing. Maybe the authorities had missed something. Jamie could have killed Toni out of revenge for her offing his father.

I put in all the search terms I could come up with and started reading. *Huh.* Yep, Tug was a nickname for Willard. If I were him, I'd use a nickname, too. He'd made his considerable money in the paper industry and had been widowed when Jamie was ten. I saw an announcement of his marriage to Toni. I saw a death notice and short article about his funeral. What I didn't find was even a shred of suspicion that he'd been murdered. So much for that line of thought.

Pursuing a few more lines of inquiry was equally fruitless. By three o'clock when the timer dinged, I was ready to turn off the soup, pick up a novel, and read myself into a nice couch nap with a cat on my lap.

Chapter Fifty-Two

Dressed for the season in a cream-colored turtle-neck, black pants, and a sparkly green sweater, I made my way to the mixer, now in full swing, by five-thirty. After chatting with the bakery owner for a few minutes, I moseyed up to my aunt standing at a high-top table. She was halfway through her selection of bite-sized spanakopita and mini-quiches, with a bacon-wrapped scallop on its way into her mouth. A gingerbread man waited on a separate small plate, its white-iced grin nearly leering up at me.

"Hey, sweetie," she mumbled around a mouthful.

"Adele, this afternoon I was looking for information about Toni and Clive." I kept my voice low. "They seem like they were an odd couple, but I couldn't find anything on the Internet."

"No surprise there." She didn't seem surprised by my jumping directly into such a question, either. "Clive is one of them Luddites, don't even own a computer. And Toni was all sensitive about her privacy." She popped in another bite.

"Do you know how they met?"

She popped in another bite and held up a hand while she chewed and swallowed. "It was at some bereavement support group over to Nashville, you know, after old Tug knocked off, and Clive's first wife died, too."

Did Octavia know Clive now had two dead wives in a row?

"The two of them just plum hit it off," Adele went on. "True to form, Toni got tired of him after about a year. Seemed like every little bitty thing he did annoyed the living heck out of her."

"He said she'd kicked him out of the house."

"That she did."

"Do you know Clive had lost his plumbing license?" I asked.

"'Course I do. Who doesn't?"

Me, for one. Of course Adele would be aware of anything going on in town, especially as the former mayor. Silly of me to even ask.

"He's a pretty nice fella, but he ain't what you call a skilled journeyman." She drained her plastic cup of white wine. "Not exactly the sharpest tool in the shed."

"How did he get a license in the first place?"

"Has a cousin at the state licensing agency, that's how. Heavenly heavens, them munchies are good. I love me some bacon with my scallops. You oughta get yourself a plate before they disappear." She leaned in and planted a kiss on my cheek. "I'm headin' home, hon. You take care, now."

"I will. You, too."

I spied Buck leaning against the far wall in a casual hands-in-pockets stance, but his eyes were alert as they surveyed the room. Would he share any facts of the case with me? It was worth a try. I made a beeline for him.

"Evenin', Robbie."

"Hey, Buck." I sipped my wine. "I was wondering if you knew the window of time Toni died in."

"A-yup." He stretched out the affirmative like a rubber band, then shut his mouth. He gazed forlornly at his three empty plates on the high-top table next to him.

I waited. When he stayed silent, I said, "Are you going to share it with me?"

"I spose I can, long's you don't tell nobody. Beltonia died sometime after midnight and before sunup."

"That's almost eight hours. The sun doesn't rise until seven-thirty or so at this time of year. They couldn't pin it down more precisely?"

"Welp, yes, they did. The time was more like between two and five in the morning."

"And? Does anybody have an alibi?"

He wagged his head right and left. "They all live by theirselves. Nobody around saw nothing."

"Except Shirley saw someone."

"Yes. That is, she *says* she did."

"You don't believe her?"

"It's one of them, you know, fifty percent of one and a dozen of the other."

My jaw dropped at his fractured metaphor.

He lifted a shoulder and dropped it. "We ain't done with the investigation by a long shot, hon." His cell buzzed from its case on his belt. "'Scuse me." He turned away to check his phone.

I glanced around the room for a moment. When I looked back, Buck was disappearing out the front door, still struggling into his jacket. Something must be happening. Too bad I didn't know what.

By six-thirty my mouth was about worn out from smiling while I networked. I knew lots of the local businesspeople, but I was surprised at how many I didn't. Part of it was that the Chamber had invited folks from the Nashville Chamber of Commerce, too. They always reciprocated with an invitation to their spring mixer. My feet hurt, and I'd run out of store business cards. The appetizers had pretty much run out, too, because they were so tasty. I stuck my head into the kitchen and asked for the chef, but my friend had already gone home.

As I turned back to the mixer, ready to hit the road for my own home, I could have sworn I heard the words, "Toni's killer" across the room. The voice could have been a woman speaking in a low register, or it could have been said by a man. But who was conjecturing about homicide at a holiday business mixer? I walked in that direction through the thinning crowd. Corrine rested her elbow on the upright piano in the corner, more or less in the area I'd heard the words, and was engaged in conversation with Jamie, whose camera was slung around his neck as it had been yesterday at the tree lighting. When had Jamie showed up? Our mayor had a fairly low voice. Maybe it had been her speaking. I veered toward them.

Before I could get there, Dr. Geller strode with his uneven gait up to the two. I hadn't seen him before now. He pointed his finger at Jamie. "I thought I told you never to show up at one of these functions." His color was high, his voice loud and strident.

Jamie's glare shot icicles of hatred at the older

man. "You don't own me, man. You have no right to tell me where I can and can't be." He raised the camera and clicked a couple of shots of Geller. "You, a wife abuser and murderer, you're the one who shouldn't be here. I'm surprised you're not locked up already."

"Hey! You put that thing down, Franklin," Geller snarled. "Who told you you could take my picture?"

"Ever hear of freedom of the press?" Jamie taunted. "I'm documenting the event for the social pages."

Geller, his face a mask of rage, grabbed at the camera with his right hand.

Uh-oh. A rerun of yesterday?

Jamie evaded him with one step back. Geller cocked his left arm, elbow raised, fist ready to strike.

I cleared my throat. "There's no need for that, Doctor."

"You want to fight, old man?" Jamie asked. "I'll show you a fight." He raised both fists and bounced on his feet in a boxing stance. They were both tall, but Jamie was younger, faster, and didn't have a prosthetic leg. It wasn't exactly an even match.

I waved my hand to distract him. "Jamie, back off."

Nothing changed. I could almost smell the smoke from their ears.

Corrine stepped smack between the two, facing Geller. "Cool it, gentlemen, and that's an order." She held up her right hand, palm out, in front of the doctor's face. With her left hand she gestured backward with her thumb to Jamie. "Enough." She did not smile, waiting until both of them lowered their fists.

Whew. Corrine to the rescue, effective where I hadn't been. The remaining networkers in the room quieted, staring, murmuring. Geller muttered something under his breath and shot me a flared-nostrils narrowed-eyes message of hatred. How had *I* earned that? He turned on his heel and limped out, pushing past a female shopkeeper so hard she had to grab her friend to stay on her feet.

Chapter Fifty-Three

I'd never been so glad to leave a gathering. I hurried toward home through the dark, uneasy from witnessing the near fistfight between Geller and Jamie. Jamie had left not long after the doctor, but not before Corrine secured a promise from him not to harass Geller or anyone else with his unwanted photographing. Shouldn't Jamie have learned his lesson yesterday? The dude was at least a decade older than me, and I had no clue why he kept trying to provoke people like that. To me it seemed like stupid behavior. I guessed some folks were slow learners.

Pans 'N Pancakes was only a few blocks away and I was always careful to stick to well-lit streets when I walked alone at night. The canister of pepper spray in my pocket was a reassurance. Abe had strongly urged me to carry it whenever I went out. I wasn't hard to convince, given what I'd been through in the past. He and I had actually practiced together, so I knew exactly how to grip the container the size of an asthma inhaler, point it straight-armed away from me, and activate it with my thumb. It was a shame to think sleepy South Lick could hold danger, but I'd had to face it more than once. I'd rather be safe than sorry.

I paused outside the restaurant to text Abe.

Leaving to walk home from restaurant. Will text you when I get there.

He was at banjo practice but texted back.

Be safe.

At least the sidewalks were still wet, not icy. The just-past-full moon had risen and was casting pale but welcome light on my path. Small blessings, and I'd take every single one of them. As I walked, I couldn't keep my thoughts off murder, though, including what I'd discovered today.

I pondered Tibor Csik's long journey. To be a concert violinist with an erudite professor for a wife and have to leave everything—family, home, possessions, language, a rich culture—to escape persecution must have been impossibly wrenching and tragic. And then to lose your wife in childbirth, and your son and grandson to prisons? I couldn't even imagine the pain. I would love to get to know the little gentleman better, if Shirley would allow it. Or even if she wouldn't.

And then there was Geller's supposed confession to Octavia about taking Kristina's body to the attic. Was that true or a smokescreen for the real story? Add to it his display of anger at the mixer and I wasn't sure what to think.

My steps slowed. What was the consistent thing about this case besides secrets? Tempers. Well, except for Shirley. She didn't have a temper that I knew of. I ticked through the other people I considered suspects. The rumors about Marcus? I felt comfortable ignoring them. He seemed sincere about dealing with his issue. Jamie was foolhardy and rude, but he didn't seem dangerous, even though he'd been willing to defend himself a little while ago.

William Geller was the one who had acted with extreme vitriol. I shuddered, thinking of the look he'd given me at the mixer. He had to be the killer. He'd struck out to protect his reputation as a doctor. To uphold what he considered his honor as a husband. And he'd definitely run the risk of gaining a criminal record, which would ruin all of it. His public behavior a few minutes ago had been a shock. Maybe it shouldn't have been, after what I'd witnessed at my own store. I didn't know how he'd killed Toni, but he certainly had easy access to drugs and might have had a key to his sister-in-law's place. I glanced around, but nobody seemed to be following me, especially not him. I would call Octavia the minute I was securely inside. I wasn't stopping now to do it.

About to trudge up the front steps of Pans 'N Pancakes, I stopped short and stared. I could swear I'd left the porch light on for myself. Inside the store the tiny white lights I'd strung around the windows sparkled, and they were on the same switch. The bulb in the porch fixture must have burned out. Still, I pulled out the pepper spray in my right hand and the door key in my left, shivering a little as the bad woo-woo feeling returned.

I tried to insert the key in the lock but it didn't go in. Unlike some, I was not a lefty. I leaned over and peered at the keyhole, finally getting it right. Before I could unlock the door to safety, a faint wisp of a human-made sound came from the darkness to my left. I sucked in a breath. I caught a whiff of stale cigarette smoke. *Smoke?* The only person I'd run into recently who smoked was—

An iron grip clasped my left wrist. *No!* I snapped my head in that direction.

William Geller's gaze of fury burned at me. "You were trying to ruin my life. You couldn't leave well enough alone."

Exactly what I'd feared. "What are you talking about?" I yanked my elbow back. He didn't relinquish his grip. My heart hammered. My palms sweated inside my gloves. An arctic chill raced down my spine. "Let go of me!"

"As if. You've been asking questions. Lying to patients. Digging, digging, digging. You women are all alike." He nearly spat the word "women." "You would wreck my career and think nothing of it. I'd be locked up and you'd go back to making your little flapjacks for terrorists. Well, I'm not having it."

I struggled to twist away. His hand was bigger and stronger than my wrist and I couldn't free myself. I didn't have enough light under the porch roof to aim a good kick. I flipped my thumb under the cap of the pepper spray, but I was too close to him. I'd practiced from farther away.

He lifted a fat syringe in his left hand. Enough moonlight reflected in to see that much.

I sucked in a breath. This was not happening. I couldn't let it happen.

"Don't worry, it'll be an easy death," he snarled, his tone low and ominous.

I pointed the canister before he could jab me. I

jammed my thumb onto the button. The *pssshhht* of
the spray filled the quiet night. He screamed and let
go of my wrist. I kept spraying a circle of the stuff into
his face as I backed away. He clawed at his eyes, at
his face.

I raced down the steps and back toward town.
After a block, I slowed to a speed walk, pulled out my
phone, and jabbed 911. My own eyes watered.

"Brown County," the dispatcher said. "What's your
emergency?"

"William Geller attacked me at Pans 'N Pancakes.
Nineteen Main Street, South Lick. I pepper sprayed
him. He's on the front porch. Send someone to get
him. He's the murderer. Hurry!"

The dispatcher started talking to me. I disconnected and pressed Buck's number. I resumed jogging toward safety, grateful for my excellent lung
capacity from bicycling and my flat-heeled boots.

"Robbie, what's—?"

Breathing hard, I slowed again and told him what
I'd said to the dispatcher. "I think Geller murdered
both twins. I called Dispatch, but please go catch him.
I don't know how long the spray lasts." I'd never had
to use it before. My eyes stung. Some of the spray
must have drifted or bounced back at me.

"Got it," he said. "Stay on the line."

I heard him give quick, terse orders.

"Where are you?" he asked me.

"I'm jogging back to Hoosier Hollow. I was at the
Chamber mixer."

"Okay. Sit tight there until you hear from me." The
call disconnected. I was in the Hoosier Hollow block
now and I slowed to a fast walk. No way could Geller

recover so quickly from having his eyes burned with capsaicin. Could he? Sirens wailed into life. Usually when I heard public safety vehicles take off for an emergency, I felt uneasy. Right now? That whooping alert was the best sound in the known universe.

Chapter Fifty-Four

I stood in front of Hoosier Hollow waiting to hear back from Buck, breathing hard. I was still warm from my escape, and the last thing I wanted to do was return to mingling with business associates. I texted Abe, instead.

Had a scare at my store. I'm fine. Back at Hoosier Hollow waiting for Buck.

I didn't want to worry him, but I knew he'd be concerned if I didn't follow through with a message about getting home safely. My legs came down with a case of the shakes as my adrenaline ebbed. The candy store next door, still open for evening shopping, had a bench in front of its gaily lit window, so I lowered myself to sit on it. I leaned elbows on knees.

Geller's voice had dripped with disdain and dislike when he said the word "women." I'd bet anything he killed both Toni and Kristina. Maybe Toni had suspected he'd killed her twin all along and had threatened to expose him after her bones surfaced. My hand flew to my mouth. Octavia had said Toni died of an injectable toxin. Now all the lab had to do was analyze what was in the syringe Geller almost killed me with and they could look for traces of it in Kristina's remains, too.

The restaurant door opened, and Corrine sailed out, calling good-bye over her shoulder to someone. She turned in my direction and halted, looking surprised.

"Why, Robbie, I saw you leave a little bit of a while ago. What are you doing setting there in the cold?" She hurried toward me.

"Can you sit down for a minute?" My teeth had started knocking.

"You're cold, hon." She plopped down next to me and extended her arm around my shoulders. "Don't you want to go back into the restaurant?"

I shook my head, pressing my lips together to keep my teeth from chattering.

"Then we're going in here." She gestured behind us with her thumb, then stood and took my hand. "Come with me, girl."

I let her guide me into the warm, fragrant candy store, into a corner at the front but away from the door.

"You look like you've been through a crisis of some kind." Corrine spoke softly but looked worried. Raising her voice, she called out a greeting to the woman behind the counter. She turned back to me and murmured, "You're safe here. Tell me what happened."

"Geller attacked me on my porch," I whispered.

Her eyes widened. "He didn't."

"He did." My voice came out in a quavery scratch. "I pepper sprayed him and got away."

"You poor thing." She whipped out her phone. "Did you call it in?"

"Yes." Now my whole body was shivering.

Corrine wrapped me in a big Hoosier hug. "You're going to be fine, Robbie. You're safe here. You're going to be fine."

After a minute or two, her warmth and mantra did the trick. The warm store helped, too. I disengaged, wiping my eyes. "Thank you, Corrine. I needed that."

She peered at me. "Get some of that spray in your eyes, too?"

"I think so."

She snorted. "One of the hazards of the sh— uh, stuff. Same thing happened to me a couple few years back when I was obliged to fend off a idiot man up in Chicago. Still, it's pretty darn effective, ain't it?"

"It is," I said as a cruiser pulled up at the curb. "That's probably Buck. I told him I'd be in the restaurant."

"I'll go get him." Corrine bustled out, returning in a flash with a worried-looking lieutenant.

He laid a hand on my shoulder, craning his head down to look into my face. "Did he hurt you, Robbie?"

I extended my wrist, now red from Geller's grip. "Only when he grabbed me here. Did you catch him before he recovered from the spray?"

"We catched him, acowering right there on your front porch. Got him locked up as tight as a too-small bathing suit on a too-long ride home from the beach.

He's not happy about it, 'course. Yelling he's innocent and complaining about every little whatnot."

The shopkeeper hurried over. "Is everything all right here?" she asked Buck.

"Yes, ma'am, thank you. Could you package me up a two-pound box of chocolate truffles, pretty please? Or heck, make that two boxes. I'm thinking my sainted wife could use some sweets right about now."

She looked at all three of us as if she didn't believe we were simply candy shopping, but she didn't ask any more questions. "Certainly, sir." She headed back to the counter.

I kept my voice low. "Can you find out what he was about to inject me with?"

"Sure's as my name's Buckham Hamilton Bird." He nodded with satisfaction.

I stared. "That's your full name? I had no idea."

"Yepperoo. Anyhoo, the doc ain't as smart as he thinks he is. Had a vial of some drug right there in his coat pocket. Hang on a little minute. I took a picture of the label so's I'd remember it. Some long medical-type name, of course." He pulled out his phone and found the photograph.

"Succinylcholine." I sounded it out. "I wonder what that does."

Corrine was already looking it up on her phone. Her eyes widened. "Says here it's used in anesthesia for surgery. Too much leads to respiratory paralysis, and if a patient takes digitalis, too, this suksenna-whatever can cause cardiac arrest."

I shivered again, but this time not from the cold. "Geller told me mine would be an easy death. Not being able to breathe is an easy way to go? I doubt it."

"Toni took some kind of medicine for her heart," Corrine said. "He musta known that. Being her brother-in-law and all."

"Look, there's Abe." I pointed out the window at him standing on the sidewalk, looking both ways. What was he doing here? I'd told him I was fine.

Buck rapped on the glass and gestured to him to come in.

Abe hurried in and took my face in both hands. "Are you all right, my sweet? I couldn't find you at Hoosier Hollow."

"I'm all right," I said, although my throat thickened around the words. "I didn't need you to leave practice."

"You didn't answer my text. You mean way more to me than playing music, Robbie." His eyes filled.

"I'm sorry, sugar, I didn't realize you had sent a message back."

"Robbie here was single-handedly responsible for apprehending a double murderer tonight," Buck murmured proudly.

Abe blinked in astonishment. "You were?"

"Thanks to the pepper spray you got me, I was able to get away from William Geller after he attacked me on the porch of my store. Buck and company were the ones who apprehended him, thank goodness."

The proprietor brought Buck's boxes of chocolates. She gave Abe a look. "Can I help you, sir?"

He smiled. "I'm with them, thank you, ma'am."

Buck followed her to the counter to pay, then returned to our little group, boxes in hand.

"Let's get you home, darlin'," Abe said. He glanced at Buck. "Can we go in the front door of the store?"

"Octavia's people should oughta be done with it by now. It's not a homicide scene, thanks to Robbie."

I blew out a breath. "Come with us if you can," I said to Corrine and Buck. "I have Four Roses." I had finally recovered enough to smile without shaking.

Chapter Fifty-Five

We four sat around my biggest table. I'd cranked up the heat and lit the tree, while Abe had started carols playing softly. We were all nibbling on the truffles from one of the boxes Buck had bought and sipping bourbon, tea, or both. Actually, nobody was drinking unadulterated tea.

"I know I told that lady both boxes of chocolates were for my wife, but I thought you deserved a goodly portion, too, Robbie." Buck grinned as he stretched out his giraffe legs toward Ohio.

"Thank you," I said. "I'm glad I'm alive to share them."

Abe pressed his knee against mine. "I am, too."

I was about to ask Buck a question when the bell on the door jangled. Adele pushed through followed by Octavia.

"I invited the detective to join us, Robbie," Buck said. "Hope you don't mind."

"Of course not. Come on in," I called to the two. Adele would have heard about the arrest on her scanner, which she never turned off.

Adele hurried over and gave me a big hug. She grabbed two more mugs from the kitchen, then sat across the table. Octavia hung back.

I stood. "Please pull up a chair and join us, Octavia." My former animosity toward her seemed to have evaporated.

Still looking a bit wary, she came over to me, hands clasped in front of her. "Thank you. I'd like to apologize for not apprehending Doctor Geller before he attacked you. We were this close." She held up a half-inch gap between thumb and forefinger. "And then he evaded the tail I'd assigned to him. He's not going to do that again, believe me."

"I appreciate that," I said. "I'm just glad I was able to get away, and that he's behind bars where he belongs."

"For the rest of his living days, if I have anything to do about it." Octavia gave a grim, low-watt smile.

"Set yourself down and have a drink, now, Octavia," Adele said.

The detective took a deep breath and let it out, then sat next to Adele, who proffered the bourbon and poured after Octavia pointed to her cup.

"So that story Geller told about finding his wife already dead was hogwash and a half," Corrine said. "I'll tell you, I'm glad to hear Toni didn't murder her twin sister."

I was relieved, too.

"I suspected the story was a sham," Octavia said. "But I didn't want to let him know how close we were. And you know, he only limped here in South Lick. To see him move around that hospital, you'd never know he had a prosthesis."

I looked at her. "You're right. When I saw him in the waiting room, he wasn't limping. That didn't register until right now." How could I have not noted his smooth stride?

"And Geller was the person Ms. Csik saw leaving Toni's half of the duplex," Buck said.

"Yes." Octavia took a small sip and swallowed, then cleared her throat. "My, that's smooth."

Corrine laughed out loud. "You never had no Four Roses before?"

"I can't say that I have. I rarely partake of hard alcohol."

"She's more the merlot type, am I right, Detective?" Adele asked with a smile.

Octavia inclined her head. "Cabernet sauvignon, but yes. I enjoy a good red wine on occasion."

"So both Clive and Jamie are in the clear?" I asked.

"Yep." Buck cupped his hands around his mug. He'd opted for his whiskey in hot tea. "I had a word with Franklin about risking a libel charge next time he writes falsehoods for publication, though."

"Good," Corrine said.

"Octavia, Jamie mentioned to me sometime during the week that you were 'trouble,' as he put it." I regarded her. "Do you know what that was about?"

She returned my gaze from behind her dark-rimmed glasses. "I have encountered very few citizens who enjoy being a person of interest in a homicide investigation. They and their movements, past and present, are subject to intense scrutiny. I'm sure it was nothing more than that. Of course, I'm not going to let a person's displeasure dissuade me from seeking the truth."

"None of us in criminal justice do," Buck added.

Adele slapped her thigh. "And boy howdy, we're glad about it."

"I'm glad about my boy Marcus being in the clear, I can tell you that much," Corrine said.

"Shirley Csik is out of the woods, as well," Octavia said.

Shirley would be relieved to hear that. I glanced at Adele. "Octavia, did you uncover anything about Shirley trying to bribe an official at the prison where Shirley's brother is incarcerated?"

Adele gave me a knowing look. Octavia blinked, but Buck nodded.

"Yes, in fact we did," Octavia said. "Ms. Csik was not charged with a crime at the time."

"We was looking at it for a motive," Buck began. "Seeing as how Toni helped her get it all put quiet, like, and maybe had decided to go public with the story. But Octavia, here, she was in pursuit of the perpetrator of homicide, not small-time bribery with love as a motive. Shirley wasn't no killer."

I smiled to myself. *Good.*

"Both murders were the work of an unscrupulous doctor with a hatred of women and access to a drug that should never be used outside an operating room," Octavia said. "We're now checking to see if he is connected to two other female cold-case victims with whom he'd had contact at the hospital. One was a pharmacist, the other a surgical nurse. Geller was clever. The pathologist who did Toni Franklin's autopsy almost didn't notice the puncture sites in the fold under her buttocks."

I shuddered. "He had so much rage against me it looked like he was going to jab that needle into my neck."

"Probably was," Buck said.

"I can see Geller killing his wife if he found out about her affair with Jamie," I said. "He'd already discovered some of the money she was hiding from him and tried to beat her for doing that. He would have been furious at her not being under his control any longer."

"And if he injected her with poison, it wasn't no spur of the moment killing, neither," Buck said. "Clearly premeditated."

Octavia nodded.

"That kind of man shouldn't never get married," Adele said. "Shouldn't be let near women."

"I agree. But Octavia, why did he kill Toni?" I asked. "Did she know about him murdering her sister?"

"She apparently suspected it after the remains surfaced right there in their house," she said. "We found a half-written letter addressed to the editor of the newspaper on her laptop, accusing her brother-in-law of murder. She mentioned her sister had finally confided to her that Geller was abusing her. Maybe Toni hinted to him she was about to go public and he took action before she could."

"And he had the gall to flip the story," Corrine began, "and accuse dead Toni herself of the murder. Yessiree, the man belongs right where he is currently sitting."

"Amen," Adele said.

"Will you be able to find evidence of the same

drug in Kristina's remains, do you think?" I asked Octavia.

"It's possible. Depending partly on luck, they might find the toxin in mummified tissues, bones, the pulp of the teeth, or her hair. A decade in a closed environment is not as destructive to a corpse as a body left outside for a much shorter period of time."

"Good luck with that, Detective." Corrine stood. "Nice work, all y'all. I best get myself home and give the good news to my Danna before she hits the sack. You girls have an early morning tomorrow."

I hit my forehead and swore. "I haven't done breakfast prep yet." I stood.

"I'll help you," Adele and Abe said in unison, then burst out laughing.

"We'll leave you to it," Octavia said. She rose and came around the table, extending her hand. "I commend you for your bravery."

I shook her firm, slender grip. "Thank you." I left it at that.

Buck held the door for Corrine and Octavia.

"Thanks for the truffles, Buck," I called.

His grin split his thin face. "You earned 'em, hon."

When I turned back to the kitchen area, Abe and Adele had their heads together. Adele saw me looking and put on the biggest fake smile I'd ever seen. What was that all about? I shook my head and went to scrub my hands. That biscuit dough wasn't going to mix itself.

Chapter Fifty-Six

The restaurant was hopping the next morning. Danna and I had spoken briefly about the previous evening before we opened.

"You must be glad Marcus is officially cleared," I said while breaking eggs.

"I never once thought he was guilty." She stared at the condiment caddies, then looked up. "And he kept his cool way better than me during the thing with Mr. Franklin on Sunday. I can learn from my brother."

I smiled to myself but said only, "Good."

Turner arrived on time at eight and I was glad he did. Everybody wanted to talk about the arrest, about the doctor attacking me, about everything from the last week. And yet we still had to cook, deliver, clear, reset, and do it all again. I tried to fend off the questions about Geller's attack and arrest as best I could. I was a hundred percent relieved the man was behind bars, but I had a business to run.

Phil hurried in with four large covered pans full of brownies and cookies. "Sorry I didn't get these over to you yesterday, Robbie." He set them on the counter.

"No worries, man. Heck, we don't need them until eleven." I smiled at my favorite baker. "Do you want to eat?"

"No, thanks. I need to do a little Christmas shopping." He poured himself a mug of coffee and headed off to browse the cookware area.

Corrine and Marcus came in together a few minutes after Turner. A four-top of early birds had left, so I wiped off the table and seated mother and son there. Adele and Samuel were next to appear. Corrine waved them over to her table. *Good.* I was sure Samuel and Marcus had already been brought up to speed on the events of last evening.

Buck set the bell to jangling next, with Abe and Sean on his heels. *Abe?* Color me confused. Didn't he have to work? And . . . what was Sean doing out of school? Maybe it was a teacher in-service day. The three of them ambled over to where Adele sat. I wiped my hands on my apron and joined them.

"Is everything okay, guys?" I asked. "Why aren't you in class, Sean?"

Sean simply gave me a mysterious smile. I glanced from face to face. Adele's eyes sparkled. Samuel had his arm around her shoulders. Buck had his hands in his pockets and a Cheshire cat grin on his face. Corrine pressed her fingers over her mouth like she was trying not to smile. What in the world was going on?

Abe cleared his throat. He knelt on one knee in front of me and pulled a small velvet box out of his pocket. My breath rushed in. He opened the box to reveal a round diamond on a simple gold band. He took my left hand and smiled the crooked smile I adored, his strong but gentle grasp delivering the warm comfort it always did. My other hand flew to my mouth. The buzz of the restaurant quieted.

"Robbie Jordan, would you do me the honor of becoming my wife? Will you marry me?"

I gazed down at this man I loved with all my heart. I looked around at all my favorite people, including Danna and Turner, who'd somehow joined the circle. Phil had reappeared, too, and was holding his phone toward us as if he was shooting video. Adele was wiping her eyes and Danna sniffed. I gazed at Abe's son through my own blurry eyes.

"You good with this, Sean?" I asked, barely getting out the words.

He gave me a big braces-clad smile and two thumbs up.

I looked back at my husband-to-be. "Yes, Abe O'Neill, I will be happy to marry you."

He slid the ring onto my left ring finger. It fit perfectly. He stood and kissed me with tender lips. I kissed him right back. The restaurant erupted in a roar of whoops and applause.

"I wanted to wait until Christmas," he whispered, "but after last night? I couldn't delay another minute."

"I'm glad you didn't," I whispered back.

We turned and faced our family, our friends, our townsfolk. I extended my left hand above my head and made a half circle, diamond out. A crescendo of applause and cheers broke out. Abe slung his arm around my waist, and I pulled Sean in on the other side for a one-armed hug.

"Thank you for letting me join your family, dude," I murmured to the teen.

"You are seriously a lot more fun than that guy." He pointed to Abe but softened the comment with a smile.

All my lovies gathered around for hugs and congratulations. Until a customer across the room lifted his mug. "Can I get me a coffee refill, please?"

Recipes

Gingerbread People

Gingerbread men (and women) pop up throughout this book. This is Sean's grandmother's recipe.

Ingredients

¼ cup butter at room temperature
½ cup brown sugar
½ cup molasses
3 ½ cups unbleached white flour
1 teaspoon baking soda
¼ teaspoon cloves
½ teaspoon cinnamon
1 teaspoon powdered ginger
½ teaspoon salt
¼ cup water
Chocolate chips or icing

Directions

Preheat oven to 350 degrees Fahrenheit. Cover two large baking sheets with parchment paper.

Cream the butter and sugar. Beat in the molasses.

Combine the dry ingredients. Add them to the butter mixture in three parts, alternating with a total of ¼ cup water.

Form into a disk, wrap, and chill for at least half an hour.

Flour a surface and roll out to ¼ inch thickness. Cut with gingerbread man and woman cutters and place ½ inch apart on baking sheet. Add chocolate chips for eyes, mouths, and buttons before baking, or leave plain to decorate later.

Bake for 8 minutes or until edges start to brown. Cool on a wire rack. Add additional decoration if desired using your favorite icing recipe.

Holly Cookies

Abe's mother makes these yummy sugar cookies for Christmas. The recipe comes from the author's mother, Marilyn Muller, via her mother, Ruth Flaherty, both of whom were talented and loving bakers.

Ingredients

- 1 cup softened salted butter (never margarine)
- ½ cup sugar
- 1 egg
- 1 tablespoon vanilla
- 3 cups unbleached white flour
- ½ teaspoon baking powder
- Green sugars

Directions

Preheat oven to 425 degrees Fahrenheit.

Cream butter and sugar in mixer until smooth. Beat in egg and vanilla. Mix flour and baking powder, then stir in until mixed. Divide the dough in half, shape into disks, wrap, and chill for at least half an hour.

Line a cookie sheet with parchment paper. Dust a clean surface with flour and roll out first disk to a ¼-inch thickness. Cut with a holly cookie cutter and place on cookie sheet at least a half inch apart. Save all scraps and chill. When the sheet is full, sprinkle lightly with green sugars and bake for 5–7 minutes, watching for browning. Cool on brown paper. Repeat for the other disk and chilled scraps until all dough has been baked.

Enjoy with a cup of tea, a glass of milk, or a touch of Four Roses bourbon. (Note: Neither Ruth nor Marilyn would have partaken of the bourbon.)

Teriyaki Chicken Wings

Thanks to Kai Fujita for sharing her mother Flo's recipe. Robbie makes these as a hot appetizer for the Bible and Brew night.

Ingredients

- 2 cloves garlic, minced
- 5 ounces sugar
- ½ cup soy sauce
- 1 teaspoon grated fresh ginger
- 1 tablespoon sherry
- 2 pounds chicken wings or wingettes (the tiny drumstick parts), trimmed of excess fat

Directions

Line the bottom of a broiler pan with foil and place slotted top or a rack on top.

Combine garlic, sugar, soy sauce, ginger, and sherry and stir until sugar is dissolved.

Add chicken and mix, then heat through in a large skillet on medium until chicken is tender, turning frequently.

Drain, move to broiler pan top or rack, and finish under broiler until crispy.

Serve warm or at room temperature.

Corrine's Beef Stew

Corrine Beedle cooks up this hearty beef stew the night Marcus is invited over, a perfect dinner for a cold winter night.

Serves four to six.

Ingredients

Olive oil
1 pound stew beef, cut into one-inch cubes
Salt
Pepper
Flour
One large onion, diced
3 fat garlic cloves, minced
2 carrots, peeled and cut into one-inch chunks
12 ounces mushrooms, cleaned. Add whole if small, in halves or quarters if larger.
2 good-sized potatoes, scrubbed and cubed
1 cup hearty red wine like a cabernet sauvignon or a burgundy
2 cups beef or chicken stock
2 tablespoons minced fresh rosemary
½ cup chopped fresh parsley

Directions

Preheat oven to 350 degrees Fahrenheit.

Season beef with salt and pepper and dust with flour. In a large Dutch oven with an ovenproof lid, add olive oil to lightly cover the bottom and heat over medium high burner. Add only enough meat cubes so they can sauté without touching. When one side is brown, turn until other side browns. Remove to a plate and repeat until all meat is browned. Remove all to the plate.

Add more oil and sauté onions until tender but not brown. Return all meat and onions to the pot and add garlic. Sauté for one minute. Add carrots, mushrooms, potatoes, stock, wine, and rosemary and bring to a simmer. Remove from heat. Cover the pot and bake for two hours or until meat is very tender.

Whisk water into one tablespoon flour until it makes a paste, then stir in stock from the pot until it becomes a slurry. Whisk slowly into the stew to thicken. Add parsley and simmer another twenty minutes. Adjust seasonings.

Serve hot with crusty bread, green salad, and red wine.

Spinach-Red Pepper Egg Bake

An easy crowd-feeder for breakfast or brunch, Robbie makes this as a holiday breakfast special because the green of the spinach with the red pepper bits looks so festive.

Makes approximately 24 pieces.

Ingredients

Four slices bacon, cooked to crisp and
    crumbled (omit for vegetarians)
1 cup grated sharp cheddar cheese
1 ½ cups baby spinach, finely chopped or
    one pound frozen chopped spinach,
    defrosted and well drained
Whites of 1 bunch green onions, finely
    chopped
1 red bell pepper, seeded and diced
¼ cup sun-dried tomatoes, diced
1 clove garlic, minced
½ teaspoon black pepper
10 large eggs
¼ cup milk
2 tablespoons Parmesan cheese
½ cup shredded mozzarella cheese

Directions

Preheat oven to 375 degrees. Oil a 9"x13" baking dish.

Mix bacon, cheddar cheese, green onions, bell peppers,

tomatoes, garlic, and black pepper in a bowl, then pour into casserole dish.

Whisk eggs with milk and pour over vegetables.

Top with Parmesan and mozzarella cheeses.

Bake for 25–30 minutes or until eggs are cooked through. Cut into two-inch squares and serve warm or at room temperature.

Peppermint Mocha Muffins

Marcus suggests adding the peppermint flavorings to these easy muffins, perfect for the holidays. Makes one dozen.

Ingredients

1 ½ cups flour
½ cup unsweetened dark cocoa powder
2 tablespoons instant espresso
½ teaspoon baking soda
1 tablespoon baking powder
½ teaspoon salt
½ cup white sugar
⅓ cup brown sugar (dark or light)
1 egg
1 cup milk
½ cup canola oil
1 teaspoon peppermint extract
½ cup mini chocolate chips
¼ cup crushed candy canes or peppermint
    candies

Directions

Preheat oven to 425 degrees. Grease a standard muffin tin.

In a large bowl, combine the flour, cocoa powder, instant espresso, baking soda, baking powder, salt, and sugars. Mix well.

In a small bowl, beat the egg, milk, oil, and peppermint extract.

Stir the wet ingredients into the dry ingredients with a fork only until moistened.

Fold in the chocolate chips and peppermint bits.

Fill muffin cups three-fourths full.

Bake for 5 minutes. Without opening the oven, lower oven temperature to 375 degrees. Bake for an additional 10–12 minutes, until a toothpick inserted in the muffins comes out clean. Allow to cool before removing. Serve fresh or store in an airtight container.

Connect with U s

Visit us online at
KensingtonBooks.com
to read more from your favorite authors, see books
by series, view reading group guides, and more.

Join us on social media

for sneak peeks, chances to win books and prize packs,
and to share your thoughts with other readers.

facebook.com/kensingtonpublishing
twitter.com/kensingtonbooks

Tell us what you think!

To share your thoughts, submit a review,
or sign up for our eNewsletters, please visit:
KensingtonBooks.com/TellUs.